sunday's

on the phone

to monday

christine reilly

touchstone

new york   london   toronto   sydney   new delhi

Touchstone
An Imprint of Simon & Schuster, Inc.
1230 Avenue of the Americas
New York, NY 10020

First Touchstone hardcover edition February 2016

TOUCHSTONE and colophon are registered trademarks of Simon & Schuster, Inc.

For information about special discounts for bulk purchases, please contact Simon & Schuster Special Sales at 1-866-506-1949 or business@simonandschuster.com.

The Simon & Schuster Speakers Bureau can bring authors to your live event. For more information or to book an event, contact the Simon & Schuster Speakers Bureau at 1-866-248-3049 or visit our website at www.simonspeakers.com.

Interior design by Kyle Kabel

Manufactured in the United States of America

10 9 8 7 6 5 4 3 2 1

Library of Congress Cataloging-in-Publication Data

Reilly, Christine, 1988–
    Sunday's on the phone to Monday : a novel / Christine Reilly.—First Touchstone hardcover edition.
        pages   cm
    Includes index.
    1. Families—New York (State)—New York—Fiction. I. Title.
    PS3618.E5644S86 2016
    813'.6—dc23   2015020850
ISBN 978-1-5011-1687-2
ISBN 978-1-5011-1690-2 (ebook)

For Mom and Dad,
and my brothers,
and for Robert, the boy on the mountain

sunday's

on the phone

to monday

part one

parents

so long, farewell

Mathilde's father, James Spicer, had been the last person she'd known to use a shoehorn and a handkerchief, archaic tools gone the way of arrowheads and telegrams. He'd been an art dealer. Mathilde's father, who'd been polite when sober, was square-headed with big and fat feet. Who'd worn a camel-colored coat and hat, which he'd always tip in elevators. Mathilde's father, who'd smelled like ash, pastrami, and melancholy.

They had a routine. Every work evening she'd hear the door unfasten in their apartment. She'd yell, *Daddy's coming home!* He'd say, *hello, Boots*, because of how he'd claim she was only as tall as the tops of his boots. Her mother, Judy Spicer, would hover in the next room like a minor character in a play.

Daddy's coming home!, and he'd open the door, and he'd come home.

Boots, he'd say, *what was the very best part of your day?* He'd pull her onto his lap. He'd squeeze between the backs of her shoulders—the place where wings would have sprouted, if humans grew wings.

Mathilde would say, *this minute*. She loved him as fiercely as a daughter could love her father, even one who was acquainted with his flaws—such as the nights he came home knee-deep in his scotch, burping, and slurrily calling her Roots instead of Boots.

Daddy's coming home!, and he'd open the door, and he'd come home. If she were lucky, he'd be sober. She wasn't always lucky. Regardless, it was good to have a father in the house.

When Mathilde's father suffered a Heart attack on the 2 train coming home from work, she'd been in the middle of a rehearsal. Mathilde was sixteen, and her father had been forty-four. She was Liesl in the Lycée Français de New York's production of *The Sound of Music*. She was lucky because Jack Jetter was cast as Rolf. Rolf and Liesl were in love.

Mathilde had always fancied Jack, who was a grade older, but truly fell in an incurable love at their high school homecoming dance. This was four months before. The song playing in the background had been the Supremes. "Baby Love." Jack had pressed his cheek against hers, half a head and a mouth taller. When the song was over, he kissed her forehead, sputtered a raspberry on her left ear. *You're going to make some man very lucky someday. I'm already jealous.*

Someday a man would love her. Mathilde couldn't imagine making anybody lucky, let alone a man. - *Maybe he loves me,* - she fooled herself. - *Except why can't he be that man?* -

The next morning, Mathilde heard the same song on the radio, her favorite golden oldies station, counting the times Diana Ross sang *baby*. There were twelve different *baby*s Diana crooned after the other, twelve *baby*s clunking like pennies, waiting to be wishes at the bottom of a fountain. *Baby baby baby*, Mathilde shimmied, at home with the silvery superfluousness of her own voice. Twelve was the magic number. If Jack's picture appeared in the yearbook twelve times, it meant he loved her. If she saw him twelve times that week in the hallway, it meant he loved her. But twelve was an unkind number, spare and rationed. In order to get to twelve, you had to go one and two and so on, and before you knew it, you lost it to thirteen.

Mathilde wasn't sure if each *baby* referred to a different beloved, whom Diana must have loved at some point but now could not differentiate from the next *baby*, or to just one sweetHeart she felt compelled to repeat twelve times over. Some wheeling form of melodic echolalia sent infections masked as energies through Mathilde's eardrum. Had Mathilde really fallen in love? Mathilde thought of each *baby* crying in her arms, twelve babies calling her a naïve little schoolgirl who should not even pretend to know what love was.

Jack fed Mathilde's fancy the next four months during rehearsals, insisting they get into character by repeating dialogue that Liesl and Rolf would have said to each other but that wasn't in the script, calling it *method*.

Liesl, Jack told Mathilde, *I love you*. Sometimes, if she really pretended, it was Jack saying it to Mathilde, not Rolf to Liesl.

Rolf, Mathilde told Jack, *I can't live without you*. His eyes were bright and uncomplicated, like bridge lights. Every minute she loved him more.

They'd been rehearsing "Sixteen Going on Seventeen" the day her father died. It was Mathilde's turn, to sing about how she needed someone older and wiser telling her what to do, and at last Jack sang, *you are sixteen going on seventeen; I'll take care of you*. That was Mathilde's favorite line in the play. Her father was dead. She had one hour left to find out.

When they finished, Jack pulled Mathilde aside and asked if she had time to go over the scene where Rolf, a member of the Nazi Party in the second act of the play, tries to shoot Liesl's father, The Captain.

Practice your face, Jack told Mathilde. *You don't look convincing enough*.

Mathilde tried to look forlorn, her teeth tingling as Jack studied her face. To limit her arousal, she thought of filth. A documentary of the Vietnam War that had been on TV the other night. Roaches the sizes of half-dollars. The girl in her grade who always said *sorry* for raising her hand in class, who smelled sometimes like clay.

Why are you smiling? lisped Jack, burbling like he would with a mouthful of pulp, *what, is this part too cerebral for you?*—the very worst of his insults. Jack's opinions were immaculate.

It's not like that, said Mathilde. *I'm just punchy.*

You can do this, Mathilde, said Jack. *You have to.* But the more Mathilde held it in, the more her pure and flustery pubertal love wanted to husk itself out of her.

They practiced the scene with Jack insisting he wouldn't be leaving until they had *no seams left.* He ministered until their guidance counselor came in. *Mathilde, your mother just called. Can you come into my office?*

the mathilde who was not herself

O f all the roles she'd ever play in her life, Mathilde's most ambitious character was a lead in a Scottish play called *Textbook Case*. Mathilde was twenty, an acting major at NYU Tisch School of the Arts, studying abroad at the Wimbledon College of Arts in London for a semester. Mathilde was Milla, a damaged, rash, and unabashed orphan placed in foster care her entire small life. To perfect her role she shut herself in her flat for at least five hours a day, accessing her darkest parts.

For if she wasn't suffering for her art, what was she suffering for?

She'd start by announcing, *pleasure to meet you. I'm Milla.* This was the ritual she'd repeat for all of her characters. After her introduction, she was jettisoned of herself, no longer Mathilde.

As Milla, Mathilde forced herself to think of her parents at their worst. The times when they'd be late to pick her up from school or parties. The moments she'd look into her father's face and register an eerie nonentity. Not enough energy for love, or not enough prioritizing that love. His life was defined by more important things than his children. (Mathilde had a younger brother, Sawyer.)

Her parents used to have earsplitting fights, as loud as the Old Testament god. Her father would say to her mother, *you have some set of morals, toots,* resorting to sarcasm when livid.

His worst words could have been misconstrued as sweet had they not been delivered with a tone that could make anyone suppurate—christening her mother *sweetHeart, baby, precious,* when their arguments were the dirtiest, forever ruining these words for Mathilde. Whenever anybody would call Mathilde by an endearing nickname, her feelings would be hurt, and she'd curdle a desire to squish her hands together.

It was too bad, for she was commonly nicknamed by innocuous octogenarians. *Here's your change, honey,* a man holding a newspaper once told her when she was in her twenties. He looked like a retired firefighter or a Depression-wizened businessman who spent his life making money for his next four generations.

- *Fuck you,* - thought Mathilde but said, *thank you.*

Mathilde figured if the average person was about 50 percent selfish, then her parents had been 75 percent: the kind of people who probably shouldn't have had children but did anyway, who did a halfway decent job but were by no means outstanding parents. Her father had vices—drinking, smoking, gambling. Her mother was more interested in being a wife than a mother. She was also greedy—the only person Mathilde ever knew who didn't believe in charity.

Mathilde poisoned herself with her thoughts for hours. - *My parents would probably rather have three million dollars instead of me. I have a life that only looks fine on the outside.* -

The troupe toured Europe and America that summer. Mathilde played Milla to different audiences in different theaters and festivals, ending in a converted abandoned hotel theater in Manhattan. While the rest of the cast went their own ways, most of them back to Europe, Mathilde stayed in New York and finished college.

There's this one part in *Textbook Case* where Milla asks another orphan, *won't you beat me, so I know I did something wrong?* These words came back to Mathilde in quieted parcels later in life. On her twenty-fifth birthday, as she opened a gift, Mathilde thought, - *won't you beat me, so I know I've done something wrong?* - At twenty-nine, when she accidentally set off her car alarm she thought, - *won't you beat me, so I know I've done something wrong?* - Once, when she was in the shower washing her hair, Mathilde asked herself, - *won't you beat me, so I know I've done something wrong?* - At thirty-six, as her mother lay in the hospital with a cancer quiet in her body, Mathilde thought, - *won't you beat me, so I know I've done something wrong?* -

not a love story
(though it tries)

As Mathilde grew up on the Upper West Side of New York City, Claudio was growing up in a wasteland suburb of Detroit. Mathilde grew up with a comfortable amount of money; Claudio with no money. When Mathilde graduated high school, Claudio was graduating the University of Michigan with a degree in business. The night of his graduation, he paid twenty dollars for a Greyhound to New York. He had four shirts, sneakers, sunglasses, three pairs of underwear, blue jeans, a well-deserved bank account, and plans to open up a vinyl store. He was sort of crying when he got off the bus, but he wore the sunglasses.

He'd been able to afford Michigan only through the scholarship he'd received. The bank account was a result of waiting tables throughout high school and college. The best part about going to college there was not needing to take out student loans or borrow money from anybody. One of Claudio's true loves was music, which made sense after having spent his entire youth saving his money. Vinyls he could borrow and lend with friends. The songs caught in his head were free. He rarely made transactions for anything tangible—never clothes, nor meals in restaurants, nor tickets to elsewhere. - *Music is air*, - he thought. - *You can recycle it.* -

Claudio had neuroses about the amount of money he spent,

feeling infelicitous if he thought about it too much. - *Why the fuck did I buy that overpriced fish dish; why did I ask the bartender for top-shelf gin?* - It always added up. To indulge himself, Claudio listened to music all the time—in the shower, as he slept, while he talked on the phone. Music made him wealthier.

Claudio grew a beard and hand-rolled his cigarettes and ate only black bread and trusted no one when he moved to New York. He wanted to appear older than he was but couldn't help attracting college students as friends, who'd come to his store and pick out records for their parties. Eight-tracks had long been out, and CDs were new, but neither sounded as good, as emotionally reviving, as the records. Claudio banked on nothing being better quality than records for a long time, risking his whole fiscal life on this.

He'd never even been to New York before. - *Get out,* - he'd told himself. - *Never come back.* - He'd have to make his own luck, which was fine. He'd never felt at ease depending on others. He'd only needed to find some people he could employ for family.

How'd you guys meet? folks would ask.

Claudio always said, *we made out at a party on St. Mark's.*

Mathilde always said, *we met through friends.*

What really happened was they attended a party in an NYU undergraduate's apartment where vodka was dispensed through feeding tubes hung from the wall. The undergraduate, a friend of Mathilde's, had bought a Hall & Oates record from Claudio's store and thought that the way Claudio smiled with his tongue sticking out of his teeth while ringing her up was cute in a grainy way, so she invited him to her place.

Claudio drank vodkas because he didn't know anybody. Everything around him started to look like glass. The apartment had two floors with a steel staircase in the shape of fusilli and narrow circular steps, which Claudio fell down, responding to his own plunge with *Jesus H.* His ass smarted. All over the wall were hundreds of cookbooks. Adjusting himself right side up, he noticed a pair of thin legs, then the woman attached to them. *Have mercy.* Mathilde looked mature. Maybe she'd be too grown up for such foolishness.

Nice rings. Claudio scanned her hands. She wore two rings, but the left wasn't a diamond, so he could try his own hand with hope. *Is that where you live?*

I'm sorry?

Where in your body do you spend the most time?

Well, my head, said Mathilde. *You?* She thought, - *won't you beat me, so I know I did something wrong?* - And then she thought about a line from a play she did two years ago, titled *Pretend It's a Party.* The line was - *I'm tired of you laughing at me.* -

No wonder, Claudio said, *you look so much in la-la land. Anyone in particular you're thinking about?*

Nobody too special, admitted Mathilde. She'd been thinking of Milla from *Textbook Case,* whom she'd left in her brain with the rest of the characters she'd played. Milla didn't know how to read or write. She had no outlet outside of her head, and fear crowded her thoughts. Considerably speaking, Mathilde was much luckier than Milla. How she missed her!

Milla wouldn't have been so shy around Claudio. By this point, Milla would have been touching Claudio's arm, laughing at his jokes, feeling his swinish body hairs stand for her attention. Claudio would have thought Milla was more fun than Mathilde. A firecracker. - *You're making the wrong choice, buddy,* - Mathilde felt like saying.

She was being classic Mathilde. Thinking of her characters as though they were friends of hers. How could she tell Claudio that the people she missed most of all weren't real or that they were part of her?

Besides, Claudio would be sure to dislike her once he found out how juvenile she was. Mathilde had light-years of maturity when it came to cognition—she could probably hold court with MENSA members—but when it came to her kinesthetic sense, she was childish. She mixed up her right and left, cried during happy moments, laughed during sad ones, and didn't know temperance when it came to corporal needs like falling asleep or needing to use the bathroom. Whatever she felt, she could not wait to do. Her body held all of her clout.

The party overflowed with people and expensive talk. Two a.m. in the city was like 10:00 p.m. anywhere else. *You need some water or something?* yelled Claudio. His word *water* came out as *waw-duh*. Lately and astoundingly he'd heard himself already start to have a New York accent, pronouncing forest *farrest* and almond *ah-min*.

Soft fingers of smoke curled around their faces, an effluvium infection of their hair and clothes. This was pre-Giuliani, a time when everyone smoked indoors and felt their surroundings made them stronger.

Mathilde suggested they find someplace quieter, and so they came across the fire escape. Claudio opened the window and pinched the loose skin between her pointer and middle finger. *Hand fat*, he joked. Mathilde stuck out her tongue.

Here, we can fit, said Mathilde.

You sure you're relaxed? asked Claudio, watching his breath in front of his face. He felt like a cool smoker.

It's New York, said Mathilde. *You get good at being comfortable in tiny and risky places.*

The time felt necessary at the end of the party for Claudio to ask Mathilde, *do you want to go for dinner sometime this week?* He squinted and shook his head, as though Mathilde had already rejected him, though they'd Eskimo kissed for almost an hour atop a pile of coats. The effort was there: Claudio made moves but let Mathilde feel like she had some control over the situation. And Mathilde minded Claudio, letting him touch the side of her back as he asked, letting his reticence fade. Touching her back felt firm, filling, sufficient.

Oh sure, said Mathilde.

Mathilde had no way to know this, but the word *sure* rubbed Claudio wrong. He thought it beget a lackluster quality, that people said it when they didn't take things seriously. Maybe he'd made the wrong decision? - *Oh, come on*, - he thought. He never really dated in New York, just had girls he'd talk to, go to concerts with, and occasionally sleep with.

The last had been a lawyer named Viola. Viola with the barbed cheekbones and the body starry with moles. She ate his leftovers, held her own at parties, and they were a fit in terms of maturity: Claudio needed to feel older, and Viola liked to say she was born forty. Viola was okay. But for some reason he and Viola had always been in a fight. He didn't know how—it wasn't as if he ever looked for trouble. How did people go about having relationships? What kind of process was it, and how organic? He would've loved to date a girl had he known precisely how.

Cool, thank you, said Claudio to Mathilde. *And don't worry. You can always trust somebody if you meet him upside down.*

Claudio took Mathilde to dinner the next night at a restaurant in the West Village. He unmercifully muscled over drinks as his inhibition eroded. He was careful at first not to talk too much about himself, to approximate the time he spent talking with time he spent listening and asking questions, to find that perfect balance between not sounding like he was giving a speech or conducting an interrogation. He suddenly realized before his third whiskey that he'd been talking about Brian Wilson for however long it took the people at the table next to them to sit down and order and get their meals.

I should just stop talking, he interrupted himself. *Especially about music. What else is there to say about music? I just like everything.*

No, marveled Mathilde, *you're fascinating.* God bless Mathilde,

and her face, which was old-fashioned, Claudio realized. Maybe
it was the eyes, intuitive and weary. She looked like she could
have been a product of one of the wars. *Well, you got me started,*
he said.

Mathilde sparkled, her spectacular mouth making punctuation: a parenthesis, a befuddled backslash. When she drank
water, her lips became ellipses. And how did Claudio's mouth
look to her, he conjectured, making all sorts of hideous shapes?
Without a doubt like the qualm of a question mark in discor-
dance with the assured crudity of an exclamation point.

Claudio set the rules for himself: - *her mouth reminds me when
to stop.* - A smile meant continue: they were on the same page. A
frown meant the same: he had to justify himself, explain, maybe
allow her to retort. A period, lips closed and ineffable, meant
she wasn't interested anymore.

Over the course of the evening, Claudio discovered that
Mathilde also loved music. Who didn't? But Mathilde liked
music that moved her. She didn't just listen to it because it was
there. Her favorite album was Joni Mitchell's *Blue*, closely followed by Fleetwood Mac's *Rumours*. She explained to Claudio how she wanted the qualification of being a person people
thought of when they listened to certain songs.

Mathilde had a chimera cat named Penelope. Her favorite flowers were sweet peas. Her best outfit was her blue bell-
bottoms, her grandmother's mink coat, and a peasant blouse
that she got in the East Village for five dollars.

Why that outfit?

Because I'd wear it anywhere.

Even to your wedding?

Even to my funeral. This dizzy chime, the urgent art of
Mathilde's laugh, overwhelmed Claudio in a safe way. *Make
sure I'm buried in it, will you?*

*I hope you've told some other people. Not because I anticipate not
seeing you again. It's just, you'll probably outlive me.*

Oh come on! She laughed like he was kidding. *This is pretty morbid, for a first date.*

It is? He wondered if Mathilde thought he was brave, deep, different. Or did he seem like a phony? Taking such a wonderful person out to dinner was a goddamn idiotic idea. If only he'd taken some sedative. Even a hit of weed would've made him more comfortable, brought him to an orbiting lull. The soft way Mathilde studied him made him feel like maybe something about him was off, like his eyes were too cocoon-shaped or his hairline too focused.

After drinks, dinner, dessert across the street at a bakery, and then a nightcap three blocks down at another bar (Mathilde aggressively ordered some specialty cocktail Claudio had never heard of before called an *adios, motherfucker*), Claudio offered to drive her home. Over dinner he'd found out that Mathilde lived with her mother and brother, Sawyer, on the Upper West Side and commuted downtown to her college classes.

I wanted to dorm, but my mom's the cheapest rich person you'll ever meet.

That's too bad. My parents are poor, but they're really generous. Sometimes too much for their own good.

You have a car? asked Mathilde. *In Manhattan?*

I mean, I sometimes even drive it to the grocery store, said Claudio. An old stretch limousine had been repaired, then for sale last year at an auto-repair shop in Holliswood, Queens. Claudio had had his eye on it for a month, buying it as soon as he'd sold enough records. It (or *she*, as he called it) was the first big thing he'd ever owned.

Claudio told Mathilde this, then all about how well his business had done in the past year, much better than he'd thought. How he spent all of his spare money on parking spaces for the car. *Seems like a waste.* Mathilde was truthful.

Well, there's nothing I can think of that I'd rather spend money on. Don't you want to save it?

I wanted to own something larger than me, said Claudio.

What about buying property?

You're kidding, right? asked Claudio. They laughed in a way only New Yorkers could laugh.

Yeah, I guess that makes some sense.

And on that note, let me drive you home.

You don't have to, said Mathilde, in the laudable way girls speak, offering not to be taken care of. Earlier she'd also held out her hands as a gesture to pay for her half of the bill, but Claudio had said, *my pleasure.*

What kind of person would I be if I didn't make sure you get home safely? clicked Claudio: traditional, bearlike.

Are you sure you're good to drive?

I'm a tank, said Claudio. *And I like living. I have some things I want to do before I die. But I get it: you don't know me. You're going to have to trust me.*

I'll trust you, decided Mathilde.

Mathilde took a toothpick and the restaurant's business card while Claudio munificently tipped the coat check girl. A Muzak version of "It's Only a Paper Moon" tolled. He opened the door, and they were hit by the city air in uprising swirls. Mathilde's ears were touching the sky. Wasn't perspective a glorious and mad thing?

Come, said Claudio. And Mathilde followed him.

He was thinking - *she hates me.* - Christ, she was tiny and hot. Parsley bangs snipped across her forehead, news-anchor skin. She'd gotten up halfway through dinner to use the restroom, and her shirt bottom swung up, a hint of split-upward unsweatered bare back just about killing his feral self. Her hip bones like monkey bars.

It took twenty minutes to walk to Claudio's parking space, pay the parking lot attendant, and maneuver out of there. All the while, Mathilde had a slumbery feeling of the uncanny. Something about the situation reminded her of something else.

As they merged onto the West Side Highway, Mathilde realized. The limo—how much like a hearse it was. Was it already
five years that he'd been living under the ground?

- *Not living,* - Mathilde reminded herself. - *Not dying either.
Everything that could have happened already happened.* - Sometimes
Mathilde would even say out loud, *he's not cold. He can't feel any-
thing.* She was always reminding herself.

You all right?

Yes, I'm okay, said Mathilde. *Just thinking.*

About what?

Um, Elvis. She didn't want to mention her dead father, feeling like she had talked about him too many times. This tragic
baggage had become part of her identity: the girl with no more
father. She couldn't help being born to him. It wasn't her fault
he'd died!

Most of the boys Mathilde dated before Claudio talked about
how they were thinking about kissing her before actually kissing her. Claudio didn't meander. She didn't know what he was
thinking as he kissed her before he even wholly stopped the car.
It was an architectural and fancy kiss. And, would you believe
it, he tasted sweet: sly, sexy, milkshakey.

Be careful. Mathilde laughed as he parked the car.

You don't trust me? asked Claudio. Those fat blue eyes.

Can I? asked Mathilde.

Outside, a fugue of drunk twenty somethings passed by.
Claudio saw one of them point at his limo and say to her friends,
fellas, my ride is here.

My mom's upstairs, Mathilde continued. Mothers generally
liked Claudio, because he was quiet and handled gently. Though
in this case, he didn't know how he'd hold his own. He didn't
feel like himself. Perhaps he was high off Mathilde's conditioner,
which smelled like apple pie. He could've eaten her hair. Fur-
thermore, she frenched the way she talked: kindly, kinetically.

This where you grew up? Claudio asked, hindering in front of Mathilde's building, a high-rise on Riverside Drive. It occurred to Claudio that he hadn't really asked Mathilde about her childhood. It was all about the present. See, he didn't know about the things you were supposed to talk about during first dates.

My whole life, said Mathilde. *That's my doorman, Isaac,* who was reading the newspaper. She wanted Isaac to look at her, grant some nod of approval or discretion. Isaac felt like a family member but one degree removed. She trusted him with secrets. He bore witness to the times she came home with rum spiced on her mouth, the boyfriends and girlfriends and joints she snuck up when her mother was out of town or sleeping.

I keep picturing you as a little girl, said Claudio.

Don't, urged Mathilde. She told him to circle twice around the block, her way of continuing the night. Claudio kept driving east.

Where are you going? asked Mathilde.

We, not you, corrected Claudio.

He drove along Central Park, then stalled. They made out in the backseat. Mathilde had never done this on a first date before. She had what she called her *jollies* but had been decent at domesticating these thrills and chills, until now.

Do you come from the inside or the outside? he asked her. She had gorgeous everything, her slinky neck, even the pits of her knees.

Mostly inside, she told him. The moon curled down in a cleaving gibbous. The radio played music from the 1950s. *Why must I be a teenager in love?* the radio asked Claudio and Mathilde and the stars up above. Claudio and Mathilde didn't answer, and neither could see the stars because they were in Manhattan. Claudio tried to remember what it felt like to be a teenager. But he kept mixing his own memory up with scenes from *Grease 2,* the movie that was on TV late last night, a reverent remedy to his insomnia. He didn't think he'd ever been in love. He sniffed her around the shoulders like a dog.

What are you doing? asked Mathilde.

I'm trying to remember how you smell, he admitted recklessly.

Who are you?

Pepé Le Pew, he joked. *A skunk. And you're the girl who's out of my league.*

No, said Mathilde. *Who are you really?* Claudio studied her mouth. Her cheeks sucked in. Her stone-fox, infinity-shaped lips riveted him.

I'm Claudio Simone, he told her. *Who are you?*

Mathilde called her girlfriend the next day and told her that she had just met the man she was going to marry. *And that's that,* she made up her mind, studying a love bite in the mirror over her wrinkling vocal cords. A small problem—a pox. She wanted to keep it for the rest of her life.

You say that about every guy you make out with. It was true. Boys fell for Mathilde, especially princely and brainy boys who liked music, aged eighteen to twenty-six. She had a history with them, taking them to her sorority formals and playing mind games with them and pretending their kisses between her legs didn't tickle. All of Mathilde's valves were open to love. She thought about how Claudio looked, with his arms like wooden spoons and eyes the color of the deepest sea. She said that they were going to get married. *And have lots of children.*

You don't even know if he'll be a good father.

He has nice arms. Good for picking up babies, Mathilde leaped, deal-sealing. *He makes me relaxed.* She thought about Claudio asking her if she came from the inside or the outside, how lovely it felt to answer. They had no problem talking about sex; that must've meant they could talk about probably anything. She felt humbly protected, like a baby inside of a house belonging to someone responsible, somebody who specifically made her to take care of her.

So, this won't be a love story. Nobody is trying to tell you something about love. This will be a story about a family.

the claudio who
was a brother

september 13, 1988

Mathilde stayed the following night on the corner of Tenth and Avenue A, in the apartment Claudio shared with his best friend, Zane. She asked Claudio the next morning, *what do you want for breakfast?*

Claudio garbled *French fries*, and then he said *two front teeth.* He opened his eyes and saw Mathilde, who was waiting for him to hold her. *Man, how did I get here?*

He jumped up and ran a shower. *I'm a water sign. Cancer.*

So am I! Scorpio. But it's nothing I buy into. I only believe in science, was Mathilde's certainty, though she did pay attention to the possibility of faith. Actually, she was a compulsive wisher. On dandelion skeletons, on pennies, in fountains or wells, on eyelashes, at 11:11 a.m. and 11:11 p.m., on birthday candles. She tried to split them up evenly into selfless and selfish wishes. She didn't even believe in them coming true and still wished.

In the shower, Mathilde left speckled love-bites on Claudio's neck and chest. He gripped her ass with both hands. A tear leaked down her cheekbone, and it tasted holy. Mathilde's clean, enchanting body. *Your body is an American wonder*, he proclaimed. *It's better than water. Better than chocolate. It's even better than hope.*

Keep hope, said Mathilde. *It's good.*

I never hope, said Claudio. *And that's why I'm still alive.*

What does that mean? Mathilde couldn't trust what Claudio said when it came to being alive. This was coming from a man who'd earlier said *I've done every drug there is* and *it's not in the cards for anyone in my family to push past fifty.*

Instead of answering, Claudio walked to the kitchen and came back with a bag of chocolate chips, pouring a handful into his palm and holding his hand out to Mathilde. Mathilde asked, *can we talk about something less gloomy?*, for she was supposed to be the shadowy, sensational one. Claudio was supposed to be her balloon, pulling her out of her rumbling, showboating despair.

I guess, said Claudio. He too had been asking himself that question for twenty-three years. *Let's talk about your legs.* He touched Mathilde's left leg. Her wet, bald left.

What about them?

About how they just won't quit.

Darling. You're making me blush. Mathilde's counter came out artificial-sounding, her voice emboldened.

I read a sad poem about legs, once.

By who?

My sister, Jane, wrote it and gave it to me for my birthday. It didn't make a very good present, because it was so sad. But it stuck with me. I still have it.

Claudio hadn't told Mathilde much about his sister, except for, *she's in a hospital.* A disquieted Mathilde had asked him what illness she had, and he'd said, *it's not physical*, so she hadn't pried. *Show me.*

Claudio turned off the faucet and dried them both off, then walked into his room. He came back in a bathrobe, holding the poem. *Okay, kid*, he said. Droplets of water clung to his neck.

Fins

He said you could do a helluva lot with them. You
    could stick
a cigar up there, he said. You can wear them to bed
or to the ball. He said god must've been generous
with my legs but also that they were trouble. Long,
    unlonely,
unsalted pretzel sticks. There for decoration.
Put anything on them and they will stand.

Cover those cornstalks with boots, somebody else said.
Cover those thighs with chaps, cover those feet
with another pair of feet.

Maybe he was a religious man or something
but he kept mentioning god like he was in the room.
He said it's like two or three of the best architects in
    the world
designed those legs. I didn't know if he was still talking
about god then, I felt like a fool for not knowing.

He said he would play one like a piccolo
if I'd let him. When I looked down
at my legs then they appeared blurred
and drippy. Like the left one was leaking
or something.

When Claudio finished reading, tracing the words with his
fingers, neither spoke. He always thought the poem was written
to keep some other words from coming out of his sister, existing in a preventative way, like the Electoral College. Finally,
Mathilde cracked the silence. *I thought we were going to talk about*
happy things.

You're right, Legs, said Claudio. *Can I call you Legs? So I have a better association?*

Boots, Mathilde mouthed but didn't have the muscle to tell another sad story. She thought of her brother, Sawyer. She could tell Claudio a story about him, a lesser catastrophe, one to commiserate over.

This would be the beginning of Mathilde's cheery, cheesecakey nickname and the predecessor to Mathilde's calling Claudio other body parts: throat, ear, large intestine. They laughed for almost an hour.

She gave him all the tools he needed to hurt her, and he did the same. Wasn't that the logic in love?

the mathilde who was a sister (& the story she told claudio)

january 27, 1983

While walking home from school, thirteen-year-old Sawyer Spicer was attacked for the way his hips stuck out like a girl's. *Let go! Leave me be!*, he choked, spitting elisions through his tears.

The pack's leader was Neil, an unjustly handsome transfer to Lycée Français de New York in Manhattan, where Sawyer and his sister, Mathilde, attended middle and high school. Neil was handsome and decisive, and had made Sawyer feel large. The night they were assigned the project together, on photosynthesis, Sawyer went home and thought about Neil coming out of the shower. Sawyer loved boys from when he was young enough to love people in general. It was just another, more specific part of himself. He liked most people, and he liked to imagine boys naked. It wasn't so different from enjoying most food but craving pad thai.

They'd finished the project in under an hour, migrating downstairs to the bodega. They were rung up by the man who had tragedy-mask wrinkles on his face and who spoke every sentence like a question, one of New York's few remaining Jewish bodega owners. Neil and Sawyer brought two pastrami sandwiches to Sawyer's apartment, where Sawyer's doorman asked them both about last night's Giants game. - *Is this a date?* - Sawyer thought, then felt his skin flush lilac. He was a dweeb!

Neil ate like a sandpiper, mashing his face down into the sandwich, consuming speedily, unbelievably. When he finished his sandwich, Neil handed Sawyer the aluminum foil wrapper the way a child would do in the company of an adult. They talked for another hour, mostly about their families and friends.

I had lots of girlfriends at my old school, but one I liked the most, said Neil. *Susan. We got to third base.*

Wow, said Sawyer, swallowing his spit, unsure of how to feel. Not exactly disappointment, because he figured Neil had girlfriends, more like he was in debt.

Do you masturbate? Neil asked Sawyer in the same fluttery voice he used to talk about the girlfriends.

Every so often, said Sawyer, his stomach cramping as Neil asked him how often.

Like about once a week. You? Sawyer asked people *you?* so regularly he sometimes forgot that he was the *I*.

Oh, when I'm bored, said Neil. Sawyer wanted to go back to their sort-of rapport, where he was comfortable, where they took turns talking, but then Neil took out his loose-leaf. He pointed at the blank page opposite their diagram on photosynthesis. The project was stellar, and Sawyer had done most of the work. They were probably going to get one hundred. *Draw what you think about.*

Sawyer didn't draw anything vulgar or gratuitous, just a body. A man. A person. Everything that there was needed to be. He drew the hands in a bewildering way: palms up, as if waiting to accept low-fives.

Neil stared. *This is hot.*

Thanks, Sawyer whispered, focusing into Neil's drippy lips, his Dalmatian eyes (the left blue more royal than the right), wondering if it was going to be the moment of his first kiss. Instead, Neil rolled it up into a tight cylinder, then bopped Sawyer on the head with it. *Later,* he said. *See you mañana,* with an overflow of accent so phony it was delicate.

Sawyer went to bed thinking about the word *later.* No matter what, there would always be a *later.* This later could be a
mañana, or a Sunday, or a Tuesday, or a never. His wrists trembled.

Neil didn't look at Sawyer the next day in class. Sawyer, in-
flicted with an obscure shame, looked down at his shirt. Maybe
he had something on it. It was red with triangular pockets. His
mother had bought it in France. - *Wrong,* - Sawyer thought to
himself.

One week later Neil chased Sawyer after school with some
boys who played lacrosse and got to third base, at least, with
girls. Afterward, they left Sawyer with his drawing, the word
faggot wedged in red ink over the pelvis. Earlier, their class had
received their graded diagrams on photosynthesis. The carbon
dioxide seeped into the plant, and the oxygen slid out. The sky
was an alphabet of blue. And all energy came from light. They
got one hundred. At least Sawyer passed something.

Mathilde put him to bed. *No,* she said. *Don't cry.* Before he
closed his eyes, Sawyer apologized to her. She felt her Heart
wobble clumsily through her chest. When he woke up after a
few hours, she reaffirmed to him, *you didn't do anything wrong,*
so they both could hear it.

Here's the thing with teenage boys, Sawyer said to his sister.
They'll eat anyone's Heart if they're told it has protein.

Groups, said Mathilde. *Someone's making a decision somewhere.
Who knows who.*

You're lucky you're a girl.

These were the words Mathilde repeated to Claudio, in his
bed. *He told me I was lucky for being a girl,* she said, *and I knew
I wanted girls for children.* Soft, mindful sisters—the kind she
didn't have. *Boys would be too complicated,* she declared, having
mercy. She didn't need more of that in her life.

dog blues

Mathilde landed a role in a play, *Make a Living*. She was to be a twenty-one-year-old girl playing a thirty-eight-year-old woman named Frances. Frances wanted a child but didn't have a partner. Most of Frances's monologues involved a loneliness that Mathilde personally felt too immature to convey. That year, for the purpose of her art and for the sake of her challenging role, Mathilde sussed every day for something that would make her cry, making so much of her own emptiness.

Before rehearsal, she'd walk into her parents' room. (She would never be able to call it only her mother's room.) She'd stick her nose in her father's clothes. Crackers and coins and cigarettes. The searing, bewildering smells of his world. Her mother hadn't given them away, which was of use for Mathilde. She didn't need much to weep, just a snuffle or two.

Who is that boy you've been seeing? asked her mother. *Someone special*, she guessed.

Just a boy, Mathilde said and said it for a while, as though he was only one of a plethora of lazy loves.

As a twenty-three-year-old, Claudio couldn't help but enjoy things that were taboo but, in his estimation, harmless—jokes that violated protocol, tenuous words. Mathilde had the luxury of mollycoddling in moods for work, and he by association experienced these selfish tempers with her. Dating Mathilde felt like going to an amusement park every day. Like somebody much larger than him was grabbing him by the shoulders and thrashing. She made him feel good in a devouring way, and this way frightened him when he thought about it.

This was partially due to his lack of experiencing anything directly catastrophic. He'd never had any misfortune too extreme to process. Never lost anyone unexpectedly (to death) or been in a war zone. His parents had been gullible, dissociative people—the type to get conned. But he had no reason to believe they weren't happy. The very worst thing that happened to Claudio was that he grew up poor. In a world where some people watched each other's heads blowing off, Claudio always described his life as *not bad*.

(But he'd never lived a life other than his own, so who was he to judge the quality?)

His sister, Jane, always seemed to be more depressed, but she lived a different life. She was a girl, which Claudio speculated was harder. Boys had pressure to grow into men, but girls had contradicting types of pressure: sometimes to show themselves off, sometimes to hide. Sometimes to speak up, sometimes to collar their speech. Jane, who had become so hard to love— maybe she was having a bad life, but not Claudio. His life wasn't bad and would never be bad, if he could help it.

Mathilde didn't understand what *not bad* meant. Things were either wonderful or appalling. Feeling felt like exercising, the terrain of an actor. She cherished crying like tripping on a drug—adored the messy, thick sleepiness that came with it, the released toxins and proteins and hormones. She felt she had more substance when she embraced calamity, going out of her way to rent the movies that drove her to snivel for days. Especially the ones based on true stories, because a story wasn't really sad unless it was real.

Claudio knew he was in love with Mathilde by their second date, which took all night. They stayed up until 7:00 a.m.

talking about their favorites: animals, days of their lives, stories, songs. Mathilde told Claudio how Willy Loman's failures taught her that good luck can get a person only so far. Claudio believed that the song "My Sweet Lord" by George Harrison almost made him believe in a god. And then Claudio thought, - *I can fall in love with her.* -

There'd been other girls, sure. But none of those relationships had to do with love. The closest he'd come had maybe been Viola or his high school girlfriend, a ballerina named Sylvie, whose dance company sweatshirts Claudio would wear. But nobody he'd ever slept with had been as open as Mathilde. Claudio was a sucker for people with Hearts on their sleeves, who honored him with life details he hadn't provided conversational momentum for. Being with them felt like eating clams with wobbly shells, or having a cashier honor an expired coupon. Mathilde made him feel like he could save her from harm. It would be easy to. Not like Jane, whom Claudio had been unable to save.

His favorite thing about Mathilde, though, was that she was the best damn listener he had ever met. Most people he knew just pantomimed listening when really they were counting seconds until it was their turn to speak. Mathilde wasn't like anybody else: she really listened.

Claudio and Mathilde spent every day together those first months of dating. Then came the weekend Mathilde traveled out of town to visit her brother, Sawyer, who was starting his freshman year at Cornell. Claudio had the weekend to himself. - *What did I do for fun a few months ago?* - He couldn't remember.

Claudio's roommate, Zane, brought a stray dog back to their apartment that Friday night. Claudio was listening to records and eating strawberry jam from the jar with a spoon. He had little willpower around sweets and was mildly addicted to sugar. He made sure there was never anyone around to witness his pornographic ingestion habits. Claudio guessed he could've had a kind of eating disorder, but how could he be certain? Eating disorders were a relatively recent phenomenon, like cellular phones or camcorders, and they were popularly diagnosed with white middle-to-upper-class girls. Claudio even liked stomach viruses when they paid off in a real way, and thought Karen Carpenter looked good until she was dead. He wasn't just into the thin-as-wineskin look, though—there were a lot of kinds of pretty, he believed.

Hey guy, said Zane. *How cute is this guy?* There were two guys: Claudio and the dog. The dog was large and silver, with pointy wolf-ears. It reminded Claudio of winter. Snowshoeing. Some sylvan place that wasn't New York City.

Where'd you find it?

He followed me home from the bar. Zane bit his lip like a tarty showgirl, just missing the cold sore on his philtrum.

How do you know it's a he? Did you check?

Nah. He looks masculine, said Zane. *I can tell.*

Come on, said Claudio.

You think I'm kidding. It's my instincts.

How do you know it doesn't belong to one of your homeless buddies? asked Claudio. Zane was one of those people who talked to everybody. He had extroversion down pat, didn't even call for a crutch, like when smokers make friends through sharing cigarettes outside.

I don't, said Zane. *I'll call the pound tomorrow, but can he stay with us tonight? And why are you eating jam with nothing else?*

Because I do this thing, said Claudio, *called whatever the fuck I want.*

It's bizarre that you're eating just jam.

Does it bother you that much? The dog sniffed the jelly jar.

Dogs don't eat sweets, said Zane.

Mathilde's cat, Penelope? She eats macaroni and cheese. You can't make stuff like this up, said Claudio.

Mathilde again, said Zane. *Don't you ever talk about anybody else?*

That night, Claudio fell asleep on the couch as Zane watched a Leslie Nielsen movie on TV. The dog charged the couch, nuzzling Claudio on the shoulder. The record player played "Walk on the Wild Side." Claudio couldn't sleep without music, though he could sleep through anything—storms, apocalypses, neighbors. *Hi, buddy*, whispered Claudio from his sleep, rubbing the dog's back with his palms.

Think we should call her Mathilde? joked Zane.

What the fuck, brother? snapped Claudio.

A hustle here and a hustle there, said Lou Reed.

But they have so much in common, said Zane.

New York City is the place where, Lou Reed said.

Both breathe air. They can both eat and sleep. The missus is a carbon-based organism too, right, Claudio? What a coincidence.

Claudio smiled back thriftily. *You've never been in love.*

You've known her a couple of months, Zane pressed. *Your feelings for her, you know what they are? They're just chemicals*, Claudio's friend said. *You fucked her. Now you think you love her.*

Zane had had an unhappy childhood. His parents didn't love each other anymore but still lived together. Claudio had heard so many stories about Zane's dad that when he finally visited the parents at their apartment he thought, *- wow, that's the father.* - Zane's father looked ordinary, with wooly knuckles and a pleasant handshake. Bald in the middle of his head, a strip of skin poking out almost obscenely. He seemed like a nice guy.

He took them out to dinner at a fancy restaurant where the French fries came in a paper cone on a metal holding tray, and told them to get anything they wanted. Claudio got the rib eye steak doused in béarnaise sauce and ate until he felt like he was consuming too much of a good thing. He'd been having that kind of luck. At the end of the night, after they all said good night, Zane turned to Claudio and said, *see what I mean?*

Not really, said Claudio. *I liked him.*

You're not very observant, remarked Zane. *Did you see how he was being? He thought that he could buy our happiness. Buy back the time he hadn't spent with me.*

If you want my honest opinion, I have no idea, said Claudio.

A man with a neat beard clasped a collar over the dog and collected him in a truck the following morning. *Will you guys give him up for adoption?* asked Zane. *I know sometimes if there are too many dogs they'll put some to sleep.*

Beats me, said the worker. The truck left.

Zane said, as though Claudio had been wondering, *we couldn't keep him. Our landlord would have killed us. It said no pets in the lease.*

How would they know?

They'd know. Plus, we can't afford it.

A dog is a lot of responsibility, agreed Claudio.

Later that day, Mathilde called Claudio on the phone, crying. *Something my brother did today reminded me of Daddy.*

Claudio was used to her summits, her debriefings and bad days. *Is everything okay?*

Nothing is going to be okay.

What did he do?

He was singing "American Pie." Tonight. We went to an open-mic night on campus. That's what we did. There were about a dozen people there, and Sawyer sang, and all of them saw me cry. Even though I definitely wasn't in the spotlight at all, I was sitting toward the back, you know how hard it is to cry quietly? I was so ashamed.

I'm sorry it happened. What made you cry? Your old man liked that song?

I'm not sure, chirped Mathilde, with adolescent inflection, *but my father had a magnificent singing voice.*

Again she was making a fuss out of a fake memory too many

degrees removed, but he nursed her. *That must hurt so much.*
With no hint of the vague indignation kneading inside him.
And then, a startling vision appeared in Claudio's mind: a dead
dog. The one he could have loved.

Will you ever leave me, Claudio?
Never.

the sawyer who was a brother

I can't believe you're in college, Mathilde said.

Sawyer had been doing well. His major was undeclared, but he liked Portuguese class. He wasn't so crazy about biology because his lab partner was an international student from Jamaica named Clifford. Clifford was handsome, long-boned, and worked on what he called *island time,* which must have been why they always finished last. Sawyer ate all his meals in the cafeteria with friends on his hall. He wrote editorials about American international policies in the school paper and played club tennis. He went to parties about twice a week and sometimes walked drunk girls home, kissing them good night on the mouth with his lips closed. He practiced kissing when he was alone, giving his knees love bites. He was going to make the dean's list.

Sawyer lived in a double with a football player named Jermaine, who was cool, and who'd made a girlfriend during orientation. *It's like you have a single!* Mathilde declared, kicking her shoes off and throwing her body on his bed in a way that many people would probably find affectionate but which Sawyer found slightly woeful.

The campus coffee shop hosted open-mic nights on Fridays. Singing in public was always a consideration in the cache of Sawyer's mind. His father had loved to sing. Sawyer thought about his father dying only sometimes. It was getting to be less and less. *I'm thinking we can catch this open mic*, Sawyer said.

How many people go? asked Mathilde.

It's a little more low-key, so I'd say about a dozen or two.

I don't know, Sawyer, said Mathilde. *It seems pretty boring. I thought you'd show me a better time.*

But you love to sing, said Sawyer. Mathilde loved to do anything with an audience. He'd bought her a karaoke machine for her birthday.

I want to meet people, said Mathilde.

There are no small audiences, just small singers, Sawyer adjusted the quote.

It'll be full of nerds.

Instead of the open-mic night, they went to a party at an off-campus house rented by football players. Jermaine was there with his girlfriend and gave Sawyer a high five, which let Sawyer feel hip. Mathilde left the room to fill their cups with beer from the keg, and Sawyer spoke from rote with several people he recognized from class or other parties. Oh god, there was Danny, six-one and smelling of biscuits, with his Earl Grey glaze in his eyes, Danny who was kind to everybody. Sawyer felt like he'd caught a cold, placing a fist to his dumpling of a Heart.

Sawyer, said Danny.

Oh and, said Sawyer, because he wasn't living in his body anymore. He was in the corner of the room, sitting crisscross applesauce, watching himself carol consonants and conjunctions to Danny. - *Suck it up, buttercup,* - he admonished himself. This was supposed to be a normal part of life.

Now he understood what people meant when they said they *needed* stiff drinks. *Necessary* was the word. Sawyer and his sister took shots, round after round, with other guys and girls. Everybody was somewhere between eighteen and twenty-two. Everybody was ready for a good time. Music and eye contact

and golden strangers. Astonishment; a collection of pedestals.
The night freckled with cold stars.

In two hours, Danny left with a girl named JJ, a psychology
major. Fussy, vanilla, and, because she was a girl, everything
that Sawyer was not. Sawyer tried not to feel too bad about it.
Time for him to check on his sister. He hadn't seen her in how
long? Twenty minutes? Two hours? He hiccupped, debauched.
He was hungry and he wanted to have sex and he wanted to go
surfing.

Have you seen a girl? Small. She looks like the girl version of me.

Finally, he found her. He found what he was letting happen, in the kitchen glutted with kids. They were laughing at
whatever was funny. Mathilde standing on a chair, giving a
monologue.

I came into this world against my mother's wishes.

He recognized this one: Miss Julie. *The most difficult and respected woman's role in show business*, she'd always said. Mathilde
was being Miss Julie in addition to this horrible production of
being herself: exposed, injured, everybody's business but her
own.

Sawyer thought about what they shared: a childhood, their
parents. For a second, he hated their parents. Even their father.
He hated them both for telling them they could be anything
they wanted to be when they grew up. It was beyond clear his
sister was just wasting her time acting. She didn't know when
to give up. Hell, she didn't even know how to give up.

We have to leave. He didn't like what he was saying, but not to
respond at all, he understood, would be catastrophic.

What the fuck, Sawyer?

Let's go, her brother said. *I'll tell you outside.*

We're not going anywhere, yelled Mathilde. Not only did
she sound histrionic, but she also managed to sound radically
old-fashioned too, with her squirty voice and overpronuncia-
tion. Like Elizabeth Taylor or an Andrews sister.

Let's go.

I was having fun.

Shut up. Shut up. A scene had been unearthed in there. And already it was something painful to relish.

But— Mathilde started crying in the middle of talking. Again? There was always something indecent about the way she cried—her tears were worth next to nothing, she expelled them so frequently.

Why are you crying? Just stop crying.

Why are you being so mean? asked Mathilde, in that worthy way of hers. She was salty, astringent, like seawater or sour cream. She was humiliating, enormous, so stupid for being his sister.

Because, said Sawyer. He signaled out to the back door, hands as commanding as an orchestra conductor's. Mathilde followed. They walked across a campus parking lot, gravel shifting and shrieking under their feet.

Telling the truth was so fucking hard. *You haven't been crying for Daddy. You've been crying for yourself.*

That's not what you were going to say, said his sister. *Just say what you have to say.*

Sawyer took a breath. - *Just get it out of the way already.* -

It's like this. Everybody in there, you know, the people you thought were listening to you? They were all laughing at you.

They weren't, Mathilde said to her slobby sneakers. She looked up again, thinking, - *they were?* -

Let's go home, said Sawyer. The walk home was all law and order and nobody said anything. Mathilde was chewing the collar on the neck of her dress. Sawyer looked at his watch, which used to be his father's. Two-thirty a.m. was a vanishing time. A time where nothing you do could ever be of good use to anyone. He said one more thing, then stopped: *I'm just trying to help you.* To teach her a lesson about what happens when you are paid too much attention.

At the dorm, Mathilde announced that she was going to take a shower. She spoke in a stung, almost haughty, tone. Sawyer made Jermaine's bed with his own sheets. She came out in a piping fog, wearing a towel. Sawyer had set his table with baby sunflowers.

You're the only college boy I've ever met who owns a vase, said Mathilde.

I love sunflowers, said Sawyer. *They're my spirit plants. When I get married, I want to walk through a field of sunflowers.*

Mathilde smiled sadly.

Both trying to salvage dignity, neither talked about the night. Instead, Sawyer asked if she recalled the time when Neil and his friends hurt him after school. *It still feels true, but distant*, said Sawyer. *I feel like I'm telling a story that isn't mine anymore.* As he said this, Sawyer tried to remember why he'd even brought this up. Because maybe it would make her feel better, reminding her of this true and harrowing story. Or at least show that he too could be at risk. Failure was a form of humility, maybe.

We suffer the same way, said Mathilde.

No, said Sawyer. *I don't think so.*

But we do, sniffed Mathilde. *We get each other.*

You have to understand: I'm not like you.

His sister quirked her chin down so her split ends touched the blanket. Whose benefit had he said that for? Mathilde's or his own?

I didn't mean it to sound like that, said Sawyer. *Look, I'm sorry.* She didn't get it. He'd only said this because, in these circumstances, indeed they couldn't be more different. Sawyer usually did everything in his power to hide his troubles. Mathilde went out of her way to *be* trouble.

Then Mathilde told Sawyer a story he'd never heard before, about how a boy in her biology class asked her out on a date as a joke. His friends had dared him to. The next day, Mathilde had found out that the friends had been six girls. Girls who doodled phrases in their binders like *boom shaka laka*, girls who wanted to know more about outer space, ineloquent girls who feared closed-mouth kisses, girls who imagined world peace. Girls like Mathilde. That was what she'd thought, anyway.

They noticed me a lot, said Mathilde. *They were good at noticing things about me that made them hate me.*

Why do you like to be noticed so much, then? asked Sawyer.

Sometimes, if something bad happens, do you ever have this craving to re-create it in a way? As though, if you could redo the bad thing, but in control, you would make it better? Mathilde closed her eyes and resisted her ballistic urge to make noise. Instead, she glimpsed out at the dorm room window in the adjacent building. It was already decorated for Christmas. A plastic pine bathed in twinkly lights. She thought, - *everything will be fine.* -

It doesn't make it go away but it makes it better, repeated Sawyer.

Some things don't get better, said Mathilde. *But you can make yourself better. You know?*

- *You don't make yourself better by acting worse*, - thought Sawyer, but this time, he didn't say anything.

OVO

After six months of dating, Mathilde and Claudio took psychedelic mushrooms with Zane. Mathilde hallucinated a dodo egg cracked from the inside, mangled feathers pushing through. Even out of her right mind, Mathilde accounted for the dodo having to be dead. Dodos were famous for being extinct. She wouldn't let this opening happen, running down six flights of stairs to a tree outside Zane's apartment and beginning to dig up Manhattan.

You have to be dead. You can't exist. Maybe back then, but not anymore.

She felt Claudio's hands on her, clammy. *Your highness*, he said, alluvial-smelling, his smile like a good-looking teacher's at a boarding school somewhere in the countryside. Girls would've tried to get him fired—that was his kind of handsome.

Help me. Please. Help me bury what shouldn't be here. Mathilde grazed her belly, embracing a Fitzgeraldian sense of sulkiness.

You're burying air. Come inside, he said. *Closer.* She was all he had, and he was all she had, and that was enough. *You're going to be okay, baby*, rubbing her ass.

Zane buzzed them back in. Claudio held Mathilde, both breathing in puny flutters. An Otis Redding record played. Zane was in the kitchen by himself, sitting on a stool, peeling figs and popping them in his mouth. He had a sunburn on his t-zone.

Every time I see you, you're eating, said Claudio.

I could easily say the same about you, amigo.

That's not true. Claudio could repudiate in an elegant way, since to his knowledge Zane had never personally seen him eat eighteen Chinatown pork buns for lunch, then starve himself for three days, etching down an estimated calorie count in his journal. Or had he? Did Claudio have a spy tracing him? He pondered, filling and offering a glass of water for Mathilde. *Drink, kid.*

Why do you guys only hang out with each other? Go mix and mingle.

Not too interested, said Claudio. When he first moved to New York, he had the feeling that he was always missing out on something. After he met Mathilde, none of that mattered. He felt bad for the old Claudio to whom it mattered—the Claudio who didn't share this pure and nesting love, who took up too much of his own time.

You have a nose bleed, Mathilde noticed about Claudio, who'd taken almost three times her amount of 'shrooms, *poor thing,* holding his hand. With his other hand, Claudio opened a half-eaten bag of chips. Instead of eating the chips, he opened and closed the chip clip like jaws.

Do I? Claudio's eyes welled. He slid the dimmer as they waddled into his bedroom. *Rest.* Mathilde closed her eyes, but Claudio distracted her. Then he oriented her, slipping a fun-size pill in her hand. Something to help her get to sleep. She wanted to take care of him, but instead he just kept taking care of her.

Who is more broken, asked Mathilde, *me or you?*

Claudio wiped Mathilde's nose, dusted with peppery freckles. Her eyelashes were like brooms. Every time he looked at her, Claudio noticed something different. *Both of us,* said Claudio.

the wedding day
(and the next day)

Claudio and Mathilde fell in love easily, and perhaps this was a result of keenness, greenness, a furious thirst. Naturally, their early, sweet-as-pie love was not the same kind they developed later in life. Within a year of dating, Claudio proposed, and Mathilde said *of course*. The fiancé and fiancée spent their evening cooking pasta, drinking Sancerre, and listening to a Ravi Shankar record. Mathilde asked what he was afraid of.

Vultures.

Mathilde said, in her therapist's voice, *they live in the desert.*

Scavengers just creep me out. Even if there's an apocalypse sometime soon, even after you think every animal, plant, and germ in the world is obliterated, I guarantee you that there's a vulture hiding somewhere under some rock, waiting to get rich off the foulest circumstances. He'll be alive, watching the end of the world, and you know what he'll think? He'll think, my lucky day. *He'll fly over the entire world and find who'd been the wealthiest guy and just pick at his Swiss watch. And he'll decide that he's not hungry anymore.*

Mathilde looked at her husband. Mr. Simone. She would be his Mrs. (He'd decided she was wife material, and how could he know? Mathilde didn't even know yet!) She couldn't get her mind past the *everyone is obliterated* part. - *Everyone will die. Everyone, already, is dying of something.* - But how could Mathilde be dying? She'd hardly had a life at all yet.

Vultures always think they need more. Claudio fixated on his fear. *They don't even remember what they have.*

Mathilde didn't want to make a big deal out of her wedding. So Claudio and Mathilde synchronized it to take place the afternoon of the last production of her play, a small production of *A Streetcar Named Desire*, set in a cramped, boggy theater in Hell's Kitchen. Mathilde played the female lead, Blanche DuBois. In the play, Blanche is raped by her sister Stella's husband, Stanley. The play's run lasted for thirty-two productions. The afternoon of the thirty-second, Claudio and Mathilde eloped at City Hall with Sawyer and Zane as witnesses. Mathilde wore a short brown Halston dress that she'd pulled out of her mother's closet the day before. It was June. The sun was stiff and saffron, pushing across the sky.

Mathilde and Claudio combined the cast party with their wedding ceremony. After, the new Mr. and Mrs. Simone went dancing until 4:00 a.m. at a burlesque-style nightclub and then to an after-hours nightclub, where they saw Patrick Swayze and where Mathilde accidentally tore her dress in half while doing lines out of the palm of her hand in the bathroom. Finally, they went to a diner facing the East River and ordered large plates of spaghetti and meatballs and talked about Cold War Soviet defectors. Mathilde kept calling Baryshnikov *Misha*, like she knew him. Cocoplum-eyed, she yawned, put her head on Claudio's shoulder. He twirled his tie and told her how soft her skin was. *Like oysters*, he said.

Is this our honeymoon? Mathilde asked.

Are you kidding? asked Claudio. He told her he'd been saving up in the past year for a trip to Europe as a surprise. They were going to see Paris, Amsterdam, and Vienna. They were going to see the opera and the Musée d'Orsay and the canals. They were going to eat snails and schnitzel and *hagelslag*.

Holy ghost, Mathilde said. *I'm lucky.*

The end of *A Streetcar Named Desire* arrives with cruel and tragic irony. In the last scene, authorities escort Blanche to a mental institution because she is unable to deal with reality. But her sister, Stella, is doing the exact same thing by not believing that her husband raped Blanche.

The morning after their wedding, Claudio called his parents to tell them the good news.

He asked if there was any way he could reach his sister, having tried earlier to call her at Pine Rest Christian Mental Health Services in Grand Rapids. Pine Rest was where Jane had been living since she was fifteen—first with juveniles and then shifting among wards like a twentysomething yuppie bouncing between studio apartments. Jane had initially been diagnosed with obsessive-compulsive disorder. Then, borderline personality disorder. And finally, schizophrenia. None of the conditions replaced the other; they veined in her all at once. Melody, harmony, and cacophony.

The administrators had said that she wasn't in the system. They couldn't tell him any more information about her whereabouts, for legal reasons. *We have to be confidential*, they'd said.

Alas, Claudio's troubling sense of culpability. He had tried every year to go back and visit her, along with visiting his parents, but now had to start saving his money for Mathilde. She was his new family. - *My wife*, - Claudio thought. How sweet this nom de plume sounded. - *My little bride. My baguette. My bluet. My coquette.* -

Your sister? She's free. His mother let out a bloodcurdling giggle. *Where were you these past six months?*

Huh? Claudio couldn't picture Jane alone, with the daily choices of eating and sleeping. There was no way. For another moment, and for the countless time, he wished he had one of those regular sisters who'd go to college, who'd love Chekhov and hang mistletoe in her room and take electives in modern dance or architecture or anatomy and physiology. Just a normal girl who'd learn how to do laundry at eighteen and who'd like to get her hair blown out at a salon. Who'd now be working in a city and go on bad dates and pay for her own electric bill. A girl who'd call her father Daddy and her mother her best friend and her brother (sometimes) kiddo.

They didn't have the funding to keep her in. They tried to put her in a halfway house, but she left.

Where is she?

Not here. I begged her to come back, but she wanted nothing to do with us. Neither of my children want anything to do with me.

Mom, I go back and visit you and Dad whenever I can. He went back during off-seasons, never during times like Christmas. It was selfish but for his own sake—and for Mathilde's. They'd spent the autumn and winter holidays with Mathilde's brother, Sawyer, exchanging earmuffs and cuff links and frames and eating at boutique restaurants with menu fonts in Garamond and the quaintest matchbooks

If you really loved us, you'd live here.

Do you know anything about where to reach her? Do you know if she's okay?

His mother gave a number. *But I never call her. All she asks for is money.*

Claudio said good-bye, jittered, dialed his sister. Jane answered on the fourth ring. *What?* She sounded winded, as though she'd been sprinting.

Jane? It's your brother. How are you? Claudio spoke kindly. He had to be chary with his phrasing or else Jane would hang up on him. He considered the necessities of the situation. Basically, he had to get her into his sight as soon as possible. Jane wasn't safe. She was free, and he had to save her from being free.

I'm okay. I'm with my boyfriend. There was something so tragic about the likelihood of Jane having a boyfriend.

Who's the boyfriend? Claudio felt his muscles smoggy and syncopated, his liminal impulses hating this man before he would know his name.

I've had a lot out here. But this one's the last one. He's the real deal. A grand slam! His name is Otis. Sit on a potato pan, Otis, she sang.

Where are you now? Claudio asked. He thought, but didn't say, - *I'll come and get you.* -

America. The beautiful.

Can you be a little more specific?

New Orleans. Jane pronounced it with a phony Creole accent, *Narlins,* a counterfeit native.

That's quite a ways.

You feel closer through the phone, she said, metaphorically or crazily.

I was thinking, do you want to come visit me in New York? Claudio thought about telling her that he had just gotten married but didn't want to overwhelm her. Besides, he didn't really feel married yet. Things were more or less the same. *We just set up our apartment. You'd like it. It's charming.*

Charming *means small, my dear,* said Jane.

- *Where does she have it in her to be snobby?* - Claudio wondered. - *What entitled her?* -

We have a guest room. We'll stock it with wooden hangers and flowers, said Claudio. *Magazines. A good reading light.*

I don't know, Jane's voice ricocheted. *Maybe.* She sounded like she had a cloud in her throat. Maybe she was eating yogurt, Claudio hoped.

Well, I already bought you a ticket, and I don't want it to have to go to waste.

I can't fly, said Jane.

Why not?

I need my boyfriend's permission.

Why's that?

Stop asking me questions, you crazy poo poo, said Jane. *Take a hike.*

Blanche DuBois's last line in *A Streetcar Named Desire* is *I've always depended on the kindness of strangers.*

the jane who was a sister

When Claudio was eleven, he snooped through his sister's drawers. He had nothing in mind he was looking for, was only curious about the person his sister was turning into.

What are you doing? Leave right now, said Jane, whose face and head smelled like anointed pomade, who'd recently gained about twenty pounds in her chest and hips. On the school bus that year, some guys made slurping noises to her, like faucets, and Claudio pretended not to hear them. It was the same deal for the nights when Jane would sound like she had a runny nose—there was no way she could've had a cold every night and be cured the next morning. With all the tulip-shaped Kleenex in her wastebasket. With her eyelids like pudding.

For some reason Jane didn't talk to him anymore; Claudio felt like he had made a mistake by growing up. Maybe he'd grown in a wicked direction or matured in a brusque way that convinced her not to like him. They were no longer a team, which both troubled and thrilled Claudio. It was only exciting because now a stranger (at best, an acquaintance) lived in his house. He knew a woman restricted and always a few feet away. The body shouldn't have belonged to Jane. She didn't know what to do with it anyway.

Two weeks before, Claudio's family went on vacation for the first and only time, to Las Vegas. They drove across the country in their father's Chevy Chevette hatchback, all of them fretting over the car's probability to crumple like crepe paper.

Eight dollars a night for their motel and they were greeted upon their arrival by two used towels in the bathroom, a drain clogged with ruffled hairs, and a muggy lock that wouldn't open for eight minutes. On the penultimate night, Claudio's father found dried bloodstains on the bottom of his pillow. *Some luck*, he said. *You get what you pay for, I guess.* He spoke out loud to nobody, but his son listened. His son decided they were a family who would never have the money to pay for more than disappointing things, that they were a helpless kind of family, and that helpless kinds of families must do whatever they could do not to get help but to also not need help.

Something had happened on their last day of vacation. It was hard to remember everything. Claudio and Jane were swimming in the motel pool; their parents were at the casino. Claudio and Jane were playing Marco Polo. The lifeguard, a teenage girl looking somehow *off*, was talking to a teenage boy on vacation with blanched blond hair and a contoured chest.

Marco, said Jane, splashing frequently, as though since she couldn't see, nobody could see her either. Pealing and untranquil. Her skin raw and creamy.

Polo, said Claudio. He'd never learned to swim the official way, with the backstroke and the butterfly and lifeguards who handed out the cards with the Red Cross on them when you moved up a level. The fastest way he moved about the water was a kind of side-scissor stroke, with his hands pushing very close to his body, like flippers. *The Claudio stroke*, he called it.

Who was that in the shallow end? Older than the lifeguards, but younger than, say, Claudio's father. Claudio remembered his beer gut and tiny square sunglasses and a tattoo on his arm of what looked like a swing.

The man had spoken first, hadn't he? Laughed messily, asking Claudio if he could ask his sister a question. Claudio remembered how he'd asked permission. He remembered how Jane opened her eyes. Claudio also remembered secretly hoping for something dangerous but not too dangerous.

That man looked funny walking in the water, mannequin-posture, sending symphonies of scrambled water to the pool's surface. But what had he done? Whispered in his sister's ear? Did he even ask her his question? His back obstructed Claudio from seeing what was going on, like his body was a vanishing point. Claudio, treading water, waiting for the moment to be over.

What happened next was easier to recall: the man, wrapping a motel towel around his waist, striding up the pool's steps. The lifeguard laughing at something the boy on vacation with no hair on his chest said.

What happened? Now Claudio felt allowed to be brave. There was nothing dangerous around.

Jane weeping. What was she saying? Claudio couldn't hear her, just remembered her shoulders popping in and out of the water. Shoulders cushy as scallops.

Claudio's nipples stood up. He didn't like his body, thought it too skinny. *What did he do?*

Jane said something, and his ears were clogged with chlorine. Claudio, whose eyes seared when he opened them underwater. Jane, who'd been wearing a bikini for the first time.

Claudio and Jane shared an eye color, a well of dark blue. Eyes that vitrified over. Borealis-eyes. Claudio suddenly saw two holes in her face. Jane had a mouth, and she had teeth, and she had a nose and skin, and she had holes that held her eyes, and she was crying. The eyeholes were leaking. Jane had a face and she had a body. She had a brain and a face and a soul and an embarrassing body. Claudio had eyes, and he was seeing her body. That bikini she was wearing was terrible. *Why didn't you help me?* she asked.

I couldn't see, said Claudio. He thought about his blind spot:

really just a collection of nerves and optic traffic. His father always griped about his own while driving. *He was in my blind spot. It wasn't my fault I did what I did*, he would say.

I'm so sorry. What can I do?

What can you do? Jane asked her brother. *Now?* Shit.

Claudio thought about the Led Zeppelin song, - *hey hey, what can I do?* - He thought about the song by Neil Young, - *hey hey, my my, rock and roll will never die.* - He thought about the Bob Seger song, - *I like that old time rock and roll. The kinda music just soothes the soul.* - He thought about the Sam & Dave song, - *I'm a soul man.* - He thought of the Bob Dylan song, - *hey Mr. Tambourine Man play a song for me, I'm not sleepy and there is no place I'm going to.* - He thought of the Monkees song, - *cheer up Sleepy Jean, oh what can it mean to a daydream believer and a home-coming queen.* - He could keep asking her questions. That was something he could do, he guessed, after not having even gone through the mechanical semblance of pretending to save her.

What did he say to you?

Jane teared more quietly. She looked soft and babyish, like a toy. - *Dolly,* - Claudio thought.

They headed back to the motel room, as muffled as the dead. When they got back to the room, Jane sat on the cold floor. She placed her elbows on her thighs and her head facedown on her wrists, facing outward, as though they were about to accept a gift. Her horrible hands were in the shape of caves with small openings. She shifted her upper-body weight through her face, one hand to the next.

I want us to be happy, said Claudio. *We're on vacation.*

An hour later, their parents came back, a tangled nexus of unnerving smells: shrimp cocktail and gin and construction debris. They'd brought back leftover buffet rolls, which her mother had snuck into her purse. *For you*, she told her children. Claudio couldn't decide if the slippery rolls were better or worse than not getting anything at all.

Their father kept asking them the same questions, so Claudio knew he was hammered. Jane's awful body made a figure eight in bed, sideways, facing the wall.

What's wrong with your sister? Jane's father was speaking about her instead of to her. The word - *invalidation* - for some reason arrived in Claudio's brain. *Did you say something to hurt her? Look at how you've made her unhappy!*

She's resting her eyes, said Claudio. He made a shush noise, hustling air through his teeth.

How was the pool?

Fine. Fine and fun.

How deep did you go?

Twelve feet. Claudio spoke for Jane.

His father lit a cigarette. He always smoked Frenchly and ergo uncharacteristically with the rest of his cloudy-dowdy motions.

Did you win any money? Claudio asked. The smoke highlighted his father's doughy head

Claudio's father laughed. *I did, and now it isn't here anymore. But we didn't lose any either. We'll go back home the exact same as we came here. Nothing lost, nothing gained.* He turned on the TV. Twenty minutes later, he asked Claudio, *how was the pool?*

That night Claudio dreamed the afternoon in the pool. Only he was wearing a shirt and used it to strangle the psychopath. He once heard somewhere that nightmares prepare the brain for potential, but not very likely, situations of menace. Deplorably so, Claudio couldn't even console himself with thinking that the nightmare would never come true because it already had come true.

jubilee

For the rest of his life, Claudio would refer to himself as *the shirtless criminal*. He'd repeat his new name, this blueprint of a lie, in his head. *The shirtless criminal is never unhappy. He is tireless. He is never useless.* Sure, nothing bad had ever directly happened *to him*, but this said nothing about everything around him. He would be lucky to escape. He threw himself into his schoolwork, convincing himself that one day, he'd leave. He'd forget about his failure to be a hero. His failure to be a brother. His failure to be decent. - *I'll get older. I'll find money. I'll find love. Trouble won't follow me anymore, not even on vacation.* -

Later in the year, Jane entered the neighborhood beauty pageant and won, becoming Miss Teen Detroit. Their mother encouraged her, having heard of this privilege from one of their neighbors. *You can get a scholarship to college.*

I don't want to go to college, said Jane. She hadn't changed much outwardly since the incident. Except her body became more like plasma or a slug, the way she dragged it around.

What's wrong with you?

You didn't go to college, pointed out Jane.

I couldn't, said their mother. *I wasn't lucky.*

Jane and Claudio's father worked checkout in the supermarket. His favorite time of year was black cherry season. He'd bring them home by the bagful. *Those three slim weeks in*

June. Come and gone so fast was a common thing he said. With sentimental quips like that out of their father's mouth, it was easy to forget that he was an alcoholic. Their mother didn't work, claiming she wasn't able to. She got frequent headaches and stayed in bed for weeks at a time. She'd declare she once breathed in chemicals from the nearby cleaning product factory, which ruined part of her brain. *The front part*, she once clarified. *The part that solves problems.*

You can go anywhere, Jane's mother told her. *You've grown into a beautiful swan, you know. Just like the fairy tale.* Claudio found the idea mysterious, how their mother could pay attention to ideas like beauty, since she wore such tattered nightgowns in the daytime and often blew her nose into her hands.

Claudio can go anywhere, said Jane. *Let him enter the stupid pageant. Claudio's free. He can walk wherever he pleases, and nobody says anything. Nobody laughs either.*

I don't understand you, child, said their mother.

So Jane competed for Miss Teen Detroit, staying after school for rehearsals, and three months later Claudio and their parents saw her compete. The pageant was held in the Rotary Club. Jane wore a red prom dress donated by somebody's older sister and spoke about saving the whales. She'd be living in the psychiatric hospital in twenty-seven days. The day she won, the prior year's Miss Teen Detroit told her to bend down for the pointy, glimmery crown. Jane's picture in the local newspaper was about the size of a thumb. It was the last memento she put in her room before she left home for good.

It was easier for Claudio to allow himself to be sad for the picture instead of for Jane—Jane's ruddy newspapered face. He wanted nothing but to erase what she'd endured. His sister, the queen for the day. She had no idea what was coming.

the jane who was free

Jane landed in New York. Before Jane's arrival, Claudio told Mathilde all he knew about his sister's recent life. *For the past six months, she's been living on her own, which I've only known for a few days.*

Jesus Christ, said Mathilde, who hadn't yet met her sister-in-law but whose reputation preceded her. By this point Claudio had filled her in on the basics (but not Vegas, never Vegas, nothing about Vegas. What happened in Vegas stayed in Vegas, and in Claudio's horrible, horrified Heart).

Claudio told his wife the details he'd unearthed: that Pine Rest Christian Mental Health Services deinstitutionalized Jane because they'd lost funding from the government. About how first Jane lived in a group home, and then the group home classified her as stable the same month they lost their endowment. Then how Jane needed to have a social worker who would speak to Jane's parents on the phone, but six months ago Jane convinced the social worker that she could do her own laundry and support herself and function the way the rest of society did. That every couple months, Jane called her parents but mostly to ask for money.

Claudio, sleuthy, dug for more of his sister's life that week. Jane made conversations a challenge and to serve as trajectories of her desperation. Claudio told Mathilde that the only thing he knew about his sister's new life was that she had a boyfriend, whom Claudio had never met.

I know I'll hate him, he told her.

How do you know?

From the way she talks about him.

How does she talk about him?

I know Jane. Something inside her is wrecked. It turned many years ago. Now she can never make the right decision to save her life.

Mathilde was a bit anxious about meeting Jane. Claudio told her, *my family is your family. And vice versa.* This was easy for him to say. The year before, Mathilde's brother, Sawyer, had met a man named Noah at a gay bar in the East Village called Eastern Bloc. He told everyone they had fallen in love. Noah was a venture capitalist. Sawyer was a translator, transforming texts from English to Portuguese and Portuguese to English (sometimes French to English or English to French—Sawyer was trilingual). Sawyer and Noah had recently moved in together to an apartment in Chelsea. The four of them were best friends.

Claudio had woken up early to meet Jane at the Port Authority. As he opened the door to their apartment when they returned, Mathilde leaned in to hug Jane after seeing her hand sticking out. She hoped this action faked a relaxation with the state of affairs.

This is Mathilde. My wife. Mathilde discreetly gazed at her own posture in the mirror, discovering she was as stiff as a collectible figurine. She shook out her left leg, cracked her neck.

Hi, wife. Then came the soft handshake. Jane was lanky, wearing a V-shaped halter top that dropped all the way down to her belly button. At first, it appeared as though Jane had drawn all over herself, but upon closer inspection, Mathilde discovered she had tiny, very thin tattoos. An ellipsis on Jane's rib cage and the words *love me do* on her wrist. She could see some of Jane's veins, like chutes, big for her body. Right away, Mathilde knew what Claudio meant. Jane looked destroyed. It was the way she talked. Her voice was loaded, like she'd always be cognizant of the awful things happening in the world.

Long time, no see, said Jane. *In fact: forever, no see. Until now.*

How was the flight? Why did people ask that? Time didn't really count on flights. When the stewardess had come around with the beverage cart, there'd been so many options Jane felt overwhelmed. But then Jane had said, *hot chocolate, please*, which the flight didn't carry. So Jane had said, *vodka please*, and the stewardess, blond with a squelchy voice, had told her it cost six dollars. And Jane hadn't remembered the last time she'd had six dollars for longer than an hour before spending it. So Jane had said, *nothing*. That was Jane's flight.

Easy.

Jane, the most passive of bedfellows, didn't want to do much for the weekend but eat and watch movies. Mathilde suggested they watch only funny things on TV, so they watched *Airplane!* and *Monty Python and the Holy Grail*. The few times Jane laughed, she sounded as though she was getting hurt. They ordered Chinese food, and Jane ate more than half of what they ordered for the three of them. She ate mostly with her lips, like they were diligent to grab and push the food past her teeth and inside her. She grabbed a six-pack of bananas from the refrigerator and ate all the cold fruit inside.

They should call it Admiral Tso's, joked Claudio. *Or President Tso's.*

How do you eat that much and stay so thin? asked Mathilde. She knew Jane was nutty, with no prudence to her deeds, but Mathilde was so eager to please Jane that she felt like her soul had stepped out of her body and was kneeling at Jane's feet, kissing her itsy-bitsy tattoos.

I'm lucky, I guess, said Jane.

What's your favorite thing to eat?
Feelings?
- *Finding refuge in eating must run in their family,* - Mathilde thought. While food was never something Mathilde felt fearful over, she'd detected Claudio's strangeness around it almost immediately. Claudio had told her she was one of the lucky ones. *I'm always thinking about it,* he'd said. *It's not so easy for me to only eat when I'm hungry.*

Claudio asked after dinner if they wanted to go out for a drink, and Jane said she wasn't feeling up to it. *I'm tired,* she told them. She looked out their window. *New York,* she whispered, *I'm in you.*

Okay . . . in that case I think I'm going to practice some guitar, said Claudio. *Do you mind?*

Whatever, said Jane. The air conditioner belched. Jane wanted to hurt her brother because he knew how to do something that she didn't.

A serious lightning that night spasmed, split the sky, woke Mathilde up. She poked her head out of the bedroom. Jane had disappeared.

Mathilde listened closely, between the thunder's half-life. Somebody was talking. Jane's voice, insipid. Directly outside Claudio and Mathilde's apartment was a pay phone. How long had Jane been out there? She overheard Jane say, *if you can't come get me tonight, maybe you can come tomorrow,* and later, *you can't choose for the both of us.*

- *The boyfriend,* - Mathilde guessed.

Jane told her brother at the end of the weekend that she was needed back home. *Work needs me,* she explained flimsily.

What do you do? Claudio hated when people asked him that at bars and parties. His second least favorite conversational segue, next to the one he dreaded most, *where do you come from?*

I help Otis out. He's a salesman. He sells sunglasses. Business time, baby.

Is that right? Where does he sell these sunglasses?

He has a store. Otis the businessman gets things done. Bada bing, bada boom!

Whereabouts? Does he have a vendor's license? Claudio was the wrong person to lie to about owning a small business.

I didn't say that. I said he goes door-to-door, Jane corrected herself.

Claudio asked if he could speak to Otis on the phone. *No,* said Jane. *I'm not a kid.*

I never said you were.

What? You want Otis to beat the shit out of you? He has brass knuckles. More and more, Jane talked like she was arguing with somebody who wasn't there. Claudio had heard her that morning in the shower yelling nonsensical phrases like *lord, I'm all cervix and blue eyes.*

Claudio was careful not to scare his sister. *You can stay here, Jane. Stay with us. We'll help you go to school. You can work from home. You can make dinner with Mathilde. Mathilde makes good tacos. Do you like to cook?* Claudio knew nothing of his sister's adult life.

Buy me a ticket home, said Jane. *You tricked me.*

For fuck's sake, said Claudio, *won't you consider it?*

If you don't buy me a ride home, threatened Jane, *you will never hear from me again.*

So Claudio bought her a one-way ticket home with his honeymoon savings and blew the rest on checks to her whenever she called and asked. *I'm starving,* Jane would say, every few months. *I will die if I don't have money.*

- What about Otis? What about his business? - Claudio felt like asking. He didn't know what his sister was spending his money on. Food? Booze and drugs? Knickknacks? But there was nothing in him that could resist sending her money.

When he told Mathilde, she said she understood. *Family is family, and family comes first.* This was the only thing Claudio could think of that contained some dim, labyrinthine potential of helping her.

Europe can wait, said Mathilde. *We're in New York, so we can get anything from another culture here anyway.* She didn't mention how *anything* would likely arrive adulterated, like all-you-can-eat sushi.

- *god bless, god love, god help, America*, - she thought. - *And god especially help 1989 New York.* -

mathilde finds
herself pregnant

autumn 1989

*W*hat a surprise, but it's wonderful news, Claudio said.
 I hope the baby has your voice and your ass, said Mathilde.
And your everything else, said Claudio.

Family's family, and family comes first, Mathilde repeated to herself. Her unborn child would be as much family as Jane was. She thought about Jane. Jane's cracked hands, Jane's filthy hair. She thought, - *my sister, Jane.* - She shivered and disliked herself.

Illness is hereditary, the obstetrician told Mathilde after she'd asked. *Including schizophrenia. If that's what you're worried about. Typically the symptoms don't surface until adolescence.*

There's still no cure yet, right? asked Mathilde, for a blue, rhetorical laugh.

No cure exists, confirmed the obstetrician, with the saddest smile Mathilde had ever seen.

normal

Jane put herself up for sale only once, as she visited Claudio in New York for the first time, detouring before she arrived at his apartment. The man had approached her on the 6 train, so it wasn't like she was seeking it out. He wasn't so bad looking and said he'd give her three hundred dollars, which was splendid money. Much more than what she earned within weeks odd-jobbing and street-singing in New Orleans. She couldn't figure out what was wrong about what she was doing. They did it in a Burger King bathroom, so it wasn't like she felt unsafe or anything. In fact, the way he kissed her neck and eyelids, he was one of those guys who could really make a girl feel cherished, even if it was just for the night or, in their case, the half hour.

He slipped fifteen twenties into her hand the stealth way traveling businessmen did to bellboys, exhibiting his art to tipping subtly. Jane could learn it too, maybe. Maybe some other time somebody else could teach her. *Wham, bam, thank you, Jane!* What if she did this all the time? Fucked her way back to her sanity, or an identity. At least she would experience some short prosperity. (Regardless, anything she'd earn *could only be* for the time being.) After her gig, Jane stopped at the Strand Bookstore near Union Square and used some of her cash to buy a book of poetry. One of the poems was called *Normal*. It went like this:

Normal
Based on a true story.

I asked him if what we did
was normal. I was naked, taking out
my contacts, my finger in my eye. He was tying
his shoes, ready
to count miles from here
to far-away with his feet.
He kissed my cheeks and told me, *Normal.*
*Fun, and all very normal.**

Jane didn't know much about poetry. It was too bad she didn't
have the tools to deconstruct the poem, which tore her apart
from the inside out with what it did not say. All she knew was
that she didn't like the word *fun* in that poem. The whole time
in New York, and then when she went back to New Orleans,
Jane kept thinking, - *what is normal?* - And did it count as cheat-
ing on Otis if it was for work? And was it validated as work even
if she didn't have a boss?

How did people work? How could so many people find the
strength for full-time jobs? To have cubicles and their own
phone numbers and the scariest kind of success. To risk making the wrong decision by making decisions. There must have
been honorable ways to earn a living, but Jane didn't know how
to earn it or live it.

After throwing the book in a public garbage can, Jane entered a deli. She ordered a glass of water. *How much?* she asked.

It's free, said the cashier.

---

*   Language is a thing in which humans can rhyme *whore* with *floor* and
off-rhyme *sheep* with *weak*. Language is a thing I fear in which people can
explain why they cry or write poems and sometimes even still other people
do not understand why this is so.

What does free *mean?* asked Jane.

It means what you think it means, said the cashier, no time to wax economic. Jane took her water and sat on the curb, which was spackled with gum. She sipped her free water like it was a spirit. She thought. She thought, - *help.* -

The taste of the book slept on her palate. Jane wished now that she hadn't thrown it out. There had been another poem about a person who fell in love with every other person who passed by. How beautiful and awful was that? There was a story in the book, but it was less than one page, about a barn owl eating a mouse. The owl threw the mouse up, and the mouse came back, but everything had changed. The body was in thirds, still all mouse. This could not have been a good sign, but he was living, wasn't he? He was nobody to have gripes about existence. He was even still alive enough to ask the owl, *so, how was I?*

Jane lifted her body from the curb. What would her brother say if he were with her? He'd want her to be sane, like the rest of them, which was impossible. He'd also want her to be happy. Perhaps he secretly wanted her out of his life, to make it easier. What would he say? He'd probably say, *go home, Jane.*

the claudio who promised

O n a night Claudio went to Zane's house, he and Mathilde had learned that week that the baby inside Mathilde was a girl, and they had named her Natasha Maude Simone. *Promise me you'll be sober when you come home*, said Mathilde.

All of Zane's parties were the same. Soaked nights. At first, kindling a high before lunch would seem Dionysian. But after her first drink or smoke or pill, Mathilde would begin to feel like a meta-version of herself—the usual way people were smashed, a little bit more of themselves. And sometimes she felt like she became too much of herself: an excess of Mathilde filling up the room, dancing, yelling non sequiturs, emitting an unsanitary mixture of crying and laughing. The next morning, she'd always regret at least one thing that her yesterday-self did. Drunken Mathilde was the opposite of a character. Drunken Mathilde wasn't slipping into somebody else's skin, she was magnifying her own—a reckless kind of privilege.

Mathilde remembered the times she and Claudio went out and argued drunk, passing out and dreaming drunk. The nights when Claudio would sweat through the sheets. When they'd wake up, and everything would smell skunky, like wet felt. That myriad of nights when she'd let him pass out in his clothes and his shoes, to teach him the same lesson. The night after her last birthday, when she'd thrown up twice in her sleep and asked him if she would end up like Jimi Hendrix.

I'll just say hi. Zane never married and kept throwing parties like nobody was getting older. He made new friends every few years, and the new friends always happened to be in their twenties. *To be honest, there's a reason why we stopped hanging out. But I'm interested in how he's doing.*

Just promise, Mathilde lingered.

Of course I'll be sober, said Claudio. *I'm going to be a father now.*

They'd relocated to a two-bedroom on Seventy-second and Central Park West (Mathilde's family money funding the rent) but were thinking of moving to Long Island, close to the beach. Last week, for the first time, they'd heard Natasha's Heart beat through the sonogram, sounding like a pen tapping against teeth. These were the things they already knew about the fetal Natasha: she was a girl, she had a meatball-shaped skull, and she felt like a turned-on blow-dryer. Claudio predicted *she's going to be brilliant, and never lonely. Never, ever lonely.*

These days Claudio barely drank and had given up drugs. He told Mathilde that it was fine when they were younger, when they could afford to be selfish. *I trust you,* said Mathilde.

Mathilde spent her night catering to herself—crocheting a scarf and reading *Curious George* out loud. She enjoyed picture books for their simple tensions and ebbing pace. She pretended that Natasha Maude Simone could understand. She boiled a pot of herbal tea, drank the whole thing, and went to the bathroom twelve times. Her cat, Penelope, piled on her lap, pupils broad and open with moonlight.

She called Zane's apartment only once, asking to speak to Claudio and saying *hi, Kiwi,* and Claudio said *hi, Tulip,* and Mathilde heard party noises in the background, and then they kept calling each other by nicknames until she asked, *when are you coming home?* and he said, *oh, soon.*

At three-thirty in the morning, Mathilde was so stressed she ate an entire zucchini in bed. First she fried it on the stove, adding garlic and salt. She cut a mangled diadem out of newspaper and wore it as a hat. She thought wearing this in the mirror would make her happier but only said to her reflection, *I look weird fat.*

Claudio came home at five in the morning. He was lucky to have made it up the stairs, let alone home. He turned on the lights, and Mathilde covered her eyes. *Your feet are sticking out of the bed. You little creepy crawler!* said Claudio, taking off his shirt. He looked like he had gotten a haircut, and Mathilde wondered who the fuck had given him one. The rest of him looked like what dies in the winter. His arms were thin tree-skeletons, his cheeks a pair of pallor-mortis-white pumpkins.

What were you doing?

I'm not sure. The usual.

What have you done to yourself?

It won't happen again. Claudio may have been drunk, but he still could do damage control.

You broke your promise, said Mathilde, one hand cupping her belly with the baby inside her and the other hand grabbing her foot, shrouded in fuzzy sock. *You've never lied to me before.*

I promise. Never again.

You're a father. Mathilde stared into her husband's crumply hair. Was it possible that she loved him even more? Seeing him hurting their family? - *Boots, what was the very best part of your day?* - She pushed the thought aside. - *I'm just reminded that I can lose him. That's all.* -

I'm sorry. I need to sleep. I was thinking about something.

What?

My sister.

A silence, for sanctity. Jane as a subject was often taboo, depending on how honest Claudio felt like being. *Did you speak to her?*

She called me as soon as I got there. Don't even know how she got Zane's number. Claudio was not remembering how after his sister's visit he'd given her the phone numbers of every residence he could possibly be at, with fear, with hope. Jane would always be able to track Claudio down, if she pleased. *Talking about how the president keeps calling her. She couldn't even remember the president's name. She called him Grover P. Rockefeller.*

Why didn't you call me? I'm here to help you.

Nobody can help me or her.

That's not true. Claudio didn't know which of the two Mathilde was referring to, and Mathilde didn't either. Big tears hung down her face. Claudio knew he didn't deserve her. She was the type of woman who deserved to live in a villa or a fancy hotel. The kind of woman you named a star after. A quaintrelle.

Claudio snored, tossing like an imported market fish. At some point in the night Mathilde flipped her husband over as though he was a record. He whispered in his sleep, *drugs shmugs.*

Wake the fuck up, said Mathilde.

Hmph? asked Claudio.

I know you're hurt. I know it's hard. But you can't pass that hurt on to me. And you certainly can't pass it on to our daughter.

I promise you I won't do it again.

You promise? Because if you do, I'll leave. I give my word. Mathilde could leave her family. Claudio had done it and rarely looked back, except on nights like this. It was a conundrum, wasn't it? Almost funny. She'd take Natasha Maude, of course. It was a perfect name for a perfect baby. Even with the Simone. She'd keep the Simone too, because she knew that even if she had to leave him, she'd always love Claudio.

I already gave you mine, Claudio murmured into her thigh. *So you don't need to threaten me.*

Gave me what?

My word.

A few thatched hours passed: of Claudio sleeping, of Mathilde awake. At 7:00 a.m., Claudio felt the jolt of the last drug and booze traces leaving his system. He turned to his wife.

Hello, he said.

Mathilde lay fallow. Her décolletage was exquisite; her skin an otherworldly, cake-flour white. He'd never find another Mathilde. No matter how hard he'd look.

I promise you, from now on, to be of my word.

All right, said Mathilde, feeling startlingly good, the pollutive kind of catharsis obtained after crying.

And I promise you, groveled Claudio, *we will figure something out.*

You will, said Mathilde, too tired to say anything else. *You will and I'll be here. For you, and if you continue, then without you.*

Can we look at this morning? He stood up, his hand out for Mathilde. Their master bedroom had windows all over the south side, one of the reasons they chose to live there. They watched the sun rise, holding hands at each window, catching glimpses of their city's skyline from a slightly different angle each time.

claudio's debt begins

may 8, 1990

Natasha slept in Mathilde's arms. So far, an easy baby. She was what they'd created with love and what Mathilde wasn't sure she deserved. *I feel like I'm going to cry,* she kept telling Claudio, but she never did.

Claudio called his sister. He was at his shop, and his wife and daughter were at home. Now was the one time he'd have privacy. *Congratulations. You're an aunt now.*

Your wife, said Jane, *is a Jezebel.*

Claudio had prepared all week for this call. So far it was the worst thing about being a father: having to worry about people other than his daughter. *Her name is Natasha Maude. She weighs six pounds and an ounce.* She was a perfect person. The third love of his life.

She's not your baby. She's the Devil's child. A breech birth. The Devil wears a velvet jacket. Me oh my. My collar smells like okay roses. You love my belly! She spoke calmly in sentences that made a sense in no context, with the precision of a comfortable articulator. The delivery contained no panic—she could have been talking about riding a Ferris wheel or buying a scone from the bakery.

Jane, I was thinking, said Claudio. *I know somebody who wants to marry you. We've told him all about you. I think he's smitten. Would you marry him? It's my brother-in-law, Sawyer.*

Why in the world would I want to marry someone I've never met?
Jane laughed. To fill her life with somebody besides Otis? Otis,
who was hard on the eyes and harder on the hands and a force
as indispensable to her as shelter?

It's what you need.

I beg your pardon?

It's what Sawyer needs. A wife. Sawyer and he had discussed
this discreetly, for weeks in Claudio's shop. Owing a favor was
the last thing Claudio ever wanted to do, but he hadn't been able
to conjure any other options. Because Sawyer and Noah weren't
allowed to marry in New York, Sawyer offered to legally wed
Claudio's sister to get her the insurance to stay in a New York
mental hospital for as long as necessary.

Sawyer translated full-time for a publishing house, and while
the salary didn't make him particularly *wealthy* by New York
City means—his mother, after discovering he was, in her words,
one of those appalling homosexuals, had cut him off financially—he
had a lovely cafeteria plan, which could extend to any legal kin.
Claudio had gone to visit Lincoln Medical and Mental Health
Center in the Bronx and thought it was fine, a perfectly decent
home. - *It'll do.* - Walls the color of Jordan almonds and dinner
mints. Nurses growing smiles wide as lichen. A hospital for
people like Jane. - *For Jane, it'll do.* -

Mathilde can't know, agreed the two living men who most
treasured Mathilde in the world. If Mathilde knew, she'd never
let it happen, for she loved her brother just as much as Claudio
loved his sister and as much as Sawyer loved her (a cyclical love:
because Sawyer loved his sister, he would help Jane).

Mathilde had already asked her mother for the money but
had been denied. Maybe it was the cancer, which had already
had its way with about two-thirds of her mother's body, or
maybe it was the eight years as a widow that had hardened her,
made her solely focus on the luxury of dying in peace and with
status. *I don't believe in mental illness,* her mother had said. *Every-*

one these days thinks they have something or other. Nobody was in therapy when I was a girl. Why can't that boyfriend of hers take care of her? It isn't my problem, Mathilde, and neither is it yours.

There was no other way Jane could be institutionalized. Claudio and Sawyer had explored every option. *She'd need to commit a crime,* said Claudio, who had stayed up late doing research until his eyes felt like they were going to split into fifths, who'd drank coffee by the pint, feeling like he was doing more dying than living those nights. *Commit a crime in order to get committed. It's almost funny. Not ha-ha funny, but, you know, uh-oh funny.*

Funny, paralleled Sawyer.

She'd probably die before the police catch her. It was the type of girl Jane was: always in harm's way but somehow stealthy enough to escape any authorities—as though she repelled them instinctively.

One other thing you have to promise me.

Anything, breathed Claudio.

Noah can't know, said Sawyer. *Either.*

Wow, um. Claudio swallowed. *I mean, are you sure?*

I'm sure he can't know, said Sawyer. *Not if we want this to work.*

Can I ask why?

It would be worse, said Sawyer, *if I asked him to pay for her. I can't do that, you see? Not that he would ever say no. No, the trouble is, he would say yes. And I'd never be able to pay him back.*

Well, I just don't know what to say.

Trust me, said Sawyer, *it would be worse if he knew.* It had nothing to do with the sting and guilt of his mother's rejection. It had nothing to do with how hazardously persuasive Claudio was. Sawyer felt as though Noah already did too much for him. This was Sawyer's decision, and he chose with his Heart. This same Heart of his was sure that neither of their lovers should ever know the truth. This frayed Heart, faulty with reticence, a timid belief that even its most pure love came with conditions.

This makes things harder, said Claudio. *I don't want you to lie to your soul mate.*

You're lying to yours.

But this would be your marriage, argued Claudio, *not mine.*

It's a temporary solution. And besides, I already can't marry the person I want to. I might as well have a selfless marriage if I can't have an authentic one. Now only to wait for the day Sawyer's mother died or until Sawyer's real love became recognized by the state—whichever came first. Or more likely, whichever came last.

Claudio just had to convince Jane to come to New York, go through with the ceremony, and bide her time until it was time to check in. Then, hope. - *We'll know where she is all the time,* - Claudio coddled his mind. Scumbags wouldn't take advantage of her. She'd have a clean bed every night. Food with vitamins. Clean water. Half-luxuries.

On the phone, Jane said, *I'm still with Otis. I don't know how happy he'll be.*

Can I talk to Otis? Is he there?

Claudio heard a shuffle. *god!* somebody yelled, And that same somebody said *yeah?*

Is this Otis?

Who's asking? Who was this man, with his pebbly deluge of a voice, with his bewitchment over Jane? Claudio imagined a portly guy with a ponytail, one of those scuzzy alphas girls somehow go gaga over.

This is Jane's brother, Claudio. There's a man in New York who wants to marry Jane.

Sure, take her. Otis chortled. *Why not?*

- *My god,* - thought Claudio, - *he's killing her.* - This was possession, as simple as it appeared and yet as intricate as a multiplicity of toxins. Filaments of rage shook loose in Claudio, the marrow of a temper he hadn't felt in years.

Then Claudio's rationality, so suffered and industrious,

arrived. - *I can't get angry,* - he thought. - *For Jane's safety, I do what needs to be done. Get the information.* - It was such a fucking useful notion. He could have cried.

Do you live together out there? he asked.

If by live together you mean for an afternoon here and there, sure. Otis laughed.

Where's she normally? Claudio usually sent the money Jane requested to a FedEx office.

Make no mistake; your sister's a wild child. I want to say sometimes in my lap, sometimes in the sewer, but don't quote me on that.

Would you hold on a second? Claudio walked over to his desk, where he kept a baseball. He threw it through the closed window. Glass sprayed across the room—splintered, evicted versions of his face on the floors. It was the poverty of being human. If only being generous meant you could be in some amount of control!

Claudio spent seconds tucking the animal back inside himself. Then in turn he tucked himself tight inside his fear, returning to the line, asking to speak to Jane again. He told her he'd send a plane ticket to the FedEx center, hanging up before his sister could say *no* or *stop* or the very worst, *please.*

He sloppily dialed the house number of his brother-in-law. A lower voice answered. Noah.

Claudio hung up. - *That was stupid,* - he thought. He called Mathilde.

I miss you, he told his wife, suddenly stricken with guilt. He'd never kept a secret from her before. Why was it that sometimes the only way to save people involved deception? A removal of truth, an amputation of freedom. Slanting them into chumps.

When he and Jane were children, they once identified the clouds in the sky with nationalities. *These are the French clouds,* Jane had said. *And these are the Zimbabwean clouds and Flemish clouds and the Japanese clouds and the Australian clouds.* They were listening to *The White Album,* making snorting sounds, sweet glossolalia, as Claudio dropped the needle. *Have you seen the little piggies, crawling in the dirt?* The record was so loud, it sounded drunk. The sky bluer than their eyes. Four eyes, opening and shutting themselves, two at a time. Every sound leaving Claudio and Jane left a fracture.

    What have you done? You've made a fool of everyone.

underling

As an adult, the most difficult thing Jane ever had to do was walk a dog.

She was twenty-four, living (funnily) in New Orleans. It was a December morning, and the air felt sticky, like there was flour in it. The sun was a bitter orange, bordered by flocks of clouds. She was wearing her bra and eating Cheerios with milk while watching the local news, which told her all about the people who died yesterday, by accident or because they weren't the right religion or through complicated situations where they didn't have a lot of money.

Yesterday, President Reagan called her and told her that Claudio was waiting for her in New York, by the Forty-sixth Bliss Street Station in Sunnyside. She told him to *forget about it*, and *so long*. Ten minutes later she wished she had the number to call him back, because it was rude to hang up on the president. Jane made many mistakes. This was her girlish life: terrifying.

Her cuckoo started singing. Twelve o'clock. Like it was practicing its scales. *La la LA la la*. Maybe the president would call back at one o'clock if Claudio was still there, or another o'clock. Jane promised herself that she'd pick up next time during any of the o'clocks, even the inconvenient, witching ones. She found a chunky woolen blanket in the closet. Jane loved covering herself, even in summer. She curled under the wimpled blanket and felt home, wherever that was. When nobody else was there, Jane was the master of her house.

Find the difference between your world and everyone else's world, they'd told her at Pine Rest, but it didn't seem fair that everyone else shared the same world. It was like a language everyone except her was fluent in.

Otis made her life both easier and more complicated. She could have been his pet or his paper clip. He ordered her food and told her when to shower. He'd been able to tell as soon as he met her that she'd grown up out of order.

Claudio was able to fix himself, but he was different. Weaker people changed him, because he had to protect them. He was so lucky to have a little girl. *Natasha Maude,* he called her. If Jane had daughters, she already knew what she would name them: Joan and Juliet. They'd have her eyes and sense of humor. Maybe as a mom Jane could learn to be mature in other ways, do things like eat sushi or own a home.

What are you more afraid of, growing up or getting up? Claudio had asked her the last time they spoke on the phone. It'd been the note he wanted to end their conversation on, the self-righteous avowal to once again place the blame off himself. She'd said, *I'm only afraid of scumbags like you,* and hung up on him.

It hadn't been the truth—Jane was scared of a lot of things—but she had her pride. And the thing with pride was, sometimes it made you lie. And the other thing about pride was, sometimes it felt good to lose it for a while.

Last week Claudio had told her, *you decide how much respect you deserve.* Didn't he know by now how much she hated deciding things? Fuck her brother. Jane had respected him more before he and the rest of their family left her in the hospital, back when she'd been just a kid. But it seemed like everyone left Jane, or would leave Jane, unless she gave whoever complete management over her.

Otis also made her drink. He'd taken her to a party at his friend's three nights before, and Jane had asked if it was a surprise party. Otis looked at her as if she was squaring a circle. But she asked only because of her dream the night before. Everybody she'd ever known, friends of Otis's and kids from childhood and people from Pine Rest, threw her a surprise party, with free dumplings and free cookies and free bagels and lox shipped special delivery, straight from New York. Jane wore a free purple leotard. There was a free cake covered in peppermints that read, in fondant, HAPPY BIRTHDAY TO THE BEAUTIFUL JANE, FROM THE PEOPLE WHO CARE DEEPLY ABOUT YOU. It had been so nice to dream. So nice to imagine being worth a party. - *There are dreams out there for everyone*, - Jane soothed herself upon waking. Dreaming was a more finished version of hoping.

Be loose, Otis'd ordered, placing the cup in her hand. She didn't think she had more than one but then again couldn't remember a thing past the DJ having long blond hair. *Play "Here I Go Again on My Own*," Jane had said. When he'd told her he didn't have that song, she'd said, *but you look like the type of person who would like that song!* Then, the icy blackout.

She'd woken up without her underwear in a bathtub next to Otis and his friend Darren. Nobody knew for certain what Darren did—some kind of bookie work, or loan sharking. Already Jane could feel some part of her being touched, before her eyes (which were two ransacked corners of the universe) opened. Jane saw and felt with her eyes.

Darren kissed her hello, and she shuddered, nonplussed. Was this her world or everyone else's? Usually the only difference between the two worlds was the voices, but she could feel the kiss through her teeth and even her sinuses. She was almost certain that it was happening in everyone else's world, especially when Otis woke up. Otis looked as though he saw it happening too, this calligraphy of tongues, Darren's mouth on his lady's mouth. She knew he saw it happening because he had a look on his face like he was going to murder Darren, and then murder Jane, and then he twirled a piece of Jane's hair.

He pulled down his pants and pushed her down facing Darren and moved in the way expected of him. Darren looked at them. Enthralled, like they were TV.

Hold on, said Jane. *I'm not ready yet.*

Ready? asked Otis.

If you could just give me a second, said Jane. All she needed was a second. Really.

What's that mean? asked Darren, spitting a little clot into the drain.

Jane lifted her body out of the bathtub by grabbing on to the towel rack, which had no towels. She went to the next room, somebody's bedroom with nobody in the bed, and looked at herself in the mirror. *I am living in everyone else's world*, she whispered. *This is important. These two worlds: they're perfectly aligned.* And this was a world where what was about to survive was hardly taboo. This was a world where barely anything was taboo.

Once, she had asked her brother, *if you had to lose a sense, which one would you lose?*

I'd go blind, her brother had said. *Anything but deaf. A world without music? That's not a world I'd want to live in*, said Claudio.

At least Jane's world still had music in it. That's what she would say to her brother, if she could now. That's what she'd say to Claudio.

Claudio.

- *Think of another thing*, - Jane gave herself good advice. With a Heart full of resurrected fear, she thought, - *and why not? It's just like going to the doctor.* -

Jane returned to the bathroom, after she'd decided to be at a point where she couldn't turn back. *Are you ready now?* Otis said, and there was a subtext somewhere in there she could not have understood. He kissed her. It was like the whole messy, miasmic world was in that kiss. Other people always got their way.

Please, make room. Please, said Jane. This strident request, as well as her prior brief deferral of what she was facing, had just been cosmetic, she knew with shame. Because when Otis wanted something from her, he'd always find a way of taking it.

When she sat again in the tub, she couldn't move her legs. They felt dead. She had dead legs and dead arms. Everything about her would be dead until it was over. And Jane decided she'd like how it felt, Darren watching. She'd let it come about because she had to, and the pleasure came with fearing for her life. She hoped that it was just happening in her world because she didn't know how to live in everyone else's world loving that.

Were there other people out there like Jane, people who felt born to be debased? Pleasure came so easy for Jane, and at the same time, felt so pitiful. Maybe if they had just given her a few more minutes she would have really been ready.

Jane let it happen until she said *stop.* And they stopped. Not at first, but eventually. Eventually, anything stops.

Otis left to smoke a cigarette, and Jane and Darren were left in the room. *Be careful,* Otis joked to his friend before leaving. *Women. They get attached.*

For a second Jane felt a prodding fright that Darren might try his hand at something else. What more did he have to lose?

But fear was just the unknown, Jane recognized, and she couldn't imagine anything she couldn't predict about what could happen with Darren. So she had nothing to fear. That meant nothing really worse could happen.

The whites of Darren's eyes were soft, eggnoggish. He had a bald spot and a thin, pilgrimy nose. But staring at him straight on made Jane's whole body ache. Instead of trying his hand at anything more, Darren talked. He talked in a way that made her feel like she was living her life backward. But how else was one supposed to live a life? He asked her if she was in love with Otis. *I think so*, said Jane.

Because you know, said Darren, *love only works if both people are equally happy. Or equally miserable.*

Jane used a few devastating seconds not speaking. It was tiring, withstanding words. Finally, she was able to say, *I don't know how to measure something like that.*

That was three days ago. Jane lived with this memory. The whole horrible time she'd been thinking not of Otis but of Claudio. What would he have said if he saw her, with her pants to her knees and her frieze-face of tears? Jane's Heart would have overflowed. Claudio was Jane's big brother. For better or worse.

And Jane loved Claudio. She loved him with everything she had.

Something was singing. *See how they run*, echoed the blustering monopoly of voice. Was this the record player in the kitchen? Or just her monsooned, moth-eaten world? The record player was as rusty as the Statue of Liberty, and found in the yard of the foreclosed house across the road. When they were kids, Claudio had played "Lady Madonna" on his record player. They would listen to records with their babysitter, a boy named James who was only three years older than Jane, who had a crush on her. James used to call Jane *Lolita* as a joke. You weren't supposed to use art that way.

Otis came in through the glass door that was still broken from the time he threw his fist through, after his and Jane's fight about the spider who called for Jane from the backyard. Jane kept meaning to replace the door. (How *do* you replace a door? Do you call somebody? Do you pay somebody?) Every morning Jane told Otis, *I promise I'll replace it tomorrow*, and Otis said, *if you don't, you're out of here.* Sometimes she did leave, for weeks at a time. She'd sleep in the shelter, or in the park with her pillow and sleeping bag. It was just like camping: yielding and cold in the companionable way that would keep her surviving.

A few months ago Jane had lived for a week in a coffee shop, eating its fusty yellow pastries after midnight. She hadn't even had to do anything but let the manager call her honey. His name had been Mohammed, and he thought she was adorable, liking her from a safe distance, like a minstrel. People could be so nice. He'd unlocked the bathroom for her, letting her sleep on its gluey floor, consoling: *lady, I get that you've been through some hard times*. Jane could sleep anywhere. She knew how to get by. She was an American girl, and most American girls can stay alive some way or another. *Wonder how you manage to make ends meet*.

The cuckoo clock suddenly screamed. Jane crawled under the couch, blanket beside her. She was a caterpillar, or a roly-poly bug, coiling her body in alarm.

It wasn't the clock.

Otis was home, a dog leash wrapped around his forearm. *I thought I told you last night. Leave*, said Otis, with agency and urgency, with his gargoyle brow. In one hand he held a pizza, and in the other he held a bottle in a paper bag.

Please don't kick me out again, begged Jane, devoid of her dignity in an accustomed way, this deficit seeming as commonplace to her as catching a virus.

Quite a mess you've made, Otis continued, ignoring Jane, pointing at the floor. It was true: Jane had spilled the coffee grounds, but she couldn't clean today. It was against the rules. Jane's scrupulous, ravishing rules, which she set for herself and which she followed as precisely as a Hasid on Shabbat. The doctors at Pine Rest had umbrelled her rules under *obsessive-compulsive disorder*, which had hurt Jane's feelings. Technically Jane couldn't clean until tomorrow, and then she'd be able to clean for only the number of minutes of the number of songs that was also the number of letters that the first person on TV

would say tomorrow morning, because those were the rules
Jane had set for herself, and Jane didn't alter the rules unless she
absolutely had to, because what then would even be the point
of having rules?

I'm sorry.

We have a lot of cleaning to do, now, don't we? It was scary the
way Otis said *we* when he really meant *you*, or *you* when he really
meant *I.*

Jane started crying as she talked. *Are you upset with me?*

Put that away, said Otis. Jane looked down and realized for
the first time all day she was bottomless.

Sorry. Jane was always apologizing. She placed a pot holder
over her front. She had nothing to cover the back but her hand.

What the hell kind of medicine are you strung out on? That was
another thing Otis said when he meant another thing.

Jane was good at crying in the way that got Otis to hug her
and say he was sorry for knocking her about or for kicking
her out. All she had to do was say *I love you I love you* over and
over until they believed it could be true. - *I do love Otis. I do.* -
She loved him even during the nights he brought other women
home with him, with Jane in the next room.

It was just because she was sick. If she were normal Otis
wouldn't do that. She knew he wouldn't! He was a good man,
taking care of her the way a good man should. *Find a good man*,
her mother had told her when she was fifteen. That was what
you got for listening to a mother who gave such blurry advice.

Jane's body raised slightly above the couch, embossed. *Would
you take him for a walk?* Otis was always telling her to do things
but phrasing them in the form of questions. The dog had curly
blond fur and red eyes with milky saltimbocca rims. *Cookies.*

Cookies?

What I call him, Cunt. (What he called her.)

Whose is he? Jane walked to the sink to rinse out a mucky glass
of Ovaltine. Last night Otis had woken Jane up in the middle of

the night and told her he'd kill himself if she left him. That he hadn't meant anything he'd said in the past. Then he clarified, *anything bad*, twisting their fingers together like vines.

Mona's. Otis referred to his other girlfriends as if Jane knew who they were. Even though the only thing she knew about them was the way they told Otis exactly what they wanted from him while Jane watched game shows on TV.

Sometimes animals spoke to Jane. On her strong days she'd remind herself that this happened only in her world and nobody else's. She had a little sign in every room of Otis's home to remind her. ONLY HUMANS SPEAK, she'd scrawled in block letters. ONLY HUMANS SPEAK over the sink in the kitchen and bathrooms and next to her bed in the bedroom. On her weak days, she'd force herself to look above the sink. *Only humans speak*, she'd repeat. Always a game of touch and go.

Jane had never walked a dog before. A leash lassoed around Cookies's neck. Otis bent down, held the dog so he was about an inch above the ground, then dropped him. The dog made a scuttling sound on the floor, his paws splayed out for a clumsy second. Cookies had crusty eyes, pupils as black as squid ink spaghetti. The oily smell of saliva filled the room.

I've never walked a dog before, said Jane. She felt half okay and about a third safe.

It's not rocket science, chickpea, said Otis. The last time Otis had brought an animal home, it had been a cat, and something had happened so it wasn't alive anymore. *You didn't see anything*, Otis had told Jane.

Jane could walk on her own two feet; certainly she could walk a dog. Why did they call it walking a dog anyway? You didn't walk for it. People really should call it walking *with* the dog. She'd do it for Otis. She'd do it because she loved Otis, which was the same thing as doing it because she didn't love herself.

Jane took Cookies outside, which wasn't hard. The first thing

Cookies did was stop. She yanked the leash. Cookies pushed down on the concrete with his front paws, sliding his hind legs in an almost-split. *Look at us*, she commiserated, *going nowhere.*

The next thing Cookies did was run. He ran, and Jane followed. From a distance, it appeared as though Cookies was the one guiding Jane by the leash as they ran from tree to tree, stopping in front of one. Jane gaped at the yellow piss pushing out of him. He didn't even bother to raise a leg, he just stood there. - *He's a living being,* - Jane thought. - *He pisses and shits wherever he wants, whenever. -*

She felt a searing pleasure, regretting not keeping him inside of the house. She could have locked him in there. Maybe he would've shat on the bed and in the bathtub, and if she lifted him, maybe he would've shat in the sink, right underneath the ONLY HUMANS SPEAK sign. Jane thought about how she was watching Cookies live his life, binded to her through poverty, and how she could change it. She yanked him in the opposite direction. This felt mysteriously, devastatingly good.

Back at home, Otis would have drunk himself into sightlessness. He'd want the same things he always did. What didn't he want? He'd talk dirty; make troublesome observations like *your cunt is in my hand.* He'd unwind her; she'd let some blood. But then he'd go to sleep. Jane trilled with anticipation, thinking of all of the things she could do to Cookies. *You little shit,* she said out loud. *I have you now.*

the otis who was
an indian giver

O tis heard Jane and Cookies come in through the broken back door. Taking care of another animal wasn't so hard now, was it? He heard that bitch yap meaninglessly. Then nothing.

What do you want for Christmas? he called out. Christmas was in ten days. Yesterday, when he went for cocktails in the airport bar with Jenny or Marlene, he picked up a copy of the *Sky Mall* catalog somebody had left behind in a booth. It advertised things Jane would have liked. Like a carbonation machine. Christmas was the time when people thought they needed things they didn't.

I want to leave, said Jane.

Leave? he asked.

Leave, whispered Jane.

You can't leave, said Otis. *I've tied our Hearts together.* He reached under the sofa for his needle and eyelash-size Baggie. In a minute, everything would turn to cloudscapes. And Jane leaving would be even funnier than it was now. She would never leave. And if she did, she would always come back.

she's leaving home, bye-bye

*H*ow'd you get here? asked Jane.

    Drove, said Claudio. The limo was outside. *You didn't take the flight I sent tickets for.*

I was going to, said Jane, and she really was, because the tickets were free and Jane couldn't resist what was given to her, but Otis had torn up the tickets before she could use them. This was a felony, but Jane didn't know for sure, as she'd had only a quick look at the envelope. And while it said her name, it said Otis's address. And all Jane had was a name, not an address.

Is anybody home?

Not for a few hours.

Can you pack a bag in a few minutes? he asked her, with a sense of urgency he normally reserved for less delicate emergencies.

Where are we going?

Home. He sounded like he knew where it was. Like it was more than just a place deep inside them, a place neither could bear to go.

Okay, she said, wandering into her bedroom, opening a few drawers. She didn't know what she needed or if there was anything. Her things were Otis's, and they called it sharing. She came back with Cookies.

Who's this?

He's mine, she said, kissing his head. *I take care of him.*

Make sure he goes to the bathroom before we leave, said Claudio. *I don't have the patience to stop when we're in a hurry.*

And why are we in a hurry? Are we flying?

Nope, said Claudio. *Driving. All the way back to New York.*

What's in New York?

Well, said Claudio, *like we said. You're going to get married, and then we'll be happy.*

Do you promise, Claudio?

You have my word.

And what will happen to Otis? asked Jane.

He's nobody, Claudio said. Claudio came to New Orleans to save his sister, not to make sure Otis got his, because he had integrity, and more important, he had priorities.

Well, said Jane, *good-bye then*, talking to the house. They had to keep moving.

- *It had been so easy*, - thought Claudio, - *for her to leave*. - Was this what you called justice? The simplest kind of justice? A more hopeful man than he would say that somebody was on his side that day.

Are you sure you're not forgetting anything? asked Claudio, the promise of destination in his face, plugging his keys into the ignition. The Beatles played. *Didn't anybody tell her? Didn't anybody see?* He sang along.

Sure I'm sure, said Jane. She was. She had everything she needed.

what love spares

Back in New York, Sawyer met Claudio and Jane at City Hall, holding a bouquet of slouched sunflowers. Claudio was the witness and the best man. There was no maid of honor.

Where's your wife? asked Jane.

Uh, sick, said Claudio.

Jane's eyes broadened, like she'd never considered that other people in the world besides her might ever be sick.

If you want, you can change into this. Claudio lifted a white gown out of a bag, a tawdry nebula of fabric sprouting from its hips. *It's your size, I think. It's pretty*, he said, in a hesitant way an unstylish heterosexual man would speak of the women's garments he thinks are necessary to have an opinion about.

Bernice, who smelled like vanilla Dunkaroos dip and who managed the secondhand store next door to his record shop, had given it to him a week ago. Bernice sometimes came in to hang out, and Claudio found her good, harmless company. She even looked like her name would be Bernice, with her obesity and filbert-shaped eyes and Kmart wardrobe. Claudio sometimes confided in her but protected his psychological discharges in cloaks of false conditions. For instance, he'd told her last week that his second cousin from Pensacola, Florida, was getting married but needed a wedding dress because she was basically penniless.

This one belonged to a woman who just died, Bernice had said. *Her mother brought it in,* flaunting the hanger like she was one of Bob Barker's beauties on *The Price Is Right.*

Isn't it pretty? Somebody could use this again after it's cleaned. Claudio had smirked at the plumage. Had it been a happy marriage? Had death parted them or something before?

You're doing the right thing, Claudio had said to Sawyer three minutes before the ceremony. Sawyer's eyes shimmered with mitochondrial-size bits of moisture. As if he didn't already know that!

Where the government fails, family steps in, Sawyer said to his (soon to be doubled) brother-in-law.

I'll repay you for this. I owe you. I owe Noah too, despite his having no idea.

You don't owe someone if you'd do the same thing in their place. Sawyer would do this, and then Sawyer would return to his home with Noah like it was just another regular day, like one of them had not signed on for a lifetime of supplying housing rights and employment rights and life-and-death rights to a stranger. He'd never lied to Noah before, not even about anything little.

Jane wore jeans and a windbreaker. She carried perfumes of the street, reedy and itinerant. Claudio walked his sister down the aisle. The aisle was just a space between rows of City Hall seats. They could fit only when they walked single file.

I do, said Jane. She started to feel a little bit married.

I do, said Sawyer. He thought to himself, - *I'm saving her life.* -

Oaths were taken. Sawyer kissed Jane with duty, a nonsense kiss, continuing thinking, - *I'm rescuing a family* - (in an urgent, dissociated way—the way a mother would call 9-1-1 and say *a boy is choking* instead of *my boy is choking*). Jane tasted like a cigarette.

- *What a family I have,* - thought Claudio.

man and wife

Marriage is supposed to be the happiest day of a bride's life. When Jane was the bride, it was the worst day of her life. The minute she saw Sawyer, she felt like lying down. She felt like she was at a bar where the bartender kept refilling her drink, more and more, even after she told him she was done, until her sleeves and hair stank of rum. Jane's old roommate at Pine Rest, a girl with a catalog of personalities named Lisa, Stacy, and Maisy, had once asked her, *would you rather be the only one sober or the only one drunk?* Jane hadn't known. She'd just known she didn't like being alone.

Sawyer was perfect. He was too handsome for her, too kind. A scholar. She wondered if Claudio had told Sawyer what he was in for. If he'd told him that she was crazy. Sawyer had sunflowers for her. She didn't know where he'd gotten them from or how big they'd grow or if they'd still grow despite being uprooted. She wanted to rip them apart because he deserved a woman who knew about botany and astronomy and perfumeries and other beautiful things.

When he saw Jane, Sawyer hugged her, breathing in belittling intervals into her neck. How did he love her all of a sudden? He didn't let her go until Jane pushed him. *It's enough*, said Jane, thinking she probably only existed in this world as something people felt obliged to tend to, no less paltry than an errand.

Now three people loved her. Claudio, Sawyer, and Otis. But Otis didn't love her anymore. Sawyer only just started loving her. And Claudio's attention throughout the years had been so erratic, it seemed like he loved her only when he remembered to. What about yesterday? What if nobody at all loved her yesterday?

She wanted to go back home and sit on Otis's lap, where he smacked her in a way that made her feel reprehensible in everyone else's world but roasting with bliss in her own. She wanted him to market his sunglasses or whatever it was he claimed to sell in the daytime, and she could polish herself all day while thinking about him hurting her for kicks, thumb through magazines in the backyard about celebrities, and eat M&M's microwaved for thirty-eight seconds so they were hard on the outside and melted on the inside. One time, Otis created the no-chair policy, which meant that Jane only could use his lap. How much fun had that been?

Before Claudio came for her, the day everything changed, she'd told Otis that she was marrying another man. Otis had laughed at her—one of those temperamental and elemental belly laughs.

She didn't know what to do. When he hit her or when he screwed her, she was all his: his centrifuge. But when he laughed at her, she didn't know what she was, except for maybe something that was funny. Barely something. If only Jane could be unfunny! Now that she wouldn't be around anymore, Jane wondered who would take out Otis's garbage. She'd been good at that. Otis didn't know what he was losing. Jane took out the garbage, washed dishes, and mopped his floors until they were elegant enough to be eaten off of, sometimes using her own spit to make them shinier.

As Jane married Sawyer, Otis waited outside the whole time, banging on City Hall's doors, telling Jane the minute she was married he was going to kill her. Chop her into pieces, throw her in the Dumpster. She wondered why nobody else was saying anything. Otis was so loud you could hear him from outer space! Sawyer was smiling and adjusting his tie. He looked more like a celebrity than her fiancé. Claudio kept holding her hand.

Maybe it was just happening in her world: Otis waiting patiently to take Jane outside and stab her. He had his floozies with him, all of them, twenty or sixty-eight or something, and they were all laughing at her. They laughed like wood chippers. What was so funny? Was it how disarmingly familiar she smelled? Still of the stink Otis had on her, some sly combination of bourbon and burgers and his abundance of other women.

The ceremony wasn't even half over, and Jane felt shattered tears slipping down, changing her face. *Isn't that sweet,* Claudio whispered to Sawyer, and Jane knew that in their own way, they were laughing at her too.

dues

may 26, 1992

The afternoon Sawyer married Jane, he went back to work in his own home. He was currently finishing a Brazilian medical translation. Noah had thirteen vacation days left for this year. Maybe in a month they could travel. - *Somewhere tropical*, - Sawyer hoped.

He opened the freezer and popped two *mochi* balls into his mouth. He put his jacket and shoes back on and went to the corner gourmet grocery store, buying steaks and truffle salt and imported pesto. Tonight he'd grill the meat and cook pasta, with a thin claret.

When Noah came home that evening, he hung up his coat and stripped to his boxers. He sniffed. *What did I do?*

Hm?

You never cook.

I felt like it.

You needed that much of a distraction, huh? Work's that bad?

I just wanted to do something nice. For you and me.

Noah kissed the man he loved before saying *my bird*.

The two of them read on the couch after dinner with Noah touching Sawyer's foot. Noah read *The Art Pack*. Sawyer read *A Book of Common Prayer*. Occasionally Sawyer thought spooky thoughts, squiggly thoughts.

- *He doesn't know who he's in love with.* - How was he going to get away with this? He hadn't thought this through nearly enough. Jesus, and what a time to realize it!

Noah prodded Sawyer's hip.

I have a theory about relationships.

Do you?

A couple needs only two things in common for it to work. The same sense of humor and the same moral compass. I'm right, right?

You make some sense.

A couple doesn't need a thing else in common. But if it doesn't have either of those, it can't work.

You're right, agreed Sawyer, forcing his mouth into an excruciating, phony smile. He would never be Noah's husband. Now he could be only his lover, if even that. His bottom, his plaything. His mistress.

I always am, aren't I?

part two

daughters

the simone family of five

*T*here were three daughters: *Natasha Maude, Lucille Margaret, and Carly Wednesday. Mathilde and Claudio had traveled to Shanghai to adopt Carly, after filling out paperwork for almost two years. The adoption officials told them she'd been abandoned outside a Kentucky Fried Chicken in South Shanghai, in a bassinet, with her umbilical cord and a note that said she'd been born three days earlier. Mathilde and Claudio flew home with Carly and told their daughters,* this is your little sister. *Then Mathilde said to Claudio,* everyone is finally here.

careers

Mathilde continued to audition for plays on her own, book-ending from one off-Broadway show to the next. When he wasn't working, Claudio saw every performance of hers. By the end of each run, he could recite the lines just about as well as all the characters. He bought his wife roses at the end of every show.

Once in her life, Mathilde acted on Broadway. She was in the swing ensemble for the musical *A Funny Thing Happened on the Way to the Forum* from 1996 to 1998. She guessed she was one of those people in New York who had *made it*, whatever that meant, but her time on Broadway felt too painless, commercial, too presumptuous of what producers thought people wanted to see. - *The goofiness of musical theater*, - she deduced. Milla had still been more challenging, the rhapsody of that character submitted in Mathilde, buried.

After her daughters were born, she became a talent agent to make more money, for her mother late in her life adopted even more of a Scrooge-esque philosophy on sharing her wealth. Mathilde couldn't help but think, - *it's not even your money! It's Daddy's.* -

From eight to six on Tuesdays through Sundays, not counting American holidays, Claudio worked in the same vinyl store he owned in Queens. The rest of the time he was a father.

Before fatherhood, the only item Claudio owned that he cared about besides the limo was his guitar, a vintage 1967 Gibson. He wasn't sure why it mattered. For the most part, he was lousy: his fingers clumsy, cosseting, uncallused. He liked the idea of being able to perfect a few staple songs. He played the Beatles. "Help!" was his lazy specialty.

Won't you please, please help me?

white cat blues

1996–1998

Lucy's first memory was of her sister Natasha fastening a pair of headphones on her and playing an old Dylan song. *A sky that cries and a bird that flies. A fish that walks and a dog that talks.*

These are your earmuffs. When you get scared, put them on.

Lucy was three. She called Natasha *Tashy*. Natasha called her *White Cat*.

White cats are all deaf.

But I hear!

You only hear what's important.

She was referencing the sixth member to the Simone family—Penelope. First Penelope lived in Upper Manhattan with Mathilde and Sawyer and their mother, then Penelope lived with Mathilde and Claudio back in Lower Manhattan, and finally Penelope lived with Mathilde and Claudio and their three daughters back in Upper Manhattan.

Penelope had white fur and eyes the color of key limes. Penelope purred a lot, usually whenever she was happy. Roughly, like a triumphant engine. But late in her life, she purred hard even when uncomfortable. The vet told Mathilde that for cats, purring was like smiling. How it was turbid and of the utmost difficulty, from happiness or nerves. That a person could smile even when something bad happens.

When Lucy was five, Penelope stopped eating for a week.

Mathilde took Penelope to the vet, who told her she was dying. Claudio gathered his daughters in their living room.

Penelope's sick. Already he felt convoluted.

We know that already, Daddy, said Carly. *She won't even eat her favorite cold food, the tuna, which smells like stinky hands!*

Girls, Claudio said. *I don't think she's going to get better.*

My throat hurts, said Natasha.

So we have two choices, said Claudio. *We can let the vet give her medicine to have her pass away tomorrow, where she's comfortable, or we can let her pass away on her own. And she'll be in a lot of pain until then.*

The vet will kill her? asked Lucy.

He can't help her, said Claudio. *She's an old cat. god bless her.*

Where will she be when she's dead? asked Lucy.

Well, said Claudio. - *Let's be honest,* - he thought. *We'll bury her.*

But she won't be able to breathe!

Kid, she won't need to breathe.

She'll be buried forever?

Well, said Claudio, *she'll also be everywhere. When you die, you go to the After, which is different from here.*

Another planet? The idea filled Lucy with woe and wonder.

Possibly.

Claudio, said Mathilde, sick with the tragedy of abstract answers. The more complicated the situation got, the more they'd have to fudge the truth. And why? Because they weren't too sure what the truth was. The truth, so vague in their hands.

Twinkle, twinkle, little star, hummed Carly, *how I wonder what you are! Uppa guppa world so high, like a diamond in the sky. Shine on, crazy diamond.* It wasn't unusual for Claudio's daughters to confuse rock and roll with lullabies. Their childish confusion with lexis was one of Claudio's favorite things, as a parent, to observe. The other day, Lucy accidentally said *Fourth of July* when she was trying to say *grand finale,* which just about killed him. Or how about the time Carly thought *bouncer* and *body-guard* meant the same job?

If she goes tomorrow, you can say good-bye to her, said Claudio. *Right now, she doesn't know why it hurts. She just wants the pain to be done with.*

This was the first time Lucy was introduced to death as a concept—the wild epiphany that not everybody lives forever. After the family meeting, Lucy petted her sick cat for hours until accumulating a little pile of stray, sooty hairs. She filled a Ziploc bag with the shed furs and kept them under her bed.

That sucked, Claudio later revealed to his wife. They were in the kitchen slowly sharing a package of microwave popcorn. It was past everyone's bedtime, and Mathilde's eyes were soggy and almost violet with kept tears.

There's no way to make it easy, she said.

Claudio could divide his life into before fatherhood and after fatherhood. Before he was a father, Claudio swore that there was nothing he could love more than rock and roll. And then he had his daughters, and it wasn't even that he loved them more than rock and roll. It was that they were rock and roll.

The following week, Claudio picked Penelope up in her cat carrier, which Penelope usually despised, emitting mews. This last time was easy as Penelope was too bushed to feel claustro-phobic. He asked his daughters if they wanted to say good-bye. Carly and Natasha came outside and petted her through the cage with their fingers, but Lucy kept her door locked.

I'm busy.

The week after, Lucy's class went on a field trip to Ellis Island and learned about American immigrants. *The immigrant mentality is when you save everything*, Lucy heard her teacher say in passing to a parent chaperone. - *Like me*, - Lucy thought.

Was it possible to be born with the émigré approach, always hoarding, even if you've never left home? After a few months, the bag disappeared and Lucy kept mum, ashamed to tell anyone in her family about the sentimental act of salvage she'd performed. The bag had been more private to Lucy than her underwear.

As Lucy entered the garden terrace of their apartment building that evening, she saw Penelope's grave, covered with a stone marker of two triangle carves of cat ears and the words *RIP CAT*. Her parents had buried her earlier that afternoon. Natasha had been witness, and later told Lucy that *Daddy said a prayer.*

What kind of prayer?

I don't know. It was like in another language. Like Hebrew or Latin or something.

In front of her cat's grave, Lucy had to resist the bizarre urge to dig Penelope up with her hands, to lift the remains of the cat she'd loved and let her ash her arms, secured by this issue of possession, this urge of compilation. Penelope couldn't rationalize pain. Lucy couldn't rationalize her collecting.

Lucy slept in her parents' bed that night. Carly and Natasha woke themselves up for school the next day, passing their parents' room, glimpsing the wishbone of Lucy's body in between them. Slight legs, open like a teepee. The holy trinity, this cozened parent-child-parent triangle. Lucy had a place in the middle, snuggled beyond her strength between either her parents or her two sisters. It was what she needed to survive. And it went both ways: she was her family's adhesive, its Heart, what kept it from collapsing.

the suburbs

Mathilde and Claudio's lease expired. Claudio sold his limo to a funeral home to buy a mortgage on a straightforward, simple Tudor house far out east on Long Island, in a suburban town called Babylon. *I guess we're not young anymore*, said Claudio. *Well, it was pretty fun.* They called their new house the mouse house. Claudio called Mathilde the house mouse in the mouse house. And they were happy, mostly playing their doo-wop records.

Mathilde and Claudio now commuted to their jobs, and the suburbs gave them some space they presumed they needed. It had been Claudio's decision to move to Babylon, which he admired in an unfamiliar and conceptual way, for its bluer-collar roots. He'd spent years living in New York City in the 1980s, delimited by urban losers who happened to be the loneliest people he'd ever met (cocaine, he decided, was a boring drug), and then living in the Upper West Side with what he called *charlatan yuppies*. These days, everything was getting more and more expensive. People were selling 212 telephone numbers on eBay. New York was changing, and he wasn't sure if it was for the worse or the better, though he wasn't sure if he had the patience to find out. Instead, he craved the typical unexciting family experience that Billy Joel sang about.

Boring's not bad, he'd told Mathilde. *It means nothing bad happening to your kids. It means space. Privacy. We could garden. We could set up a basketball court.* Mathilde knew he'd hoped for boys but never spoke about it (so did she, as a matter of fact, harboring that everywoman fantasy of molding a kind and brave boy from her rib). Besides, daughters mellowed him. After they adopted Carly, he said their family was finished. *Everyone is finally here,* they'd said.

They'd been living in mouse house one week, when Uncle Sawyer and Uncle Noah took the Long Island Rail Road out to warm it, where the inflections on the Long Island Rail Road amused them: *o*'s blanketed with *aw*, a parasitical sound.

Welcome home, Longuylanders, Sawyer mimicked and handed his sister a bottle of Veuve.

This is our new nest, Mathilde protested. It wasn't just a commuting place: it had insulation of its own. *Not even a real suburb,* she argued, Long Island was a community that served itself.

Home sweet home, agreed Claudio. He cloistered his lips together, looking like James Dean.

Do you like it?

Well, it's a lot less expensive, so that matters. And the schools that are free are pretty good. There are no kindergarten entrance exams.

How old are you again, pipsqueak? Noah asked Natasha over dinner.

Ten.

Thank heaven for little girls, said Sawyer. He needed daughters and sons of his own; at least three. Maybe even six or seven. *Where can I get some? I want to be a dad too.*

So you'll be the daddy and who will be the mommy? Carly asked. *And what will Uncle Noah be?*

The other daddy, said her mother. *They won't need a mommy.*

We should invent a mommy, said Lucy. *Just in case. Then we can have an aunt. Jack C., in my class, his aunt Beverly came to the planetarium with us on our class trip.*

Claudio wanted to rip himself into pieces. Her daughters didn't know they had an aunt. Claudio visited his sister every week. He kept Jane a secret. - *The more people involved, the more of a possibility for things to go wrong,* - he supposed.

Would he ever be able to tell them about Jane, and how could he explain why he'd been keeping her a secret? There'd be no pretty or okay way to say this. It was hard enough explaining why their uncles couldn't be wed.

What will the baby look like? asked Carly. *Will it be tall, like Uncle Noah? Maybe it will have brown hair, like Uncle Sawyer? Or will it have a tanner face, like me?*

Sawyer wondered if Carly would ever feel resentful of her adoption by such different-looking people. He understood the self-tension elected when one's way of being wasn't fully accepted. If he'd had his way, he'd have teenagers by now. Sawyer was a homebody and thought he'd be a decent family man. He wanted the kind of life where he and Noah would host Thanksgivings and walk a golden retriever.

Noah was six-five and the type of handsome that only got better as he aged, with white hair and a face that could salt the earth. People compared his features to the Paul Newman on tomato sauce jars. If they'd ever had kids, Sawyer would insist they use Noah's sperm. Sawyer had won the mating lottery— Sawyer with his face like a baby's, with fudgy brown eyes, a scalloped-simian nose, and cheeks like bundt pans. Noah was not a sucker for aesthetics like his partner.

Hopefully more like Uncle Noah than me. Sawyer laughed.
Why?
Your uncle Noah is much handsomer than me. Sawyer winked at the man he loved. *Everyone's going to wonder how a fella like me snagged a silver fox like him.* Noah and Sawyer, who weren't married but who shared a love as rejuvenating and percussive as a downpour.

Stop, said Noah. *You're the handsome one.* When you're in love, you believe in a version of the world, and this is all that matters to you, even if you know it's just a version.

Why is it hard to marry? Lucy asked.

It will make more sense when you're older, but not too much, Mathilde purported.

For some people, it's even harder to stay married, said Claudio, *but you never have to worry about that with me and Mommy.*

You should worry, said Carly, *because now I'm going to marry Mommy. And then I'm going to marry pizza.*

That's what I call devotion, Claudio told his family.

carly's foible

S anta Claus brought Natasha, Lucy, and Carly a pregnant Barbie doll that Christmas. The Barbie came with a hole in the stomach and a detachable belly, with space for the tiny rubber newborn. Carly grabbed the doll first. *This baby's name is Carly. And the mommy's name is Mom.*

It was the year of Carly's impulse to draw pictures of mothers giving birth, in bathtubs, wearing hospital gowns, wearing pajamas. Mothers screaming, stick figures, thought clouds, speech clouds. *It's a boy! It's a girl! Ten fingers and ten toes.* Mothers with premature babies, blaring babies. That May, she drew a stillborn baby, and her teacher asked Mathilde for a conference.

I'm concerned, the teacher told Mathilde, slide-rule jawed, showing Mathilde the art. *Ded,* Carly had scrawled, her muse's limbs covered with a burgundy cloud.

Of all my students, I worry about Carly. Her name was Miss Berry. Really! When she smiled, she crinkled her nose. Mathilde suspected it was on purpose, not something her face did organically. Miss Berry smelled like Toaster Strudel, probably bled milk and honey, and knew that she wanted to be a second-grade teacher since she was born. Mathilde wondered what Miss pristine Berry was like outside of the classroom. Did she go on roller coasters? Did she have a secret? Was she a tough customer? Did she know how fucking twee she was?

You don't need to worry about her, assured Mathilde, to which Miss Berry only nodded.

That evening Mathilde sat Carly down on her bed and asked why she drew birth.

I like the idea of it. Carly raised a shoulder up and down. *You're mad at me because I didn't come out of you.* Mathilde hugged her daughter and told her again that she was just as much a mother to her as she was to Natasha and Lucy, which of course Carly already knew.

talismans

march 31, 2004

ommy died, Sawyer told Mathilde through the phone.
The news was a lazy trauma, as neither could pinpoint
the precise moment their mother had begun dying—for the last
few years, at least, the cancer rolling through.

Oh!

Are you okay?

I'm. I'm. Mathilde felt light-headed with pity. *I'll be okay. Are you?* She'd expected his words; they'd electrocuted all the same.

I'm fine, said Sawyer. The truth was, for the past few months Sawyer had gotten used to the idea, and for the past hour he'd been thinking of all the ways his life was now easier. He would finally be able to divorce his wife, alleviate himself from his marriage. Because of money, what could have been the worst day of Sawyer's life was also the most relieving.

When Mathilde and Sawyer's father died, he left all of his money to their mother. When their mother died, she'd left the trust to her children. It was the thing to do. The decent thing.

Though Mathilde had already given up her crying for pleasure, it was clear she wouldn't be the same Mathilde for years. The beta-Mathilde had the type of depression that remained in the back of her throat, like a lodged, cashew-size pill without water. She didn't always notice it, sometimes too consumed by her daily trivia, but the grief was always there. She avoided listening to certain music and reading certain books and cooking certain foods that reminded her of her parents. Shutting off the radio when she heard Elvis or Frank Sinatra. No more movies with Jimmy Stewart. Both her parents had loved Jimmy. Her mother's death brought back her father's death, as death's quality is timeless.

When Mathilde turned sixteen, her father gave her two antique rings, one for each ring finger: a pink-gold and diamond ribbon ring, and an Italian cameo with a shell-carved silhouette. *I was waiting for the day your hands grew,* he told her. *Now you have woman hands.* Mathilde wore the rings all the time, even when she slept. Claudio's marriage proposal had thwarted Mathilde, carried the unconscious reckoning of space needed for her engagement ring and her wedding ring. She'd purchased a safe-deposit box in a vault and placed both there, hoping the space wouldn't be too cold or claustrophobic for them. She'd hoped for daughters too, to pass the rings onto.

But Mathilde's rings didn't have nerves, and Mathilde now had three daughters and two rings.

And so the insight that Mathilde would soon need to draw up a final will and testament, divide her possessions among her daughters. Every year, she planned on meeting with her lawyer, then found an excuse not to. She should have known better. Both of Mathilde's parents died of natural causes, nothing like murder or an accident, but her father died before he could retire, before he could witness the woman Mathilde became—before her soul matched her hands. Mathilde outlived her parents the way a daughter was supposed to, but this didn't make things easier.

Wealth felt marvelous. The inheritance allowed Claudio's dream to come true: he'd be able to buy his sister upper-crust health insurance for the rest of her life. Sawyer and Jane could discreetly split. Sawyer cited the mental illness, and Jane's living situation was proof, so Jane didn't have to sign anything.

Mathilde hadn't found out, nor had Noah. They knew of Jane's postconnubial whereabouts, only because at the time Claudio explained that his own father happened upon a large sum of money acquired through some illegal means—gambling? trafficking?—whose happenstance Claudio had not questioned, for he was just so thankful to acquire the sum that would ensure his sister's safety. Claudio and Sawyer had hoped it would be a story that repelled the possibility of further questions from either party, and it was indeed. *It's enough money to last us until . . . well, until you get your money,* Claudio had said, and the idea of this repulsive time arriving had distracted Mathilde in that same very way.

Jane hadn't found out either, for that matter: nobody told her she was getting a divorce. They didn't need to.

When he reached the point where he didn't have to lose sleep over income, something curved in Claudio's brain. All this money! Scary money. He didn't know how to control it, or himself. It made him feel dumber, not shrewder—like those tragic Powerball winners he'd read about in the news, who'd lose everything after a couple of years.

After spending his whole life forced to be not only concerned but also downright afraid of his economic situation, Claudio gave away his twenty-, fifty-, and hundred-dollar bills, as though he needed to remit his money to remind himself that he had it, tipping inappropriately and exorbitantly after receiving less than satisfactory service. The first time, Mathilde argued. *Why did you just tip that busboy fifty dollars? He was kind of a jerk.*

Spite spending was all Claudio could come up with.

Oh for the love of, Mathilde said, but wouldn't say who the love was of. - *You watch where you're spending Daddy's money, -* she thought.

How can I explain this? Claudio had asked himself out loud. *By giving money away to somebody I don't like, I'm showing that I'm the better person.*

He's fifty dollars richer, and we have the wrong appetizer. It was only after she'd met Claudio that Mathilde realized she barely thought about money while growing up. She wondered if this meant that her parents did a responsible or foolish job of raising her.

Claudio tried to think of another way to justify his expenditures to his wife, but this would lead him to his hopelessly dark place. Las Vegas. Jane's eyes. How Claudio wanted more than anything to give that creepy man a free flight back to wherever he came from, first-class. Claudio and Jane would laugh, feel sorry for him. *Enjoy your flight.* Then they'd fly off in their private jet. Somehow the wheels in Claudio's brain told him that giving to people also degraded them. Sponsoring somebody was the dirtiest thing he believed he could do.

(And was this not exactly what he'd done for Jane?)

seven minutes in heaven

october 31, 2005

Natasha was a French kiss for her first Halloween party. She wore a beret with a piece of crepe paper labeled HERSHEY's KISSES on it, and a black leotard with layers of aluminum foil curled over it. It wasn't like her, but it was Halloween! Her best friend, Molly, came over and they got into costume together. Molly, dressed as Swiss Miss, had braids and carried a mug of hot chocolate.

Her sisters, twelve and eleven, were sure they were too old to go trick-or-treating, but nobody their age threw Halloween parties. Lucy and Carly planned on watching *Hocus Pocus* and eating Reese's Pieces bought from CVS. *Somebody cute is going to kiss you*, predicted Lucy.

In the opening hour, Natasha played her first game of seven minutes in heaven. *Heaven* was the backyard. Ben Greenstein went fourth, and picked Natasha.

Natasha had barely even noticed Ben in school. Ben joked about everyone else's mother and made obscene gestures with his mouth and fingers during class pictures. He was a chore to be near. Once he'd gotten suspended for threatening his PSAT prep class teacher, *eat my ass*, and then had the chutzpah to contest to the principal: *I didn't say ass. I said shorts.* But the way Natasha's mind worked was that she typically noticed quiet people more than those who relished attention. It was like training yourself to hear quiet more loudly than noise.

By that point, Natasha's aluminum foil had plummeted off in angel-hair-thin layers. She was left flimsily in her dance leotard as Ben grabbed her hand by the wrist. His thumb and pointer finger overlapped. He was almost a head shorter than she.

The party got weirder. He called her *babe*. Natasha thought - *me?* - He kissed her with his blubbery, polyps-y lips. The logic didn't hold up: this first kiss felt like nothing, like bumping into somebody while taking public transportation. Any setting when touching would make her feel neither pleased nor violated.

Take off your shirt.

Pardon?

You heard me.

I'm not comfortable. And plus, I'm wearing a leotard, not a shirt. Natasha had been taught that in a situation where she wasn't comfortable, she should let people know. Though how could Ben not know? Natasha was blinking twice the amount she usually blinked. She kept brushing her sleeves, as though invisible beetles creeped on her.

Come on, said Ben. *You want to.*

Not really, Natasha said, chilly and ticklish. How could heaven be the backyard? Why was heaven so cold in October? She knew she was a bright girl, but she still had so much to understand. She wanted to learn how to enjoy winter and how to be fine with people like Ben.

Come on!

I don't feel good. Natasha always had a stomachache. At least this was what she was used to telling her parents when she was blue or humiliated. *I can't go to school today. I can't play with Lucy and Carly. My tummy hurts.* Natasha could never admit that she didn't want to do anything, just that she was physically incapable of doing it. In reality, Natasha's stomach worked quite well. She had a fabulous metabolism and digestion.

I have a stomachache.

Don't be a dyke. Ben would go back to his group of guys and hyperbolize that he'd gotten to first and a half base with Natasha, and Johnny Rivecchi would say *who?* and Ben would repeat, like her name was an exposed pipe, *Natasha Simone,* and Jake O'Malley would say *Natasha Simone? That girl always seems sad.*

Oh please. She went back inside through the sliding doors of the basement.

Molly put an arm around her best friend. *How was it?* She was wearing perfume that made her smell like a burning-down cookie factory. Underneath the sweetness, she smelled mealy-sweaty, like Band-Aids.

It was all right, said Natasha, in a grimy moment. She didn't want anyone to think she was a prude or a dyke. But what was so wrong with being gay? Uncle Sawyer and Uncle Noah were gay. - *Maybe it's different for girls,* - she thought. But the more she thought about it, the more she knew that it wasn't.

- *Am I gay?* - She'd thought she liked boys, but couldn't really picture liking anybody. Maybe she was asexual like the fungi and plants they studied in science class. Something she didn't have inside of her, the way some people didn't have internal compasses.

While the rest of her grade took turns going to heaven, Natasha watched *It's the Great Pumpkin, Charlie Brown* upstairs in the living room with a boy in her class named Raj, who'd moved last year from Sri Lanka, who hadn't wanted to play any kissing games either. Natasha sat mutely with him, waiting for her father to pick her up at eleven.

Nobody ever asked Raj about his life before America. It seemed to be about identity: Natasha's whole class, tepid with foolhardiness, convinced themselves they had nothing in common with Raj. In their eyes, they were American, and he hadn't been, so he'd never be. Even sitting next to him on the cornflake-stubbly couch, Natasha didn't expect amity.

Did Raj get homesick? Last year, Natasha went to astronomy camp for two weeks and cried into her pillow every night, making lists of all the things she missed. *Lucy's hair. Sitting on the kitchen counter eating pineapple. The sculpture of Icarus in our bathroom.* This homesickness granted her a self that she'd never grasped before, for leaving home allowed her to understand what she had. Maybe Raj was the most self-actualized person her age, with regards to his personal diaspora. Raj of all people, with his useless mother tongue, who died in a trifling way when he came to America. He may as well have been an adult.

At 10:00 p.m., Raj scratched his lip. He had cheekbones engraved in his face, a handsome nose. Natasha wanted to kiss it. So maybe she wasn't asexual. *What's Sri Lankan food like?*

Fuck off, said Raj. Two months of being ostracized at school had left him hardened and suspicious of anyone who asked him a question with a purpose other than transactional. He yawned noisily.

Why are you people so obsessed with ethnicity? he asked her.

I don't know, said Natasha.

It wasn't meant to be answered.

It isn't what you think. My family's not like everyone else's. My sister, she's from China.

I could care less.

- Did he mean to say that he couldn't care less? Maybe he does care a little. -

There wasn't any more conversation. Natasha wanted to like Raj. More important, she wanted him to like her.

Her father rang the doorbell. Natasha didn't know who he was supposed to be. He was wearing a giant furry Russian hat. He wore that hat all the time. It wasn't even a costume! Jesus. Natasha was being punished. *Let's go,* she said urgently. Her father opened her car door. After her, he gestured and walked around to the driver's side. He'd been listening to old Halloween music loudly in the car ride home—the B-52's. Everything in Natasha's life suddenly felt condescending.

Turn it off, Daddy.

Something wrong?

I hate you.

Why?

Why did you have to pick me up so late?

Isn't this the right time? Did something bad happen?

I had a stomachache.

Claudio reached into his pocket. *Tums?*

Natasha paused. She didn't know what could happen if she took medicine on a healthy stomach. *It's gone.*

With his eyes on the road, Claudio reached over to disturb Natasha's hair. She ducked.

Don't. Besides, you're going to have an accident.

Peanut, I used to drive a stretch limo all over New York City, said Claudio. *You don't need to worry about me driving.*

Accidents happen all the time, said Natasha. *That's why they're accidents.*

Lucy and Carly ran to Natasha upon her arrival with Yves Klein–blue tongues, wearing ring pops. Carly asked her, *did you kiss a person?*

Somebody, but don't ask me about him. I can't remember if he's cute.

What was he dressed as?

The Monopoly man. Actually, Ben had been dressed as a vampire, but vampires brought to mind sucking and sex and lousy YA literature. She wanted to picture Ben as a fat old man with a monocle and two giant bags of money carried over his shoulder like a tramp and his bindle.

One week after she had her first kiss, Natasha started volunteering at a retirement home, playing checkers with a nonagenarian named Roy Stern. She had to complete ten hours of community service per semester as a requirement for her middle school's National Junior Honor Society. Every few minutes Roy told Natasha that she was the prettiest girl he had ever seen.

You're so sweet!

I love you.

You have pretty hair.

Are you married?

Natasha noticed that he had a wedding ring on.

Samantha, he told her. *Fifty-two years, we were married. Cancer took her away.*

Sorry to hear, said Natasha.

Cancer schmancer, said Roy. *It's like jury duty: eventually, you can't escape it. I have it now. They say it's slow-moving, though. By the time it'll get me, I'll be dead from something else.* Sunlight through the window lay in his purling, slumbery hair, as though it could melt the white.

Oh, said Natasha. *I'm sorry?*

Pretty girls help, said Roy. *A girl as pretty as you, why, just giving me an afternoon here and there is so nice. Ain't nothing wrong with an afternoon here and there. But I'm all done with love.*

Natasha was mature for her age. A lot of girls in her grade probably would have laughed at Roy, called him a pervert behind his back or even to his face. Natasha could see in his face that he missed his wife terribly. She pardoned him: *that's really sweet.*

Roy smiled. She was close enough to smell him: a tremulous cocktail of mulch and marmalade.

Do you ever get lonely?

Once in a while. Roy breathed in a crumpled, noisy way. *Then I think about being buried with her. It's not so bad, thinking about that. We never had children. Maybe it would have made this a bit easier. I'm forgetful, and every time I think of her she gets more and more fuzzy.*

Memory can be like medicine, prophesized Natasha, though she didn't have enough of it to really know for certain.

Mine's all I have left.

Of her? asked Natasha.

Yeah, or of, you know, me.

I see, said Natasha.

There was a difficult but necessary pause, and then Roy said, *don't worry, my life wasn't bad. Even now, you know, it ain't bad.*

ethics

The year before, in her Health and Politics class, Carly par-
took in a debate on abortion and when, precisely, does a
zygote become a human? At fourteen, Carly considered herself
anti-abortion. Her lofty moralizing (and such is the way with
most didactics) had been unable to prevent itself, a part of her
Heart. Her sisters disagreed, tried to engage her in information
about a woman's right over her own body. Carly had no capacity
for this. - *Doesn't everybody have the right to exist?* -

The dilemma was, when exactly did existing happen?

Mr. Vora wrote on the board, *when does a human being, in the
stages of pregnancy, start to live?*

*You see what that is, folks? That's a free idea. I want you to think
about it, because now it's your responsibility.*

Carly's voice jumped first. *At conception.* Materializing being
as simple as cell meeting cell: this was Carly's conviction. Her
idea of life was poetic.

Her classmate, a girl named Betsey, countered, *At birth.*

Moderate suggestions were given: *When it starts to look like a
baby. After the first trimester. After the second trimester. When he
or she is wanted.*

- *Wanted*, - Carly thought.

The debate ended on a settlement before the school bell
trembled: *when the Heart begins to beat.*

the heart

L ucy had water in her right lung, was drowning in an imper-
ceptible and plaintive sort of way. Doctors at Good Samaritan Hospital Medical Center, Children's Ward, told Claudio and
Mathilde that their daughter had about nine months to live if
she didn't get a transplant donor in time. The real trouble idled
in her Heart.

In May, just six months before turning seventeen, Lucy felt
her breath reducing even during untaxing activities like opening envelopes or washing her hair. Her feet and ankles amplified to bulgy proportions. She coughed all the time, and her
belly engorged. She noticed her whirlybird pulse all the time,
hovering.

Mathilde had taken her to the family pediatrician. Lucy
loved going to the doctor. She never told anyone this. It was a
purposeless and curious infatuation, she understood on a level
one degree removed. Growing up, she'd often daydream about
her most recent checkup and her doctor's voice, making her
feel safe. She felt a similar feeling talking to technical support
operators on the phone. She loved how present they were, how
sincere they could sound. The *is there anything else I can take care
of for you, Miss Simone?* and the *you have a good weekend. You take
care now.* It could all mean something.

What mattered was the way the doctor made Lucy feel comfortable. Lucy always had to wait at least an hour in the waiting room before seeing him, because he gave patients his time. She adored how he said the word *we* even though he referred to only her body. She liked how he opened her folder, which had every detail of her medical history, and looked over it without showing her. He made her feel passive, as though her health was entirely in the hands of professionals, not anything she'd ever have to be responsible for.

Her doctor gave his minimal yet intimate salutations: *Hi, Lucy. How are we doing today?*

I think I have the flu.

After a series of EKGs and EEGs, Lucy learned that she had dilated cardiomyopathy. The doctor described her condition terribly: *I'm so sorry to say, but it can be a very serious condition where your Heart becomes weakened and enlarged. Eventually it won't be able to pump blood like it's supposed to.*

How could this have happened?

Didn't your grandfather have a Heart attack?

Yeah. I never knew him. Was he asking her to blame a putrid gene?

I also have a Heart condition, Lucy's mother intercepted. *I was diagnosed with preventricular arrhythmia when I was in my midtwenties.* This was a fairly common ailment, particularly in women, with no fix nor real danger. The average human Heart beats about 100,000 times per day, and Mathilde's Heart beat about 110,000 times, and her doctors growing up had told her not to worry about it. Mathilde had chalked it up (at the time of her diagnosis) to being in love. A harmless, hummingbird kind of disease.

It was the era before Lucy's pediatrician cast Lucy away to some specialist in the Heart of Long Island. Lucy knew her problem required a cardiologist, but a part of her felt deceived. Her cardiologist was in her fifties, with hair so red that it seemed eggplant-colored when the light grabbed it. Lucy didn't want to trust a doctor with purple hair, but she had to.

Less than a month after the diagnosis, Lucy developed a *drowsy lung*. Only she ever called it that, christening it affectionately, like a pet or a joke. The cardiologist had listened to Lucy's breathing, then put the buds in Lucy's ears. *Hear those crackles in your lungs?* In fact, the sound of Lucy's breathing eclipsed her weak pulse.

So this means . . .

Your decreased Heart function has begun to affect other parts of your body. She delivered the news in a purely expedient arpeggio—high, then low.

This was Lucy's left lung. She felt pity: a small, paper cut, hair-in-soup pain. She'd never before bothered to distinguish her lungs from each other. Lucy silently named her lungs while she listened to her doctor tell her what was wrong with her body. Blackbird was the right lung. Hermione was the left lung, the drowsy lung. And then, she named her Heart: Face.

That week she dreamed about Face more than about real faces. Face in her dreams resembled a Georgia O'Keeffe painting. Something swollen and slow. Yellow, with a melting-mashed texture, filled with quiet. Lucy reached out to touch her Heart. Tender, fleshy. A hive.

She and her sisters loved to share dreams. Carly had a chronic dream of being pregnant and going into labor, but never felt any pain. *How strange*, she'd say, *I don't feel pregnant*. The doctor would always ask her how she knew she was in labor, and she'd say because it said so on the calendar.

Lucy swore before this that she never had a recurring dream that she remembered, all of them seeming to flurry in from and out of left field. Her dreams were visionary on one day, apocalyptic on another, obvious on the third. Lucy dreamed about her nose getting bitten off, volcanoes, Jean Valjean. She dreamed about turning into Super Mario and turning into a Teenage Mutant Ninja Turtle and her sisters turning into middle-aged intellectual men with clean hands and big noses. She dreamed about loafers and owls and rotary phones.

Dreaming that week, Lucy had the body of a whale, and beached herself at dusk. Whales who beach themselves die slowly. They don't know any other way to die. Air settled down on her as the weight of her lay. Crowds came by. They called an ambulance, but what did they expect, for the ambulance to lift the many tons of her and take her to a hospital with nothing to offer whales? The ambulance slipped in anyhow, for ornamental rationale, and parked.

The cordon of humans designed an enormous garbage bag for her. A mournful welling brewed in Lucy, harmonizing with the whine of the ambulance. This was the way it happened.

She felt Face twinge as she woke up. Releasing a symphony sigh, Lucy rolled over and called out to her mother.

How's it feel? asked Mathilde.

Like it's dragging. Like an ellipsis.

You're a poet, you know that? Who else compares a Heartbeat to a piece of punctuation?

Of course I know it. I'm a poet! Lucy smiled, hijacking her mother's tone.

Mathilde's cell phone rang. She retrieved it from her pocket. *Hello?*

Who is this? asked a jumpy voice. Jane. Mathilde mouthed *somebody from work* to her daughter, then walked upstairs and shut her bedroom door to talk to her secret sister-in-law.

Mathilde put on one of her voices. She was the type of person who designated certain voices for certain people. This didn't make her bad, she rationalized, but wily. *So wonderful to hear from you. How are things?*

Things are unkind. Unkind, and dangerous.

I'm so sorry to hear that. Would talking to Claudio make you feel better?

Nothing can make me better. I have a fever and I yawn a lot and I cry and I have infections and a blubbery belly and I'm pale and I throw up and the book I'm writing is too quiet.

Mathilde looked at the phone in her hand, feeling wistfully feeble, the way a father would after walking his daughter down the aisle.

You're writing a book?

Yes, and I'd love for you to star, when it turns into a movie. Use those acting chops. Claud brags about you.

He says nice things about you too, Jane. He didn't, because worrying about a person wasn't the same as saying nice things about a person.

That night, Mathilde told Claudio that his sister thought she was writing a book. Claudio rubbed his eyes and asked his wife to repeat what she'd said. He looked puzzled, like he'd forgotten he had a sister.

She says she's writing again? I'll try to look for something next Tuesday. Tuesdays were the days Claudio visited Jane. *But I sincerely doubt it.*

She always talked about writing when I first met her. Remember that poem? Something about the body, I remember. More spooky than sexy, though.

She used to write all the time. Little things. Poems, thoughts. Not cute stuff, admitted Claudio. *Dark stuff. But that's Jane. That's just Jane.*

the mathilde who
was a mother

The next morning, Mathilde traveled to work. Her co-commuters typed on their cell phones and listened to their music through earbuds. Technology was linear, with little room for nostalgia or circularity. Nobody grieved beepers or VHS players. Life went on for everybody, including her.

Mathilde worked at Thirty-fifth and Eighth, which was unspectacular, not her New York. The New York, New York, Mathilde was wild about was the timeless kind where the Woolworth Building and the Chrysler Building poked out through the sky like elbows. Where men with coats soft as sheep walked across Grand Central Station, holding open the door. Where they still had a Gimbels. Mathilde's Manhattan had no crime, only rent-controlled apartments and a soft smell of pistachio. Her lifelong Manhattan love affair (even though she'd grown up there, even with her family's money) was a fantasy thin as tissue paper.

As she walked to Penn Station she noticed a full moon suspended above the Peep World and Sbarro buildings. A woman on the sidewalk sliced mangoes and sold them in sealed Ziploc bags. The moon and the stone fruit shone the same yellow. She thought, *the moon is my night-light*, pining irresistibly for it to shroud her, imbue her with safety. This moon, with the same face she recognized from her childhood, peered primly over a dynamic world. Mathilde remembered reading *Goodnight Moon* to baby Lucy, who'd smelled like Johnson & Johnson shampoo and milk of magnesia. With her hair swirly like pinwheels in the wind and a snoozy, sublime dream-flush on her neck. The comeliest, most tuneful, baby.

She took the Long Island Rail Road home. Familiar cadences in the recorded voice sounded. *This is the off-peak train to Babylon. This train will be making stops at Jamaica, Rockville Centre, Baldwin, Freeport, Merrick, Bellmore, Wantagh, Seaford, Massapequa, Massapequa Park, Amityville, Copiague, Lindenhurst, and Babylon.* Mathilde mouthed the stops; hers was the last. She loved trains, especially at night. Riding them felt smooth and sleepy.

From eight-thirty in the morning to seven at night, Mathilde collected headshots and arranged castings for thespians who quoted Stanislavski and Bertolt Brecht more than they spoke their original thoughts. Spending most of her day interacting with strangers, who called themselves actors, was why she usually didn't get lonely on business days.

She didn't recollect much on her youth and thought she'd wasted too much time as a girl dwelling in sadness. What had been the point? After actualizing a family, she learned how much better life could be when it was simpler. Crying gratified but also taxed amounts of her energy and time. Her sorrow detached her from everyone she knew, and she never wanted her daughters to cry. She quit completely and abruptly. There'd be no more submission to this puerile habit. She couldn't keep pandering to herself, needed to stop encouraging what had been her own essence. It was for her own good.

- I have a husband and three daughters. I have a lovely brother. We can sleep when we're tired, and eat when we're hungry. We can be warm or cold whenever we'd like to be. There's no reason to ever

be sad. - Mathilde would never have believed her own wiring could change until the day she decided to change it. And the Mathilde who was a mother wasn't needy, didn't hunt for tragedy. It seemed as though tragedy would detect her, during the portion of her life she'd decided to be hopeful.

.

the procedure

The name *Lucille Margaret Simone* was placed on the National Heart Transplant List. Lucy would move up on the list if somebody before her received a Heart from a dead donor or died of Heart failure. Somebody was always dying no matter what. This was good news.

There were ifs involved. *If* somebody in the United States was to die young, perhaps from an accident, and *if* (s)he'd been declared brain-dead with his/her body still on life support, and *if* his/her Heart remained intact, and *if* (s)he had agreed to volunteer his/her organs to be donated, and *if* the Heart was a swell match of similar tissue, then the Heart would be shipped to Good Samaritan Hospital Medical Center, Children's Ward.

The cardiologist gave Lucy a beeper, which would beep when a match was found. It could go off at any time, like a bomb or deranged person. Lucy would need to go to the hospital and wait while the doctors prepared her body to receive the new Heart from the person who died. Lucy would be put into a deep sleep with anesthesia, and the surgeon would cut through her breastbone. Lucy's blood would be circulated through a Heart-lung bypass machine to keep her blood full of oxygen during the surgery.

Lucy's old Heart would be removed. Her new Heart would be stitched into place. The Heart-lung machine would be disconnected. Blood would flow through her new Heart. Tubes would be inserted to drain air, fluid, and blood out of her chest for many days. This would allow both of her lungs to fully re-expand. For the rest of her life, Lucy would need to take anti-rejection medications in order to ensure that her body would not disallow this new piece of her.

Your body is smart, the cardiologist told Lucy. *The immune system detects something new and wants to get rid of it.*

My body isn't smart, Lucy deadpanned. *It's dumb.*

There were risks. *You could have a bad reaction to the anesthesia. You could have problems breathing during the procedure. You could bleed heavily or get an infection during the surgery. You could get a blood clot. You could have damage to your kidneys or liver or other body organs from the anti-rejection medications. You could have a Heart attack or a stroke. You could have Heart rhythm problems, or wound infections, or an increased risk for infections from the anti-rejection medications.* The cardiologist sounded like the side-effect voice-over in a medicine commercial, reciting very quickly. Lucy half-expected to see attractive, SAG-member sexagenarians playing Frisbee with dogs through the doctor's office window.

Lucy asked, *these are all possible?*

Well, not too probable, the cardiologist reassured.

Phew! Lucy laughed. Lucy loved to agree with people, no matter her turmoil inside. Playing along was one of her worst habits.

When she got home that night, Lucy wrote everything the cardiologist said to the best of her memory in her diary. *I could bleed heavily . . .* She searched Google for *what does a Heart transplant feel like?* She lost herself in Wikipedia holes. Then she reread what the cardiologist said at least twenty times. It was hard to believe the cardiologist said this. It was even harder to grasp that what she said might actually happen to her.

She looked in her bedroom mirror. Her symmetrical body and face. The idea of symmetry comforted Lucy. For instance, heaven forbid, if her parents ever lost her, they'd still have Natasha and Carly: an older daughter and a younger daughter. It didn't mean things would even out in the end, but it came close.

- Get over it, - she told herself, and closed her eyes, touching her head of glorious, fabled hair. Hair the flush of cider ale. *My hair is about eighty percent of my personality,* she used to joke, figuring she probably had ten times as much as any other girl. Carly's was thick and funerary. Natasha liked to keep hers short. *All-business,* Natasha would describe, never letting it grow past her chin.

Lucy and Natasha shared penny-size noses and heavy cheeks. They puckered their lips when they thought hard. Both had eyelashes veiling their crescending noses, blushed cornmealy shades, and gave identical looks when bothered. Their body hair grew fast, legs fuzzy after a day's neglect. Lucy and Natasha were both blessed with chests filling C-cups and asses their lewd-rude-crude classmates worshipped in a slanderous, expropriating way. Despite their curvature, Lucy and Natasha barely had fat—lanky as Giacometti sculptures. Their gay friends wrote *OK model* and *stop* on their Facebook profile pictures.

Carly's body was taut and androgynous. She needed to shave only once a week. Her whole life, Carly had been two full heads shorter than her sisters. Her security was that *short people can hide easier.*

I want to be short, Lucy sometimes said because they always wanted what the other had.

Whenever they ate alphabet soup, they'd spell out words and phrases until the soup turned the temperature of the room. One afternoon, Natasha spelled out *celluloid,* letting her twin *l*'s kiss. Carly wrote *maroon.* And Lucy assembled *CPR,* which as an acronym technically didn't count, but her sisters forgave her because she'd been hungry and most of her letters were inside her, shyly digesting. Round two was phrases. Carly spelled *blind animal.* Natasha wrote *meteorite blue.* And Lucy wrote *my perfect body.*

Perfect? Please. Carly grabbed a fingerful of her sister's hip skin. What propelled this lack of finesse: they were all skinny enough to call each other and themselves *fat* without having it be of any emotionally destructive value. These had been their problems, and they'd been so lucky.

Well, it works, doesn't it? Lucy shrugged, back when she was healthy.

brilliant natasha

august 20, 2010

The moment Mathilde was no longer able to help her daughters with math had been defining. Lucy was in sixth grade. Mathilde stared at the homework problem like it was at the bottom of a highball glass. This was beyond her. She felt pitiable in a newfangled context, like a grandparent with a smartphone.

They teach math differently these days.

Why?

Beats me. How about you show your sister? Mathilde was thankful for Natasha, who never needed any help with numbers.

So Lucy showed Natasha, and Natasha explained it in a way that was both smart and reachable to her younger sister, and Lucy aced her homework and the following test. She learned that her mother didn't know everything. But maybe Natasha did.

When she was seven Natasha asked her parents where heaven was on a map of the world. When they tried to explain how it was more of a transcendental state than a literal place, Natasha said, *I don't get it.*

Try to picture it as a state of mind, said Claudio, *instead of a place with angels sitting around and playing harps.*

Sometimes bad things happen in my head, said Natasha. *So do bad things happen, even in heaven?*

Little lovebug, I don't know, her father said, *but probably not.*

Is Janis Joplin in heaven? asked Natasha.

Um, said Claudio. *If not, it's not a heaven I want to be in.*

Maybe we can all hang out in heaven together, said Natasha. *Or if heaven's not real, then we won't exist together. And when you're dead, maybe that's kind of like hanging out.*

When you go to heaven, will I get a new daddy? asked Lucy.

No, Claudio laughed, *but hopefully it will be so far into the future that you won't need one.*

Huh? asked Carly, sideswiped.

The next year, Natasha found out from some drip in her class the truth about Santa Claus. Her parents told her yes, the presents under the tree came from Mommy and Daddy, but Saint Nicholas was once a person in history. He delivered presents to children a while ago.

So he's dead, then, yeah? asked Natasha.

He can still be real in your guys' imaginations. Claudio heard these words come out of his mouth, then cowered. Who was he, Mr. Rogers? (A grammatically incorrect Mr. Rogers.) But Saint Nicholas had been real, and probably a nice guy. Just like Jesus Christ.

Natasha said, *imagination is the most pathetic thing I have ever heard in my life!*

But Natasha did have an imagination, assiduous and ruthless, like the rest of her. There were so many things Natasha knew. String theory. Gilbert and Sullivan operettas. The Arts and Crafts movement. She could recite Greek mythology tales with detail and pathos. Nobody in high school knew the tale of Persephone and Hades better than Natasha, down to the etymology of their names and who celebrated their harvest festival in Sicily. She even knew the operations and mechanics of flying a plane. *And* she had a grade-A memory, correct and organized.

Lucy once likened her sister's memory to a filing cabinet. *One fat with papers,* she specified. Natasha loved nostalgia, inventing and playing the *remember* game.

Remember when Mom played Miss Hannigan in that off-off-off-Broadway production of Annie *and we had a crush on the boy who played the apple seller and his only line was* apples, apples, two for a nickel? *And we tried to get his autograph after the show?*

Or *remember the time during the elementary school winter chorus concert when they made us sing that song about Kwanzaa to be politically correct and that kid Jerry Lamins sang the solo and we called him Keebler because he looked like a Keebler elf?*

Or *remember that one winter when all it did was blizzard and we watched that old 1990s show* Felicity *rented from the library and during one episode Noel said,* guys, not everyone has a beeper, *and we thought he was funny for dating himself?*

In school, Natasha was eminent and discreetly discussed for being the *hot but boring girl with no life.* Nobody at school thought her looks (her squid ink hair; her structured, sensical face) fit her personality. She wasn't a cozy girl. She didn't mind being touched, even welcomed it with flattery, but didn't engage the authority of assuming such comforts with anyone else. Her sisters were contrarily physical—brushing each other's hair, leaning their heads against the other's lap or shoulder, invoking the other's synaptic summon. Carly was a self-proclaimed *hugger*, even deprecated herself: *god, I'm such a hugging whore.*

For Natasha's whole life, she'd believed herself to be the prodigal daughter, reciting the alphabet before she could walk and knowing the names of almost one hundred dinosaur species when she was five. She took enriched classes at the middle school every morning in elementary school and enriched classes at the high school every morning in middle school. Natasha was supposed to have a lush, refined future. She was supposed to ace her SATs, earn a top grade point average, go to an Ivy League school.

Natasha took the SATs twice and applied to twenty-five colleges. She got into all of them, compiling a three-ring loose-leaf binder with her acceptance letters. When she felt unhappy, she glided through the first line of each already bygone acceptance letter.

Dear Natasha, Let me congratulate you on behalf of . . . Princeton, Harvard, Yale, UPenn, Dartmouth, Amherst, Brown, MIT, UCLA, Cornell, Northwestern, University of Chicago, Columbia, Williams, Georgetown, Berkeley, Williams, Duke, Swarthmore, Boston College, Tufts, Michigan, Colgate, Lafayette, and Johns Hopkins. She knew little about them. Her family had gone on tours but the knowledge—campus traditions and dorm sizes and preference for which of the chirpy wayward-walking tour guides—pooled in her mind.

The news about Lucy arrived the month Natasha needed to place her deposit. She gave her money to Princeton because it was both exalted and close to home without being *too* close. She took out student loans, which made her feel like she must have a future if she was expected to pay them all back. And then she delayed her acceptance for the following year. This decision demanded a number of family discussions, but eventually, her family understood Natasha's apprehension.

Perhaps next year would be the year she could leave home. Now was her gap year, and for the first time, Natasha had nothing to do, nothing required of her.

Natasha put down her hairbrush to pick up a pair of her underwear. She'd been doing nothing the past half hour but brushing her hair, like a tragic Marcia Brady. This afternoon she accompanied Lucy to the hospital and met the cardiologist for the very first time, who'd raised her eyebrows at both of them and told them what pretty sisters they were. The cardiologist's voice sounded as though she was expecting them to apologize for being called pretty, for hearing words they'd heard all their lives—words that this frumpy, aubergine-haired doctor would never hear, perhaps had never heard, objectively.

The hip-huggers had phantom black lace. The tag read

STRUMPET + COQUINE CULOTTES. Lucy and Carly gave her the pair for Christmas last year. Her sisters loved fun and frivolity. Lipsticks and French macarons. But fun and frivolity weren't intuitive for Natasha, who'd never been one for underwear that served a purpose of anything other than to uncouple her ass from her pants.

The hot but socially awkward girl with no life. Natasha was still herself even when her stakes were highest, she was beginning to realize. Her inelegance continued to overpower the caring, resourceful girl she guessed she was supposed to be, whom she had hoped to be. Whenever somebody she knew mentioned death or illness, Natasha would feel her cheeks emblazon a shade of fig, something in her belly rock. - *Are they thinking of my sister? Do they know about us?* - How condescending, this small-change focus! She deserved to be in the penalty box for coping, or precipitated grieving, or whatever it was that she and her family were doing.

She brought the underwear to her bathroom sink, loosely dousing it with water. Was she supposed to wet silk? It seemed fragile, perishable.

Perish: a slipshod declaration that brought to mind cities more than humans. But people could perish too. Three years ago, Natasha had been at a classmate's house, trying to work on a project about ancient Rome. Tommy Chase instead showed her a video he'd been making on his computer.

- *What's Tommy Chase doing now?* - Natasha wondered. She pictured him nocturnal, drinking Mountain Dew and writing racist things on message boards just because he could, continuing to be that loquaciously unsteady kind of person.

A title had blinked. ULTIMATE SNUFF FILM. Before Tommy pressed play, he said *beware*. A compilation of .gif-splices of the deaths of Benito Mussolini, Saddam Hussein, Paul Johnson, Kim Sun-il, Eugene Armstrong, Jack Hensley, Kenneth Bigley took over the screen. He fast-forwarded. Natasha in a regular-motion voice told him that she knew about most of those deaths already. Even though she'd never seen them firsthand, she could recall how each one was killed or how each killed himself stringently based on her memories of history books and newspaper articles.

We all know you're smarter than everyone, Tommy piqued her, letting her look.

The picture glimmered difficultly as the camera shook, like the camera was crying. A man lay in a wooded area. Another man held something the shape of a slot-machine arm, inside of a plastic bag. Natasha watched him smash the object into the first man's face nine times. Her insides squeezed, like fruit in a blender about to be pumiced.

Another man leaned in to poke out his eyes. He stabbed him in the stomach with something sharp. Like a rotable bezel on a timepiece, the man on the ground was awake and then not awake—a tympanic twisting between conscious and unconscious.

The first man smiled at the camera. He whacked the slot-machine-shaped object one tidy, sure time. The two living men walked to a car. A lengthy road appeared not far from the wooded area. One of the men said something in another language. Russian?

Natasha thought of her own name. *Natasha* meant "birthday" in Russian.

The two men washed their hands and the object in the plastic bag that Natasha now recognized as a hammer with a water bottle. Slushes of laugher leaked through Tommy Chase's speakers. The man behind the camera laughed too.

I should be recording you right now, Tommy said to Natasha. *One of those YouTube videos where we tape your reaction to the video.*

You're so disgusting and retarded.

It's just a video. It's not like we did anything ourselves. Whatever happened, happened without us. We're just witnesses. Actually, we're not even witnesses. We're just, like, watching TV. Tommy gave an acute smile with his eyes pushed together, looking as though he was thinking hard about something that mattered to him only fleetingly, like a crossword puzzle. *People like stuff like this. It's part of human nature.*

Because people are sick, Natasha so neatly put it, showing him how she would not be afraid. Smatterings of perspiration rained down her neck. *We're all sick fucks.*

Yeah. There probably aren't even enough doctors for everyone.

- *This is almost porn,* - Natasha thought. And porn was a civil right. She wasn't naïve—every adult had some experience with porn. Like going to the bathroom or arguing: some unglamorous way of getting it out of your system. The vital difference between porn and a crime was consent. And people, most of the time, want to live.

the family who took a vacation

The Simone family vacationed out west, renting a house for a week in Wyoming. When Mathilde planned the vacation, she was delimited by her hotly compulsive neuroses: - *my daughter may die, sooner than later. This may be the last vacation we ever* - and then she'd cut herself off by forcing herself to think of Milla or Blanche DuBois or one of her other characters. - *I have a family,* - she thought. - *We're all still here.* -

Lucy, too tired to pack her wardrobe of outlandish and undigested outfits, wore Natasha's clothes: uncomplicated pants and a shirt colored a pedestrian taupe, the tint of the seat belts on the plane. They covered most of her body, letting her appear not to have a body. This was nothing beyond a decent way to dress. If she'd felt up to it, Lucy would've packed her short skirts or skinny jeans with bangle bracelets and mukluk hats. She used to tell people that her fashion inspiration was Sgt. Pepper, as in the Lonely Hearts Club Band, and that if she were a car, she'd be Isaac Hayes's 1972 gold-trimmed Cadillac El Dorado. Natasha, on the other hand, would be a practical sedan, and if she were to use a Beatles album as her style icon, she'd pick *The White Album*.

Twilight curled shyly into night on the fourth dusk of their holiday. A croissant-molded moon, which resembled an enormous disco ball stuffed with burlesque, loose stars, broke the Wyoming sky. Here, the stars dipped to sea level, fooled people into believing they were reachable, even in walking distance. The entire family was supposed to go on a hike. *I'm tired,* said Lucy. *Go without me.*

I'll stay home too, said Natasha. They sat on the porch swing, mute, moonbathing, the wind slanting its neck. - *Silence,* - Natasha thought, - *is a myth.* -

Say something.

Old people have special powers, Lucy said.

And what the h-e-double hockey sticks does that mean? Natasha picked a hangnail on her ringless ring finger, used to Lucy practicing her serious feats of non sequiturs.

When we were little, we were at Grandma's, singing some song with Carly. It was very long. We rhymed the words violet *and* triolet. *Remember how proud we were of ourselves? The song was about snails and cats who snorkel in Middle Earth. And there's this moment where we all just happened to pause, I guess because we forgot the next part of the song, and Grandma interrupts with* see, this is why I call you young people. Old people don't do stuff like that. *But she didn't mind being old. She had lived this long, good life. I mean,* Lucy's neck flushed, *she was living. Still. You know what I mean. Anyway, it was pretty cool.*

I wonder what my face would have looked like with wrinkles. Tears swam down Lucy's face, skin ecru against her cheek muscles. *Then it's Mommy and Daddy I worry about. They made me, and how could I die on them? Remember how Mom and Dad used to call the time before birth the Before, and the time after death the After? She was with me in the Before. She* was *the Before. It will just be me all alone in the After.*

Can you stop talking about this?

It will be even bigger than here. I might get lost. You might never be able to find me again.

Natasha felt Lucy's hands on her throat. They were cold as hell—antibacterial cold, supermarket cold. Her fingernails spotted with a calcium-deficient white.

Oh my god! Seriously, what is wrong with you? Natasha yanked a gripful of Lucy's bouquet of hair. Lucy's nails, Lucy's hair. They were dead but needed upkeep.

If Lucy had been well, this would have been normal. A healthy bear-cub type of healthy fight. A quick way of cinching a dilemma. A single, polar tear laid on Lucy's cheek. *I can still hurt you*, she said, terrible and sure.

carly and stephen

S tephen Edson had a face you couldn't blame for anything, a face that made sense to people. He was sixteen and famous for his premature hair: black, with tufty flecks of gray. His skin blue-white as milk, his frame unobtrusive and long, - *like*, - Carly thought, - *a bicycle.* - He chewed gingersnaps in class. An extrovert, friends with everybody and nobody at the same time.

Two Fridays ago, Carly had walked out of her sixth-period SAT prep class, crying due to something about her sister's worsening condition. Now, two weeks later, Carly couldn't even remember what it was that had gotten worse, because things were always indistinct and bad—long story short, Lucy was suffering and would never be healthy until she had surgery. Everything hazed together in Carly's Heart, like a rug with loosened weaves. *My sister's Heart*, were all the tidings Carly had been able to congregate. *It's not doing well.*

She wept this when he followed her red eyes out of class, calling, *Carly*, carefully unswaddling a white tissue like a reverse navy man with a flag at a funeral.

Thank you, said Carly. It was hard to blow your nose politely. Stephen absolved her: *people need help.*

I'm usually not so bad, said Carly. *Not so lonely.*

After school? I live on West Barrow Street, next to that veterinarian's office? Do you have any pets? I don't. Well, I used to, before

I moved here. You can always stop by whenever. Whenever you want. We can play card games or like, video games. He recited his address, and Carly entered it into her phone.

Carly felt the prickle on her body on a school night two weeks later, ordering her to leave the house and find a friend. Lucy and their parents were at the hospital again. Lucy's lung was being examined. Natasha, who'd gotten a job babysitting for a neighbor, was working.

You're here, he accredited.

You said. Carly suppressed herself from speaking more, feeling frumpy.

You're right, said Stephen. *I did say.*

He complimented her hair. Carly thanked him, then asked if anyone else was home.

My parents work until like nine or ten. I just finished dinner. He led her into his room. There were some trophies and a poster of *Dark Side of the Moon.* Stephen picked up a cassette player. *Cassettes just sound better.*

- You don't know what you're talking about, - Carly wanted to say. *My father owns a record store,* she said instead.

Dope.

Are you any good at massages?

What? asked Stephen.

My back's killing me.

You've come to the right place, said Stephen, but he wasn't any good, and after a few minutes, he turned her around and gave her a short, deep kiss. His massage had been soft and lousy, but he wasn't so bad of a kisser. Her mouth accommodated his.

What if Carly pretended her sister's situation was worse? It would have been nice for Stephen to remind her that she could be taken care of. *- Many people want other people to care for them, -* she rationalized. Though she maybe was taking it too far? Purposely placing herself in a situation in which she would need to be saved?

Want to? she asked, trying to sound charming in a croupy fashion, like the women in the movies.

What?

You know.

Nope, he said thickly.

Do you have protection? whispered Carly.

Are you serious? he asked, a sodium window-light bathing his eyes.

I don't know, said Carly.

Listen, I dig you. I don't want you to think I don't like you.

- *Everything's so easy-peasy-mac-and-cheesy in your life,* - Carly thought. She hated the moment, hated Stephen for his felicity, for probably having a healthy sister who'd have not a thing go wrong in her adorable life.

Who cared if this habitually happy sister didn't exist; she'd probably thrive in a small, expensive private college, experiment with prescription drugs or unsafe sex a couple of times, laugh it off when she was in her midtwenties with a straightforward job at a law firm and a Manhattan doorman-operated apartment. She'd probably have the same chic name as an East Side avenue—Madison. Parker. Lexie.

Binge drinking and drugs! I could have died, this sister would grieve over brunch to the man she'd later marry. They'd secrete muffled chuckles before fighting over something like whether to tip 15 or 20 percent and forgetting about the idea of living or lack thereof. But they wouldn't stop doing it. They would go on living, while Carly's sister would probably be underneath the ground, and there'd be nothing anybody could do. But right there, there were a few things that Carly could do, with Stephen. She wasn't sure if she was in the right place at the right time, but she was in *a* place at *a* time, which was a damn lot.

Stephen took his shirt off. What was that above his hip bone? Looked like a smudge. A tattoo! The word *Lux* in cursive. She lifted herself over him, one leg on each side. He steadied her and laughed from the bottom of his throat. Put a hand to her chest. Her response: a scrap of Heartbeat.

Six minutes later, Carly asked, *can you?*

Can I what? Stephen said. He picked up her tights, which were inside-out. The label read DANSKIN, GIRLS SIZE 16. Holding them made Stephen feel like he'd just beat up somebody who couldn't take care of herself.

Carly pined. They'd both seen it happen to him—this insensitive geyser. This hormonal, unconstrained boy. Her urges were, and would be, inscrutable. This hardly seemed fair. *Can you?* she repeated.

Do you want to go home? Stephen gently asked.

Okay, said Carly, the moment leaving her unsure of anything that made her happy. Still, as soon as one hour after this, she'd daydream about it, shielded with the naïve mysticism of romantically fractured recollection.

She wasn't going to tell Lucy and Natasha. Fooling around with a boy she barely knew seemed selfish. She pushed her feet into her flats, every bone in her feeling buried alive in skin and cartilage and clothes.

Outside in front of the vet's office, the leaves were flaky, cornstarchy, and the mealy-apple smell of domestic animal lay in the air. Her body felt like a rest stop bathroom. - *Am I alive?* - she thought to herself. Then: - *Am I a boy?* - Then: - *Who am I?* - And lastly: - *Run! Run! Run!* -

Carly ran sloppily home, at last reassured that her body still worked properly. A cold fog hid her, rendered her unseen. Sprinting gave her time to consider a virulent combination of thoughts. How did her mother and father fall in love? Her mother had told her that they'd met at a party. That Daddy had been nervous. Her father would have never taken advantage of an unfathomably sad girl. Maybe Stephen had been just as confused as she, but Carly was doomed to probably never meeting a guy as kind as her father. It was the worst thing about having a father who loves you that much.

She'd made a terrible mistake. Now all Carly could think about was the future. Her future self talking to somebody. - *I was immature. In some web. My sister was sick. I was all mixed up.* -

After Carly arrived home, she washed herself with a paper towel. Her soap was gingerbread-scented. - *I'm a baby,* - she thought in neither an optimistic nor a distressing way. Then she logged onto her social media accounts and found Stephen online. She looked through his profiles, trying to find a movie he liked that she hated, a book she thought was in poor taste, a reason for his being hopelessly wrong for her. She clicked through all 634 of his childish, mildly endearing photographs, trying to find an unattractive one. Stephen skiing. With braces. At camp. With a girl (??). There weren't many, but there were a couple. She saved them to her computer, labeling the folder HORRIBLE PICTURES OF STEPHEN. She didn't want to like him. She had never planned on that happening.

She clicked back to his general information. His birthday would be in fourteen days. She smiled. - *Maybe this was his birthday present.* - Her eyes trickled.

There were hard people out there, and there were the people soft as pullovers. Hard people seemed like they had power. But really, Carly knew, it was the soft people who were at an advantage. Soft people never had to pretend to be strong; people would always want to mind and nurture the soft.

Carly was the soft. Hard was impossible to defy: wishbones, violently hot baths, the unapologetic way of a monochromatic outlook. Hard was something she respected, something she'd never be. Carly, who tried to be the sister who could bear anything, was becoming the most libertine, the most colloidal. Strength and wildness were not synonymous—they could even be at odds. What else was Carly?

- *I'm not my family's color.* -

Every year, Erica Woo had been placed in Carly's class. It was the same for Joey Bates and Majustice Miller and Sloan Ludmila, the two and a half black boys in their grade. Studies showed that children performed better, academically and emotionally, when they were placed in a class with at least one other person who looked like them. Carly always pictured a faculty meeting with teachers passing around student name cards and putting them into class boxes. Racial poker. And so, it was better to group the children of color together. Had her parents known about this when they decided to love Carly, to take her into their home?

In Wyoming, everyone had been white. In Wyoming, there'd also been more cows than people. On their final day of vacation, her family had stopped at a local farm to pet and stare at these heavy, drowsy animals. One, the color of tobacco, stood wholly still. Her nose flapped open like the inside of a flower, sobbing brassy bubbles, spattering in the Heart of her face, into her mouth, her isthmus of muddy hide.

She has a cold, Lucy noted. *Poor gal.*

Doesn't matter, Carly said, *she'll be a hamburger soon*, picturing cuts of meat—prime rib or skirt steak, grinded into hamburger with some food coloring added, sickeningly pretty, left out well past the date it should have expired.

freewheeling

october 12, 2010, 7:41 p.m.

Natasha dropped the sandwich bag on the coffee table, laughing loosely. Her college applications and high school career
were done. Natasha spent her afternoons babysitting and the rest
of her days reading library books, doing household chores, and
watching documentaries on her computer. She was bound for
college after this gap year, and her sister was dying. So why not?

Can I join? Carly asked.

Um, no. You're too little.

I've done it before. As a matter of fact, Carly and Stephen were
already smoking weed together Fridays after school in his car.
Stephen had a New York Knicks lighter and glass bowl. They'd
play Air or Moby and drive to the convenience store two blocks
away, where they'd pick out snacks. Once Carly cried because
she counted over twelve different kinds of Oreos.

Really? I had no idea.

With a friend of mine. Carly's voice sailed.

A dude?

I said he's a friend. Carly chewed a shirtsleeve.

And you say he's just a friend, but you say he's just a friend, sang
Lucy.

It doesn't mean a thing, said Carly.

Guys and girls can't be friends, explained Natasha. *Unless one
or both is gay.*

Just because you don't have any friends doesn't mean other people don't, said Carly.

I'm sorry, did you say many friends or any friends? Natasha asked in a treacly-sweet voice. *Just tell me, he's not like a pothead or anything, right?*

He wants to be a veterinarian. He's a good human. Do you trust me? Have you got it bad!

Leave Carly alone, said Lucy. *If she wants to tell us about him, she'll tell us about him.* She'd never tried pot before, though she recognized its feverish smell from parties.

Natasha had tried it a couple of times with the friends she used to have. They were all away at college now, but her connection with them even began to fade the previous May, when Lucy had first been diagnosed. It was the way they'd stop all of their conversation to talk about Lucy's Heart, as though Natasha couldn't enjoy conversation about movies or eyebrow shapes any longer.

Her final month of school consisted of cumbersome lunches, Natasha sitting down in the cafeteria next to a group of girls whom she used to feel easy calling her friends. *Hola. Sorry I'm late. What were you just talking about?*

Nothing, said Keila. She was wearing too much lipstick. *We miss you!*

- *Girls miss each other too much,* - Natasha thought. They said such shiny words all the time. How could they really miss one another after just one class period or one vacation? Nothing they said made sense. *You were talking about something. Was it a secret?*

No way, said Molly, her throat blushing. *Secret? Natasha, you're so random! How is Lucy?*

She's fine.

Did they find a donor yet? asked Jaclyn. Natasha glimpsed Jaclyn's hands, Jaclyn's fun nails that looked like miniature checkerboards.

Wouldn't I have told you about it if they did? Natasha shook her head with her wrists folded on her thighbones. *Tell me what you were talking about.*

It's not really important, said Christina, whom they all called Tina.

The white noise of the cafeteria took over. High schoolers yelling, high-fiving, paying for food, and making flimflam negotiations. Everybody was young and could afford to waste her or his own time.

TV, Molly finally said. Mad Men. *Who's a hotter old dude, Don Draper or Roger Sterling?*

For the rest of the lunch period, Natasha found herself gauging an internal battle about how to participate in the conversation.

Have you been keeping up this season? asked Tina.

Not really, said Natasha.

Girl, said Molly softly. A mammoth silence followed—never before had Natasha felt the spindling tornado of clamor and anticlamor this strappingly.

About to get high with her sisters, Natasha thought about Molly, who was only a senior in high school, since she was a year younger than Natasha, but who might as well have been going to the University of Siberia, considering the frequency with which they'd kept in touch. When she had been in high school, they'd discuss for hours particulars that Natasha would normally pay no attention to, like flirting etiquette or bralettes or Britney Spears. When she was with Molly, Natasha had opinions on certain subjects she'd never contemplated before. Where would these opinions go? It was the tree-falling-in-forest quandary— would she lose the opinions, or were they in her forever? And what about the opinions she carried within her but had yet to realize she had, since she never would confer with Molly?

They'd been the type of friends who touched unconsciously and constantly, while they were talking or doing homework. It was foundational to their amity: Molly's lovely hand on Natasha's arm, tickling itsy circles. A perky foot plopped on the other's. Molly's calf crashing on Natasha's until Natasha's cramped. Cheap and kind communication. Natasha was really only comfortable touching with Molly, since Molly's touchiness was bossy, almost vulturine. Natasha had to let her—how she loved that flaccid but still personal sensation.

Molly's new best friend was her boyfriend, Matt, who played drums and had a little sterling silver earring. Matt was on the shorter side, with the kind of dreamboat face you want to take a hard look at. With fleecy chest hair stretching NW and NE out of his shirts, like somebody reached down to pull them out. When he lifted his drumming arms during their high school's Talent Night last year, Natasha could see the same tiny tresses growing in sprigs below his belly button. Matt and Molly would walk down the halls of school with Matt's body trailing behind hers and his fingers in her front pockets. Natasha wasn't jealous, but all throughout her senior year she had caught herself looking at them more and more. Sometimes she wanted to be Molly. Sometimes she wanted to be Matt. She wanted something, that was for damn sure.

Natasha and her sisters brought the bag of pot to the kitchen. Lucy feared for her drowsy lung, so instead of smoking they baked banana bread, mixing the greens in with the butter. The kitchen reeked. *It smells nature-y*, said Lucy.

Their parents worked late. Lucy thought of her father with a stirring of weepiness, picturing him in his store, hurting to sell a few more albums. When she and her sisters were kids, her father gave them lessons in rock and roll after school, teaching them about how to seal and care for vinyls.

Money had been more of a hot topic before their grandmother's inheritance took care of most of the hospital bills, but how long could that money pile last? To Lucy's knowledge, a desperate time calling for a desperate measure hadn't arrived yet, but how would she ever know? Family funds were a taboo topic, the way her parents never spoke to their daughters about it. The other day, she witnessed her father eat an entire pan of blondies after the hospital bill arrived. *What was in that pan?*

Money makes me hungry was all her father had to say to her.

Is something wrong?

No, no way. It's nothing you ever have to be concerned with, Peanut. I worked hard my whole life just to be sure my children wouldn't spend a minute stressing about money. It's just not my favorite subject to think about is all.

That afternoon, LJ had given Natasha the weed. LJ, which stood for Leonardo John, had blond hair and brown eyes, a diver on the swim team at school. He lived down the street, harboring a consistent crush on Lucy since he was five. *For Lucy,* LJ said as he gave the bag without charge, *the best.* LJ's parents were both doctors, well-to-do but rarely home, unaware of LJ's after-school job as a drug peddler.

Sometimes Lucy, Natasha, and Carly went to his meets. Once they made a sign on poster board with Magic Markers. WE LOVE LJ, with one *L*, *ove* longitudal and *J* latitudal. When he came out of the water, stripping the goggles off his face, pressing his chlorinated eyes, he smiled so widely it looked like his mouth was going to fall off his face. He came in first place.

I'm hungry, said Lucy, about forty-five minutes after they ate the banana bread.

Let's eat.

Something French. Toast, or fries. Lucy twisted her body into a pretzel, her cheeks papaya and glistening, illusively nourished. Natasha thought of Lucy's blood working inside of her, her good lung and how it pushed the drowsy one. They were all working for her. And then Natasha thought of the word *casualty*. Natasha felt in control with the meaning, being that she read the newspaper every day. The word pertained to a world different from hers. Places where boys and girls hoisted ammunition over their shoulders. *Casualty* signified death and hurt in quantities. Often the word *casualty* was used involving statistics.

Let's call LJ, said Carly.

Fuck that, said Lucy, starting to feel the humid sense of delay in her responses. Carly had already dialed LJ's number on her cell phone.

Hey. It's Carly. Oh, you know. Yeah, we tried it. Hid it in banana bread. She laughed. *Lucy was wondering if you'd like to hang out . . . Statistics test? Come on, tool. What's more important?* She hung up. *Come over, he says.*

Lucy Febreezed the house and left a note for their parents. *We're at LJ's. Love Lucy.* As an afterthought, she scribbled *and her sisters.*

Ladies, said LJ to the three of them as he answered the door of his family's palatial, corner house. Predictably, LJ was the only one home. He was shirtless, a towel around his slippery waist. Poreless skin. A pubescent Adonis.

Pete jumped on Natasha and licked her cheek. Pete, a tow-bodied golden retriever, belonged to LJ.

The pool's open 'til whenever a.m.

They played Marco Polo, which gave LJ an excuse to make Lucy his, wrapping his arms around her until she said *cut it out!* They relay-raced. After an hour, LJ gave them bathrobes. - *The host with the most*, - he thought as he opened a bottle of Pinot Noir and put on EDM music, sparkly and weird ribbons of sound.

For the four of them he ordered grilled cheese, macaroni and cheese, a croissant, three bagels, a turkey burger, a hamburger, an omelet with hash browns, a milk shake, and a large hot chocolate with whipped cream from the twenty-four-hour-delivery diner. While waiting for the delivery, they ate some mixed nuts from the glass bowl on the table. LJ brought back cherry and grape Popsicles from the freezer.

My mouth's cold, said Lucy, looking at a framed picture of LJ's mother, who was attractive in a fancy way: plucked, French Riviera glow, pearls. *I'm so cold. Is there a draft in here?*

LJ hugged her, pressing his face into the dip of her neck. *Best friend*, he called her, even though she hardly was. LJ sometimes just said things. *You smell like Mrs. Fields.*

Pick a movie, said Carly. *What's on TV? Anything good? I like nature shows or cartoons when I'm high.*

They watched *The Lion King 1½*, joining each other at different points in sleep, their bodies lying level as sleds on the couches. When Carly woke up, the end credit music was playing, which made her homesick for a moment she wasn't sure occurred. She turned the channel, stopping at an infomercial. Natasha's head, drenched with a waning cuddliness, stayed on Lucy's lap as infomercials on the television about juicers and ab-crunching machines looped. Lucy's beeper sat calmly at a side of the room next to the girls' shoes. Lucy on occasion let loose a static cough.

The TV said, *call now. Time is running out.*

Carly clicked again, finding a rerun of *The Nanny* on TV Land, wrapping herself in the pile of fur thrown on the sofa. LJ stirred. He tousled his own soft-as-a-Fair-Isle-sweater hair.

Do you have any cigarettes? She knew he would because LJ had everything.

Mom's, said LJ, still with sleep in his voice. He linked his fingers and stretched his hands, a gesture of a forty-year-old. *Be right back.* He left the room, returned minutes later with Marlboro Reds.

These are the worst. Mom really should know better; she's a doctor. Grown-ups and their weird vices. Sorry if you get cancer after smoking one, said LJ, before realizing what he said. *Sorry.*

It's cool, said Carly. She could take jokes, even bad ones. They were just jokes, after all. *Light?*

LJ, very close to her face, smelled like lozenges. A pierce of warmth called attention to her mouth. *Thank you.*

Let's go to the kitchen, by the windows. So the smoke won't stick to the floors.

LJ rose and opened the enormous fridge. LJ's family had a state-of-the-art kitchen, existing in the disposable and unsure way that objects belonging to the wealthy did: clothes worn once, technology replaced in a matter of months, renovated walls dotted with paintings by upper-crust contemporary artists. He took out a juice box, punctured it, drank it until his entire mouth turned red. He took the cigarette from her and alternated between smoking and drinking juice, between looking middle-aged and babyish. He started to clean up around the house, stacking the beer and soda cans up in the recycling.

Sometimes I imagine what the world would be like if every boy I knew was a girl and every girl I knew was a boy, said Carly dazedly.

Right on, said LJ. LJ, who was so nice and enthusiastic for people, sometimes irritatingly so, because people who supported everything meant nothing.

LJ turned the channel to one that played only music, to "There Is a Light That Never Goes Out," by the Smiths. LJ stared at Lucy in the next room. *She's really something, isn't she?*

She sure is.

Can I tell you something?

I guess, said Carly.

I'm kind of thinking about giving her my mom's diamond hoops.

Whoa, really? Why?

Just that I want something of mine to be with her. Forever.

That's kind of a tangled idea.

How?

I mean it's pretty aggressive. Or uh, I guess, romantic? What was that Carly was feeling? Jealousy? She squeezed her own spartan, unpierced left lobe.

Before she got sick, I never cared about her this much. I always just thought she'd be there. Of course she would. Lucy who lives down the street. Why wouldn't she not be around, always?

Please shut the fuck up, hissed Carly. She conjured an image of girls who used to make fun of Lucy's hair and outrageous clothes in middle school at Lucy's future funeral, calling her sweet and kind. They were already starting to call her that. The closer Lucy came to dying, the more people would love her.

LJ turned plum, startled. *Huh?*

This is a terrible conversation.

How do people fall in love? Is it a matter of circumstance? Did LJ really love her sister, or was he just romanticizing her infirmity? Was he bold enough to admit he loved her only because he assumed that she was going to die soon? And would anyone ever be bold enough to admit he loved Carly in a romantic way?

Carly thought about Stephen and how he'd seemed to her that afternoon. They'd kissed and touched like new athletic hobbyists: unsure. Did she love Stephen? And if she did, why? In a reverie? Because he was there? Because he sat with her that one afternoon and didn't say anything? *He's just a friend. It doesn't mean anything,* she had told her sisters. Of course it meant something.

She still hadn't told either of her sisters about what had happened, her and Stephen's weird alchemy, their fragile ballet. And yet she loved Lucy and Natasha, more than anyone, much more than she loved Stephen. Her uncle Sawyer always used to say, *you can't choose the family you're born into. You have to love them.* Carly didn't love the family she was originally born into. She didn't even know the people who made love and made her, what spices they cooked with or what bank they went to or if they believed in destiny or why they gave her to somebody else. She was only three days old when the Simone family chose her.

How are you feeling? LJ asked her.

Me? I'm fine. And you?

A little bored, he said. He reached out and poked her shoulder with his index. - *He's lucky,* - Carly thought. Flirting techniques came easy to LJ and would get him far with people.

Bored? she asked. It seemed like such a selfish emotion, if it was even an emotion.

Can you think of anything you want to do? asked LJ.

Carly blushed. - *Eat? Go for a walk? Look through your parents' medicine cabinets? -*

We can play Hot Seat.

What's that?

Like truth or dare, but no dare. We ask each other questions. We have to answer honestly.

I guess, said Carly. *But what if we aren't honest?*

That's not the point. This is a game about trustworthiness.

Sure, let's play.

You go first, declared LJ. *Ask me anything.*

Okay, said Carly. *What are you looking forward to most in college?*

Um. I want to start an a capella rap group called Tone Thugz and Harmony.

Okay, but really, said Carly. Just like him to give counter-productive information. That's all jokes were: impossible answers. She stared at LJ's wall-size fresh and saltwater tanks, with actual didactic panels besides them listing the species inside, in case the family forgot who they were. Koi. Rosy barbs. Fancy guppies. Ghost catfishes. They were moving paintings.

Okay. I want to learn how to work really hard, said LJ. *High school has been too easy for me. Yeah, my life is busy with meets and homework and SAT prep, but it's nothing I can't handle. I want something I can't handle, does that make sense? I want to know what it's like to really want something.*

So people don't think you're a jerk? asked Carly.

I just think it's depressing when you get what you want after trying very little.

Then it was LJ's turn. *What's your least favorite thing about yourself?*

I feel homesick way too much. Sometimes even for the length of the school day.

That's really sweet. It sounds more like a best quality than a worst quality to me.

Well, said Carly, *sometimes our gifts undermine us.*

Oh! LJ bit his knuckle. *I have another one. Can I ask you real quick? Then you can go. Before I forget. What possession would you keep in your life if everything else got destroyed?*

Uh, this picture I took with my sisters on the first day we took the train into the city alone. We ate lunch at this burger place in Chelsea. Natasha and I got hamburgers, but Lucy decided to order sushi for some reason. Lunch lasted for almost three hours. We saw the guy from The Princess Bride *who says* inconceivable *crossing the street. We took a picture on the ice. Lucy has both eyes closed. Like she's sneezing. And I'm looking in the wrong direction, not at the camera but at my sisters. I really like that picture. We don't look like we're posing for a picture. We just look like ourselves. On my perfect day, that day in the city, we went to the Central Park Zoo after lunch. At the zoo, the parrot asked us,* how are you? *and the panda wasn't a panda bear. We'd all forgotten there were other types of pandas. What about you? What would you keep?*

LJ held up his wrist, showing Carly a twenty-four-hour gold timepiece he'd snapped on as soon as they dried off. *From my grandpa. I hate that I can't wear it underwater. I don't like not knowing the time.*

That's funny, said Carly, *I feel the opposite.*

About water?

About time.

Oh. Why?

I don't know. It has no mercy, time.

the claudio who left, then came back

october 13, 2010, 1:04 a.m.

I have to tell you something, Claudio said to his wife.

What's that? asked Mathilde.

And that something was that he'd been at a strip club some towns over, in the frailer Copiague, earlier in the night. Nothing drove him but the wickedness of an itch. He set his watch timer for ten minutes. He never thought he would ever come here, but he felt itchy. What frightened Claudio was that maybe this tingle was merely a type of desperate boredom.

The place had been tame. There was a table with three aluminum catering tins of baked ziti, but no blue fires underneath the food. Claudio resisted the urge to light the tins. A woman caught his eye.

Hi, how are you? The woman wore heels. She was very pretty. Mathilde was milk-and-honey beautiful, and this woman was another kind of beautiful. A more vulgar beautiful, with the bones in her cheeks like a Russian czar's. She made his stomach ache.

That's one hell of a pair of shoes, said Claudio. Flan-blond highlights and big brown eyes. She had a little birthmark on her left ribs the size and shape of a Froot Loop. Claudio had always loved large breasts. But then again, who didn't? He imagined taking her to a hotel and fucking his pain out. It was a similar urge to the one that plagued him at banks or restaurants. *Order everything on the menu. Empty my vault. Tip everyone I see.* This transferable romance was drastically different from the high he felt at concerts, which came with no strings, no chance for regret.

The stripper raised a shot glass and toasted him. Drinking on the job seemed encouraged. Claudio wondered what could get you fired here. *I think I'm getting a little too old for this kind of thing,* he confided.

It was Claudio's first time at a strip club, never having even been to a bachelor party. Back when Claudio had been a bachelor, all he cared about was obtaining money for his freedom. The only time he'd ever even thought about strip clubs came with an assortment of associations with areas consisting of 99¢ stores and pawnshops and gas stations with bulletproof-glass-covered teller stands. Towns that virtually ran on fast food, with closed-down, burglarized grocery stores. Skeleton houses.

- *What circumstances made sex a transaction?* - he thought, though he already knew the answer: circumstances without love. Lately he'd been speculative of all indigent parts of life. Sawyer was a sucker for beauty; well, Claudio could have been a sucker for ugliness. Not that it appealed to him, just that sometimes it was easy to find the beauty in such ugliness, even easier than it was to see the discreet ugliness in opulence and privilege. Sure, there had to be upscale strip clubs too, but he guessed they weren't nearly as interesting. As he thought this, Claudio felt shame at his condescension, the sexiness he found in desperation. Then again, Claudio knew a thing or two about desperation.

Claudio stood and wondered. - *Could a past possibly excuse a journalistic lens?* -

The last time Claudio had gone back to Detroit was the year his parents died. He had refused to let Mathilde or his daughters come with him. Both of his parents had died within months of each other, when Claudio turned forty. Within two months, he took two plane trips. Two trips to the morgue to identify the two people who'd made him.

No services, besides Claudio standing in the cemetery, listening to a Catholic priest (belonging to a local church he looked up online) pray prayers he hadn't heard since his child-hood. If his parents had kept any friends since he'd moved away, Claudio didn't know where to find them. He figured they'd at least have wanted a priest, right?

Hell, he didn't even know what they wanted when they were alive. They'd been unfortunate people: generous at their best, cartoony and livid at their worst. They hadn't wanted much, letting the world screw them over only until it did physically and finally. He was going to bring Jane, but both times after she'd heard the news she'd refused to leave her room at Lincoln hospital. Standing at both of his parents' graves, Claudio had felt like an only child as well as an orphan.

In all honesty, Claudio hadn't anticipated his parents living even that long, what with the constant worry, the toll of living life with the quality it had in Detroit. His father had been sixty-nine and his mother, sixty-seven. That hadn't been too old, not in this day and age. They could have lived longer. They could have lived better.

The only people he knew left in Detroit were his various friends, classmates, and neighbors, people who never once seri-ously thought of leaving the city that doomed them. Many sold drugs and stole in order to live. The Detroit police would only respond to murders because of the high frequency of crime. *If you want to commit a crime, Detroit is your place*, his childhood friends would always say.

Every time Claudio returned to his hometown, he'd expect the close world around him to lose color. A volta of black and white. He'd have the song "Fast Car" stuck in his head, which wouldn't leave until he did. There'd been a Dunkin' Donuts on a corner right by the highway, which closed down because

too many people had been murdered there. It was next to a
liquor store, which was (obviously) still in business. Packs of
dogs roamed the streets. One time, Claudio even saw literal
tumbleweed.

He wanted to help people. Yet he wanted to stay alive. Back
home, there hadn't been many opportunities to attempt the first
without taxing the second. Was this hopelessness the same as
selfishness? Or was selfishness a result of retired hope?

The residences gave Claudio the worst feeling of all. Many
of the yards of the abandoned housing areas had been void for
so long that sometimes he'd see a front lawn that looked more
like a forest. Every time Claudio saw an abandoned house with
a mowed grass plot, it meant that the house next to it had neighbors. It meant that the neighbors didn't want anyone to think
that the house was discarded, so they'd tidy up the place in the
hopes that no crime would be committed nearby. Claudio used
to pass a house that he concluded derelict, in the strongest sense
of the word, on his way to school, until he saw one day that someone had put up Halloween decorations. Claudio felt his insides
smoldering. Whoever lived in that awful house had children.

Not his house. Never his children. - Not bad. Not too bad. -
Claudio swore that his life wouldn't ever be bad. Even if it wasn't
good, it would never be too bad. Disaster would be yielded for
a man who worked hard and spoke up when he saw injustices.
The only part of Claudio needing reassurance was the idea that
he was this man.

The dancers' backs, asses, and legs struck Claudio with melancholy. They had the same parts as Mathilde. They had the
same parts as his daughters. They had the same parts as his
sister. Every stripper was somebody's daughter. He knew that
chestnut. Daddy issues et al. Everyone he knew was so quick to
throw her or his opinions about strippers around. People always
mentioned sex trafficking, like how easy it was to mention drug
addicts when talking about drug use.

He left the club after three minutes, deciding this wasn't who he was. Though it wasn't like Claudio to declare himself enough of anything to feel cognitive dissonance. He left because being there was exhausting.

You just got here, the host said. To maintain his baseline of pleasantness without needing to converse, Claudio reached inside his wallet and gave him fifty dollars. This was when he felt contrite. Of course he'd tell his wife. What would she say? It wasn't even a matter of forgiveness; it was a matter of belief. He was still the same Claudio, and she had to believe him. On the drive home, he stopped at a twenty-four-hour bodega and bought his wife some refrigerated flowers. They weren't glamorous, but they were still alive. White roses, her favorite.

I left after three minutes, he said again. He didn't have any more explaining to do, so he kept on saying the same things.

Mathilde answered in her loping, dazed way. *What do you even want me to say, Claudio?*

I really don't know, said Claudio. He kissed his wife's fingers.

You went alone? That's the worst part. You could have at least gone with Zane.

But you hate Zane!

There is something so creepy about you going alone.

I didn't realize this was a situation where there's safety in numbers.

Mathilde had kept an open mind her entire life, even welcomed the sensational appeal of strip clubs in the same way she enjoyed Funyuns and Yankee Candles. (After all, who didn't appreciate Night Ranger and Warrant? Shots? Beautiful women with strong upper bodies?) But what had her husband been doing there alone? What other disappointing behavior could finally put his demons to rest? *Can you explain to me why?*

I'm sorry. I can't. He knew he would've never done something like that if he had to explain it to somebody.

Claudio scratched at his temples, the first place he noticed he'd been going gray. Claudio received his first silver hair at thirty-six, and a full-on, seasoned white reached him by the time he was forty. *It was as though I had seen something scary*, he told friends of his whitening hair, still as thick as it was when he was twenty, like cirrus. Every time he felt like he'd been living too long, he scratched the backs of his hands. Mathilde had been the one to point that out. She knew his mannerisms by Heart, the same way he was intimate with her veins and freckles. He assumed that, since he didn't regularly care to look in the mirror, Mathilde had probably seen his face more times in his life than he had. Wasn't that something?

Do you remember the time I flew to see my parents when Lucy was an infant, and I wouldn't let you guys come?

Yes, said Mathilde, still hurt, still deciding how to react. She had never been a distrustful wife, but that was only because he had never really given her a reason to be before.

I was hoping to spare you.

You kept telling me you couldn't bear to run into your family's old milkman.

Claudio's old family had received milk every Friday from a man named Timothy. Timothy, who wore glasses with wire rims and called people by their names at regular intervals in conversation. When he said *good morning, Claudio*, Claudio felt a self-centered and attaching kind of love for this extra-effort-taking man. When Claudio was six, he noticed that one of the milk cartons was leaking. He told his father, who called the supermarket.

Timothy was fired and never came back to the Simone house again. The piece of Claudio that survived and grew into a man remembered this. His Heart felt like jam as he considered how families drank different concentrations of milk. Timothy had delivered them 2 percent.

It is impossible to substitute one Heart for another Heart. The family Claudio took part in forming, the family he committed to, drank skim. It was a different family from the family he had grown up with: Mom and Dad, little Claudio and little Jane. This time, this family was Mom and Dad, and little Natasha and little Lucy and little Carly. Big Mom and Big Dad. Big, strong Claudio. Nobody would hurt the people he loved. The people he lived his life to protect. He knew all about class warfare, but Claudio figured that humans could inherently be divided into two classes: the weak and the strong. Claudio came from a crappy home, but at least he would save this family.

crime

The Lincoln hospital in New York was different from the Pine Rest hospital in Michigan. This was how Jane knew she'd matured.

For instance, at Pine Rest, she'd fallen into jeopardy easily, flashing her chest to the orderlies and the other patients. But she'd only done it because they would tell her to. Usually *they* were the government workers, who called her on the telephone or through the radiator. Once, through the eggcup in her breakfast. One time her governor called her, and instead of asking her to vote, he told her to sing for the king and queen. She could borrow a coat from James Dean. So Jane started to undress, but before she could even look for the coat, she was in trouble.

Her Pine Rest doctor asked if she ever felt like somebody else, and Jane told her no. Though sometimes she felt so much that her insides could have filled two people. Yes, she could be more than one person, but whatever extra people were also Jane. Jane and a half, she felt like calling herself on those days.

Jane had been scared every day at Pine Rest, but at Lincoln she learned how to carefully differentiate her world from everybody else's. The Lincoln doctors told her that in everyone else's world, which was the same, people usually talked only one at a time and never through food or the radiator. And that the government rarely contacted people individually. And that Jane only thought they were contacting her because she had delusions and hallucinations in her brain. Hallucinations were the voices screaming *JANE! JANE! JANEJANEJANE!* Delusions made her question to whom she would surrender.

The Lincoln doctors told her that she thought it was the government because she was trying to make her world exist with everyone else's, mark harmony out of the situation. This was how Jane knew how much she'd grown: the doctors told her that some patients never realized this. But she could and would, and things would hurt less soon. Very soon, if she continued to learn and grow and take her cocktails of antipsychotics. Thorazine. Clozapine. Librium. Who decided these medicine names anyhow? The stuff she took with Otis had easier names. You got high, you had a good time or maybe fell asleep, ached for more hours later. That was all. Nobody kept a file on you or approved tailored dosages.

Every time Jane was fed her pills, she'd say *pay day* to make the nurses laugh, but one day they just stopped laughing. Someone either told them not to encourage her, Jane guessed, or else they just didn't find her funny anymore.

On good days, her doctor would say, *let's see if we can try a smaller dosage.* On bad days, he'd say, *I'm sorry,* and after supper they'd feed her more of what made her feel like she was made of soft-serve ice cream, more of what made her hibernate for about fourteen hours a night. And on the worst days, Jane could barely speak of what happened. Nothing hurt, but everything was scary—they'd strap her to a table, feed her something to relax her muscles, then nothing. She'd wake up and wouldn't be able to remember the morning. Sometimes she'd forget her brother's name, the hospital's name, the town she came from. And then it would return to her. The memories always came back, but who could tell when? Time taunted her.

Jane felt blessed. At Pine Rest she hurt in ways she couldn't explain to those who didn't share her world, the way the voices built up on each other and gnawed on the drums of her ears. Termites. But now things were getting better for Jane. Like the song off *Sgt. Pepper*, her favorite album, the one that went, *it's getting better all the time*. She was hearing fewer voices. She was getting to be a lovely grown woman, to quote Dr. Stein, her new doctor, who was so much more patient than her doctor back in Michigan. Dr. Stein was always saying things in Yiddish. *No shtupping*, Dr. Stein said, which meant, *no fucking*. This was after the incident with the night nurse. *That's bubkes!* Dr. Stein also said. Which meant, *that's nothing!* Jane wanted to learn Yiddish, but Dr. Stein said it was mostly a dead language. *What you need to learn are the curses.*

And maybe now that Jane was mature, this meant someday she could forgive Claudio for telling her she'd have a better life with Sawyer. She never got to go on a honeymoon with Sawyer. Never got to *shtup* him. Never even got to really kiss him. They drove her to the Bronx the first day she was a wife and left her there. Maybe Claudio was doing a favor, protecting Sawyer from her, from realizing she'd make a bad bride.

Before bedtime, Jane would think of her husband. *Come*, was all she wanted to say, *be with me*. She'd imagine Sawyer lying beside her in the twin, turning her over so they shared a forehead. His arms glued to hers, soft as plants. She'd be in such good hands. Sawyer would say, *are you okay, Jane?* Or, *I love you even though you are sick*. Or, *I love you more because you are sick*. This most reckless of daydreams tortured Jane's weak prayers out of her, swelled her with humility. Or was it humiliation? Jane was too old to have crushes, even if the crush was on her husband.

As a little girl, Jane had been as ugly as a toad. Everybody at school had told her so. And when she'd said to her mother, *Mommy, I'm ugly*, her mother hadn't disagreed, only said, *next time you think you're ugly, just picture how you look on a globe*. Her mother had said things like that. What did it mean? - *Maybe something about how small it is to feel ugly,* - Jane thought. But that didn't stop her from feeling it. Even after she won the beauty pageant. Being told she was beautiful somehow made her feel even uglier.

Now Jane didn't care about being pretty. These kinds of things didn't matter to her anymore. What mattered were only being alive and staying semi-sane and finding that ambitious balance between safe and free.

Sawyer only visited with Claudio, and barely! What kind of husband was he? Nobody gave them any privacy at Lincoln. Maybe if Jane kept trying, if she kept blocking out the voices that layered on top of one another, if she stayed more in everybody else's world and chewed with her mouth closed and buttoned her shirts all the way to the top, maybe next time they'd give them some privacy and leave her and her husband alone.

Claudio alone visited every Tuesday without fail. Since she left New Orleans, she'd never had a Tuesday without Claudio. Sometimes he even came twice, thrice a week. He'd been the one to tell her their mom died, and then two months later he'd been the one to tell her their dad died. But it wasn't a prank. Claudio carried the news inside him. Most of his visits would pass by without her letting loose a single word. *Tell him I hate him*, she'd tell her nurses. But Claudio would never leave. Didn't he have better things to do? She knew what he wanted: to reupholster whatever had busted inside her.

Last week her asshole sister-in-law visited too, which she only did once every couple of years, claiming to be busy with her daughters, with her own family. The visits were always worse when Mathilde came, all faux-naïf and filled with sorrow for Jane, *you look beautiful, Jane*, like Jane was an unseemly charity.

The last time Mathilde visited, a week ago, Jane had asked about her husband. *Does he not want to see me?*

Husband? Mathilde smiled at Jane with her teeth, looking unutterably concerned for her.

He's Sawyer, said Jane. *Sawyer Spicer.*

My brother? asked Mathilde. *You've met my brother?*, looking at Claudio and not Jane.

Of course I have, said Jane. *I married him, didn't I? In City Hall—me and Claudio and Sawyer and some sunflowers. Claudio said you were sick. Maybe you were here. In this hospital!*

Sunflowers, said Mathilde.

You're being a cunt, said Jane, *because you think you could marry into my family, but I've done the same. You may be a Simone, but I'm a Spicer.*

Mathilde shook her head.

When can I meet my nieces? Jane pushed.

Shortly, Claudio promised, feeling as counterfeit as a bounced check. *When you feel better, Jane.*

I feel good now, Jane would say. She'd touch her thighs to check. Same old trustworthy thighs, soggy with cellulite and still hers and still thighs, which made her feel good indeed, still a someone.

Soon.

He'd given her school pictures of the girls, every year. Jane collected their faces. She'd put them out of order, then in order, like an agitated librarian.

Do they ask about me?

Every now and then, Claudio would say.

Well, what do you tell them?

I say you're in a different place.

Better?

Sometimes, Claudio's eyes would unspool, *sometimes better.*

Someday, but definitely not today, Jane would forgive Claudio for tricking her. And then she would forgive him for everything else, like for getting the milkman fired, like for not sticking up for her on the bus, like for not protecting her when the man on vacation stuck his finger in her eye and told her he was going to find her later that night and make her feel good. It was hard because so much time had passed, and that was precisely the era when Jane first started to slip into her world. Those days were the most confusing because she didn't know she lived in a world that was different. So who was she to say what had actually happened? Who was she to say what was right and what was wrong? *You're not the crazy one*, they'd told her at Pine Rest. *It's the delusions that are crazy.*

love means

october 20, 2010, 4 p.m.

After they left the hospital, Claudio beat his wife to address-ing the elephant that had been in the hospital room: *strange of my sister to say that, huh?*

Yes, Mathilde said, hoping to believe whatever words would come out of his mouth rather than to trust her instincts. *Espe-cially the sunflowers. You know, those are Sawyer's favorite, right? His spirit plants.*

I don't remember.

How did they even meet?

Let's talk when we get home.

That night, after each truth had been exposed, Mathilde left her house. Claudio followed her out to the car.

Where are you going?

Stop.

She drove back to Manhattan, to her brother's apartment. She'd never felt more duped, and by whom? god. Tears col-lected, slunk down her face. People in nearby cars and pedes-trians were looking at her, and not in a way that fed her. While driving, she imagined the conversation they'd have.

How could you keep this a secret from me? she'd ask. *We're fam-ily.* (Yet, she realized, disgustedly, they'd *all* been family with-out her knowing. For eight fucking years!) *We're blood,* she'd plead. Blood had to be more important than flimsy contracts.

Shamefully, she thought of how Sawyer and Claudio had just proved to her how blood was more important than marriage. This meant that Claudio had to love his sister more than he loved his wife. Well, Mathilde could just as well love Sawyer more than Claudio.

To her dismay, it was not Sawyer who opened the door but Noah. In any version of her predictions, it would never be Noah who opened the door, whom she'd have to confront, as Noah was their small family's breadwinner, working twelve-hour days and paying for four-fifths of their cohabitating lives, making the sacrifice while Sawyer could pleasurably pursue what he loved.

Mathilde! Noah squinted at Mathilde's artful and lucky parking spot, right in front of his building, right where they both could see it. *Did you drive here?*

He was still wearing his suit and thick woolen socks and holding a glass of orange juice. So different from Mathilde, whose routine it was to change into pajamas immediately upon arriving home, even if it was still the afternoon. Noah dressed in his clothes seemed magnificently adult of him. Noah was the type of person who dressed up when he was having a terrible day, to make himself feel nicer.

Come, sit down. He brought her to their living room. Mathilde moored her left hand to Noah's forearm.

Claudio went to a strip club last night. Mathilde laughed.

What? Why? With friends?

Claudio has friends? asked Mathilde. She hyperventilated a clumsy mixture of laughter and hiccups. Her hands shook, now hidden between her cooled knees.

Noah curled his arm around her shoulders.

Something else has happened.

And then Mathilde told Noah the secret, feeling it ram out of her accidentally-on-purpose, bulimic-style. And then she added, *they're divorced now. When Mom died, they divorced,* which felt like pressing a Band-Aid into an amputated arm. *I don't think*

Jane even knows about the divorce. But hey, she knew more than we did, which is saying something, huh?

Noah said *what?* many times. *Wait, tell me everything.* She told him what she knew. He left the room for a while. Mathilde shoved her face into a throw pillow. Three tears tracked her face, clear as vodka.

Eventually, Noah came back. He had changed clothes, and the skin on his face shone. Then, *I don't know what to say.*

I am so sorry.

I could have paid for her health care. I would have too.

Yes, breathed Mathilde. Noah hadn't come from much money originally but earned a great deal each year. Much more than Mathilde and Claudio. He and Sawyer could afford a gorgeous Chelsea apartment and stunning furniture and vacations multiple times a year.

Oh god, how could they have done this? And why? Why keep a secret from me? It was *me* now, Noah only, in the typically self-absorbed way of fraught people in the wake of bad news, and Mathilde felt an astonishing relief. It was easier to take care of another than oneself.

The man you chose to love. The man I happened to love, said Mathilde. *Both would rather lie than ask us for favors.*

Noah understood from a place deep inside himself that she was right. Noah took care of Sawyer. They had no agreement, no binding contract besides their love. In his mind Sawyer must have thought that his actions would have been less damaging than asking Noah to pay for one more thing while Sawyer spent his glorious hours with what he loved, changing another culture's tongue into his own.

Slut, said Noah.

Jane? asked Mathilde. Jane didn't seem like a person anymore so much as a tax. But that was the end of Jane's role in the conversation. There was nothing else to say about her and nothing left to feel.

He's weak, said Noah. *Sawyer is a weak man.*

Because he kept the truth from you.

Not just because of that. Noah stood.

Because he was too cowardly to ask you to pay for her health care.

Not just that either. I just don't think he'd have the strength to do what I'm doing. Right this moment, which is knowing that the person I love most in the world has exchanged vows and rings with another person. Noah sat down. He loved Sawyer so much, he'd do anything for him. He'd test himself like this. - *Test,* - he soliloquized internally. - *It's just a test.* - It soothed him. Noah had always been an excellent test-taker. In college, he always dressed up to take tests too.

Mathilde held the side of Noah's clammy chin, treating his face like a classic car. She'd never touched him in that place before, this confidential zone of his—where a wife was supposed to touch her husband. In spite of it all, she felt a little charge, and that charge made her happy, distracted. *Oh god,* Noah said. *What else has been kept from me?*

They think they've done something noble, said Mathilde. *They think they've saved our family.*

Family, Noah repeated, mockingly. What was family? Just a set of people who thought you were obliged to them, for whatever reason. For helping you exist—or not.

a father's job

october 20, 2010, 9:00 p.m.

Claudio didn't know the whereabouts of his wife for the first time in his entire life. He poured himself a glass of tap water and lay on their bed, on Mathilde's side. He put her pillow over his face and bit the case's corner. He was everything he tried and then happened to be: a good father, a good husband, a good brother, and a terrible person.

When Claudio signed on to be a father, he agreed to take bullets, be the type of man who'd die for his wife and daughters, but his circumstances hadn't demanded that. So he honored his next task as a father: the logistics, taking care of what was messy. When his daughter got sick, he researched organ transplants, spending every one of his spare hours ensuring relations with the best doctors, the best health care they could afford.

Déjà vu was exerted, because even before Claudio could afford to keep Jane safe, he'd resorted to fraught measures. The worst part about that was involving Sawyer. His whole life, Claudio avoided depending on anybody but himself. It wasn't that he didn't trust people, more that his character was chiseled by his sovereignty. This was a matter of pride.

His wife and daughters cried on awful days, filling themselves with their coagulating emotions, but Claudio didn't let himself, for it was his job to keep the family going. That job was even more imperative than his other, to serve as the family's supplementary source of income. After her mother passed, Mathilde's trust took care of most of their needs. Christ, Claudio even viewed his day job as a luxury, so damn lucky that music was his bread and butter. How many people could say that? The only detail he ever deferred to was the hope that people would keep listening to vinyls. He often feared technology; what if one day something was made that produced startlingly better sound quality than records? He'd have to work with it, he guessed, for that was the way you worked with time.

Unlike Claudio, Mathilde barely thought of money, having recently said, *money means nothing to me except another way to pay the hospital bills.*

You say that because you've been comfortable your whole life.

When my father died, said Mathilde, *that wasn't too comfortable.*

I understand, said Claudio, *but we're talking about different things.* Could she not recall their prior arguments about money, cementing the makeup of their connubial history, their tapestry made stronger through fights and forgiveness? Here was a woman who'd continue to perplex him, after years of marriage.

Yes, said Mathilde, *and there are things more important than money.*

You act, said Claudio. *It's something you want to do. I'm lucky to work for myself. Before I saved the money to open the store, you know how I was cleaning vomit out of toilets on Friday nights. How I cleaned cars that cost more money than I made in a year.*

Mathilde paused for a long time, before saying, *god, what do I know?*

Claudio remembered the different pain that came with growing up in poverty. Sure, it wasn't as bad as what was happening with Lucy, but there was a particular kind of undignified sadness that came with deciding between foods funded by stamps as other students his age decided between colleges.

There are people who have it a lot worse, Claudio used to lecture his daughters growing up, and now he wished he hadn't. There'd been no need to make them feel guilty for what they had—that guilt was just as useless as complaining about what you didn't have. Time had complete control over luck. Times changed, and you worked with it. *There are kids starving in Africa.* His mother, of a different generation, used to tell him, *there are kids starving in Europe.* There would always be kids starving, all over.

you're gonna carry that weight, carry that weight a long time

There are two kinds of people in this world: those who, when duped, seek confrontation with their swindler, and those who seek redemption for their naïveté through calling attention to all truths surrounding them, no matter how harmful these truths may be. People who feel before they think tend to fall into the latter camp. *There's somebody I think you have to know about*, Mathilde told her daughter.

Lucy's Heart strummed at the indication of her mother's imperative pitch.

Your father has a sister, and she lives in a hospital. A psychiatric hospital in the Bronx. She's lived there for most of her adult life. I used to visit her, and then . . . after you guys were all born, well, it got too hard, you see? It wouldn't've been appropriate to bring children to see her. She's like a time bomb, you see?

Is this a joke?

And your father preferred you wouldn't know about her until she got better.

And she hasn't gotten better, Lucy guessed.

No, said Mathilde. *Not yet.* She had a picture of Jane in her pocket, and she showed Lucy, to make her aunt seem more real. *See how she and Daddy have the same eyes?*

- One set of eyes for two people, - thought Lucy. She said, *so he's waiting for her to get better.*

He visits her every Tuesday, Mathilde defended her husband.

It was no wonder. On Tuesdays her father often came home late and in an awful mood. Lucy and her sisters usually avoided him for the rest of the week, it was that bad. Engaging with him was always bothersome, like having an argument with a sore throat. Now it would be easier to understand how hard it must be for him. But maybe she would never fully, since neither she nor her own sisters was sick in that way.

Well, maybe I can visit her too? One of these days with him.

Oh, said Mathilde. *No!*

What?

She's not like us. Mathilde abused that excuse. Whenever she tried to set an example, she would say that nobody was like their family. *Republicans, they aren't like us. Democrats, not our people.* It was always the same story with most groups: drug users, hipsters, warmongers, religious people, socialists, blue-collar folks, white-collar folks, surfers, city people, country people, athletes, intellectuals. Their family identity was defined by what they weren't and what they didn't have and what they didn't care about. It appeared as though the Simones were like nobody.

Maybe . . . she'd be able to relate to me.

Mathilde arrived at a truth: *you're already related.*

Do Natasha and Carly know?

No, said Mathilde. *It's just you, for now.*

But can I ever talk to Daddy about this?

You can't. He doesn't know I'm telling you.

Well, why are you?

For the first time in their conversation, Mathilde had no more words to say. *Do you think it's right that I told you?*

How should I know? I've never met her! You're supposed to be the grown-up.

You're right, said Mathilde, her regret blinking inside of her. *I am.*

i will say the only words
i know that you understand

october 23, 2010

Lucy would meet her aunt Jane for the first time, visit her at Lincoln Medical and Mental Health Center in the Bronx. Natasha would drive her. Lucy of course told Natasha everything she knew, that night of her conversation with her mother, not being able to stomach a secret so large. (- *How unfair*, - she'd thought of her mother, - *to lay such a weight on the weakest child.* -)

Natasha's reaction was as Lucy expected: logical, and in search of an answer. *Well, what do you want to do?*

I want to visit her, said Lucy. *To see if she's real.*

Natasha sighed with relief, for she could certainly be a help with such logistics. She looked up the address of the only mental hospital in the Bronx and called for its visiting hours: 4:00 p.m., every day. They went on a Saturday, telling their parents they were driving into Manhattan to see the newest exhibit at the Guggenheim Museum.

What shouldn't I say? Lucy wondered, on the car ride over. She looked out the window, at the sky messy with clouds.

Probably anything scary. Their aunt Jane was a different kind of sick. One could never know how she'd react.

When they arrived, Natasha parked, unbuckled her seat belt, and took out the memoir of an eighty-year-old shepherd who made dulcimers and lived in the Swiss Alps. *Are you sure you don't want to come in with me?*

I'm okay, said Natasha immediately. Sensible Natasha, who figured whatever was kept a secret from them probably had good reason to be, held Lucy's hands. *Promise me you . . . will expect anything. And be okay with anything happening.*

I promise.

The day was cold, even indoors. Lucy didn't want to take off her jacket. A bulb above her burned as she signed in.

You're Claudio's little girl? asked the nurse.

Yes.

You are! Well, this will be quite the surprise for Jane. You've never met her, have you? Your father is always talking about you. Is Daddy here too?

No—Lucy breathed—*he's not.* She thought about her father discovering she not only knew about Jane but had also visited her. - *But then,* - she thought, - *who would be in trouble for not telling the other?* -

You've come at a good time, the nurse said as she guided Lucy to Jane's room. *She just finished lunch.* This was kind of a cheerful place, relatively speaking—a silent, surprisingly warm smell in the hallways, something like shortbread or lattes. Lucy ogled the some infantilized, some outwardly normal sights in each room they passed by—a drooly, braless bald woman talking to her nurse. Three men wearing sweatshirts and playing cards.

Guess who's here to see you? the nurse announced in a preschool-teacher voice. *It's your niece! Your Lucy!*

I don't have a Lucy, said Jane to the wall. When she turned her head to the doorway, however, she opened her mouth. She peeked at Lucy's feet.

I'm so happy to meet you, Aunt Jane, said Lucy. *I've missed you.* She thought about whether she authentically did miss her aunt Jane, without having known she existed, then decided - *yes.* -

I don't believe this, said Jane.

Lucy carefully stayed for an hour. They talked. *You're so young*, Jane kept saying. *You look younger than I thought.*

Oh, said Lucy.

You know, said Jane, *your father says we're so much alike.*

He does, agreed Lucy, while thinking - *he does? -*

- *Imagine being Aunt Jane,* - Lucy thought. Poorly structured Jane. Would Jane enjoy being Lucy? Or would she think it was boring?

Do you count? asked Jane. *I count everything. Helps me keep track of myself.*

You mean like calories? asked Lucy. *Kind of. You know Skinny Cow ice cream sandwiches? They're only like, a hundred calories each. But then I eat six of them at once.*

Six, five, four, three, two, one, negative four. I love people only between four and five a.m., said Jane. She let loose a yawn so loud her soul could have fallen out.

Then Jane showed Lucy all of the pictures she'd collected of Lucy and her sisters throughout the years, which gave Lucy a morbid, idol-ish feeling: somebody knowing about her so long, and so frequently, before there was reciprocation. - *I'm really not that important!* - she felt like saying.

I'm so happy it's you I got to meet first, said Jane. *Natasha looks too much like your mother, you see? I was never a fan of Mathilde. And I don't think I would trust Carly. What's she, Chinese or something?*

Chinese-American, corrected Lucy. *She's adopted.*

So Claudio and Mathilde rescued her? asked Jane. *Aren't they scared of her parents coming back? Taking her back to the Communists? Making her wear shirts the color of glowing blood, the sum of skin and tears?* Lucy said nothing. *I've scared you,* said Jane.

No, said Lucy. *Her birth parents don't know who we are, and we don't know who they are.*

What more to talk about? Lucy didn't want to tell her about her own sickness. Nor could they talk about Jane's disease. But then Jane solved their problem.

Claudio told me English is your favorite subject.

He did?

I'm a writer too. That's something else we have in common. You know, you don't really need to go to school to be a writer. You just need a lot of life experience.

Yeah, said Lucy. *It's kind of like acting. You know?* She was thinking of her mother.

I hate actors, said Jane. *Actors are all phonies. Well, except Rick Moranis. You know he retired to take care of his family, right? Anyway, right now,* said Jane, *I'm not writing. I'm revising.* She motioned her niece over. *I'll show you what I've got.*

This is a blank sheet of paper, noted Lucy.

I keep erasing, said Jane, *what I think I can say.* She raised her eyebrows at Lucy. *When I was your age, I had the best handwriting too. I was so proud of it.* She said it in a way that suggested she would never see her own handwriting again, or her own writing again, or her own hands again.

My handwriting looks like a baby's or a boy's, said Lucy. *You're lucky.*

What comes out isn't as important as what stays here. This is where I keep the real stuff, said Jane, then tapped her skull. *All of my stories. You want to hear one?*

a discount

Hello, hello, said Jane. *Is this on?* She was speaking into her hand, which warped into a pinkish fist. She was wearing a garbage twisty-tie in her hair. This was the second time Jane and Lucy were meeting. Natasha drove her again and refused another invitation to visit, enjoying the company of her weighty book on the anti-intellectualism movement in America. Lucy still didn't know why she was visiting her aunt—all she knew was that she wanted to.

Cool! said Lucy.

No, said Jane, *it's not cool.*

Sorry, said Lucy. *I don't know why I say the things I say.*

You're like me, Jane said to her niece. *You're not afraid to apologize.*

Nobody said anything.

Are we monsters? asked Jane.

Uh, I don't think so, said Lucy. *I'd say I'm pretty human.*

I hope so too, said Jane.

We're, Lucy corrected herself too late, mortified by her ego-centrism. Who was the real monster here?

Why haven't your sisters visited me?

Because they only just found out you existed? Because they are afraid of you? Because they probably have more time than me to? None of these answers worked. Lucy said, *they'll come soon. We want to get to know you one at a time.*

Can I tell you something? Usually whenever Jane spoke to people, especially her visitors and *especially* her family, outside noise would pile, like popping balloons and animals braying, but this time only a surplus of silence lingered. This silence had an intensity of a different kind, the silence of an authentic experience, which made Jane angry—made her feel like half-prisoner, half-marauder.

What's up? asked Lucy.

I'm married, but I miss my boyfriend, she said, as earnest as Dolly Parton.

Boyfriend?

Yes, Otis. Jane blushed whenever she thought of his name, in love and so unhappy. She was dying to tell somebody about him. In a gauche, middle-schooler way, she said, *he's from Ipswich, Massachusetts.*

Ooh, said Lucy, handling the news like the little girl she was. *That sounds like Chipwich. You know, the ice cream sandwich with cookies?*

Ipswich is one of the oldest towns in America. But Otis is not so old. In fact, he moved to New Orleans when he was only fourteen.

I wish I had a boyfriend, said Lucy.

Of course you do, said Jane. She folded and unfolded her legs, closing her raw blue eyes. *When you miss someone, and you're not allowed to miss them, it's a rotten feeling,* said Jane. *It feels like you've lost a baby.*

Lucy didn't ask her aunt how she knew how that would feel.

Otis has big dreams for the two of us. Bigger than Jesus. Your dad doesn't like him. They haven't even met.

Doesn't he want his sister to be happy? Lucy felt rebellious toward her father, even though something was telling her that her father probably had good reason to mind whoever this was.

Indeed. He should get to know him.

That Dad, said Lucy, hinting and disturbingly fixed for Jane's approval, *just as annoying a brother as he is a father.*

Otis would play with my hair and sing the Turtles. He'd sing, Janey Jane gee I think you're swell *to the tune of "Elenore." You know the song? You're probably too young.*

I know the song, said Lucy. *That's a great song.*

He would sometimes buy me makeup from the drugstore and wipe it off my face at night. He taught me how to whistle. He was always gentle when he shaved me. He'd shave me, and I'd smoke a cigarette in the shower, and life would be like a Bertolucci film. These were all honest things. Jane swore they were. She remembered them. The caring hadn't always been so brutal.

Maybe she missed Otis only because she missed everything from the time she was with Otis, not because she missed Otis as a person. It was the type of missing she knew how to do. She missed the fitful freedom (the only way Jane could enjoy freedom was from the inside) of New Orleans: the long days she had to fill, doing anything she wanted. On days the voices weren't too loud, she'd mosey around the city in no meticulous direction.

Sometimes she'd pick out a person and follow him or her. It was usually somebody who looked indecisive, someone who looked like he himself had no idea where to go next. On a free day, Jane followed about ten to twelve people. She'd never been caught.

Whenever the person passed a store that looked like it had something to offer Jane, she'd ditch the person and go inside. At grocery stores, she would ask for a cookie from the bakery. At department stores, there were all sorts of skin care and makeup stations that gave away free things. Discounts and birthday gifts. Every day was Jane's birthday. And with whatever money Jane had, she bought things, strictly following her impulses and confusing them for intuition.

If a clerk asked something at once innocuous and suspicious, like *may I help you?*, Jane always said, *just looking around.* She loved it most when they touched her, when a salesgirl handed her a free pastry or the cosmetologists gave her a makeover. She'd try to look and smell her best on those days, the days she'd be touched, like she was worth more than just being accidentally bumped into.

You like this! One counter girl coquettishly smiled at her. It was true: if Jane was a cat, she'd have been purring. Sometimes Jane would say *sorry* on her way out, squirreled with her free samples. Usually she wouldn't, because likely the salesperson would already be moving on to the next potential customer, forgetting the shape of Jane's eyebrows. And it would be okay, because Jane would already be putting out of her mind the lessons she'd learned about goldening the apples of her cheeks, concealing by blotting with her fingers. So nothing lost, nothing gained—until next time. Jane loved her rules as much as many people loved religion. The rules let her be a lonely, abiding prophet. The rules left her alone.

Spending nothing proved, Jane believed, that beauty could exist outside of money. Though this verification muzzled Jane like a tyrant.

Back when she was free, Jane kept a little notepad with her in her pocket: her to-do list. Usually it looked something like this:

<u>To Do</u>
- Don't do 18
- 24
- Walk 3.5

Counting took control of her mind, conditioned her, made her safe. Most important, it gave her meaning, an anchorage in the freedom filling her (killing her?). Like a machine, she tracked herself with this kind of code. This particular list meant that she had to get 24 free samples and then not go home for another 3.5 hours. And the numbers decided were just serendipity: sometimes Jane would count the number of jewelry on the first person she'd see outside or how many MISSING ANIMAL posts were listed in the newspaper, and those would be her numbers for tomorrow. But since she made up the rules, she could change them as often as she liked. She was her own boss. And she had the whole world inside her.

Jane alternated her free days with her working days. She worked when she heard the voices. These days needed Jane. She'd start them by reaching for the tin can underneath Otis's bed. She'd leave the apartment and start following somebody who looked like they had someplace to go. She'd take the bus to wherever he or she went, transfer when the person transferred. When the person would reach his or her final destination and Jane would see him or her getting off, the voices corking her brain, she'd get off too, and stay there. She'd stay with her tin can and find a populated space and sing songs all day. She'd sing for change or whistles or sometimes cigarettes. She was a pretty good singer. She sang James Taylor and Leonard Cohen, male vocalists, so she could change the keys around and not feel like she was turning them into jokes.

Jane earned more money than most street performers because she was young and good-looking. For the most part, she didn't think it had anything to do with how good she sang. At the end of the day, when the whole city turned cold and blue, she'd collect her money. The money made the voices die down, like she too could buy quiet. She'd make eye contact with the social fauna in bars until a conversation would be born. It was easy. Jane was pretty; people wanted to talk to her all the time. Being treated like she was wearing a glittery shirt reading possibility was nothing new. Maybe this was the case for every girl spending her whole life being watched by people.

Then at last she could go home, where she'd sleep like mad. Unless Otis woke her up. But there'd be only hours until the next day. In New Orleans, in the daytime, Jane had been the property of no one—the good old days.

The next day, which would usually be a good day, and therefore a free day, Jane had to spend however much money she earned the previous day. She bought small, disposable things she didn't need. Mostly food. Alcohol, drugs. Sunscreen and eye cream, because looking like you're twenty when you're forty could soften the blow of worrying about things like rent or safety. Clothes from the thrift store that fell apart after three washes. Ten-minute ten-dollar massages at the immigrant-owned nail salons. A wrapping paper caddy from the drugstore. The key back then had been getting through the day, seeking ways to splurge her time, buying things to feel better. An outsider might say that Jane's life was a pointless circle. But Jane believed this was better than the alternative—a life path the sanest of people often chose—a life of nothing but taking, a hole dug.

Come to think of it, Jane's New Orleans life wasn't too different from her later days at Lincoln, except then the voices were too much and she had more options. Too much freedom, it made Jane cry, like the song "For No One" by the Beatles (that was off *Revolver*, she knew, that dreamy, magic record) or the day her favorite seafood place closed for the season. The restaurant was called Cloquet and her favorite waiter's name was Eddie. She always ordered the crab, and he'd call out to the back, *an order of crab and hush puppies! Make it happen!* And whoever was in the back made it happen. There was something so playful and appalling about being completely powerless while food's being made behind your back.

Back in Jane's hospital room, Lucy considered her aunt's eyes, masquerading as sane for the pithy moment. They were withering and a seamless lapis, just like her father's. She tried to use a logic Jane would understand. *Did you ever think about divorcing Uncle Sawyer and marrying him?* During their discussion Mathilde had informed Lucy about the fake marriage, and the real divorce, and Jane's ignorance of the real divorce.

Yes, said Jane, distant, like a tragic character from a Russian novel. *Sawyer doesn't love me too much. I feel like I know you better than I know him.* She laughed.

Otis, though. Otis loved me. And when I'm out of here I'm going to find him. I already picked out our children's names. Two daughters, Joan and Juliet. They'll do all those things that you kids do. Take lessons in shit, watercolor and swimming lessons. They won't need help deciding anything.

I can see them now, said Lucy, swayed by pretense, for playing along was one of her bad habits.

It'll be far off, said Jane, *in the future. We'll fly cars. I won't be ready for children 'til then. I'm just a kid, like you. Older. But still just a kid.* She sat on her hands.

They'll be ravishing and thoughtful. With blue eyes and ribbons in their hair. And . . . what kind of hair does Otis have? Lucy felt like a solvent. The rhetoric of idealism came easily enough.

Short. They'll have enough luck for a third world country, continued Jane. *They won't need extra candles on their cakes. They'll never be the types of girls who would try anything once, or twice because they didn't trust themselves the first time. Don't you worry. Joan and Juliet will be different.*

Aunt Jane, said Lucy, *I need to tell you something.* She hadn't planned on telling her but figured now would be an appropriate time if any. Jane seemed cogent to her. Craziness was relative, right? It wasn't like you could hold it in a measuring cup. *Something you need to know about me, is . . .* She frowned.

Is that I'm sick. Too.

Honey, said Jane, *who isn't?*

I need a Heart transplant, said Lucy. *I'm serious.*

Otis's hair is light brown, said Jane. *Like Cinnamon Toast Crunch.*

I don't want to think the worst, but I could die soon. So much for defusing the moment.

You're kidding, said Jane. She wondered if this was also happening in the world, or in the clutter that was Jane's world. Maybe Lucy was in on it too. Maybe they were all gaslighting her, this farce of a family, taking advantage of her obvious damage. The other day, Jane asked Claudio to bring her a globe, and he did, a cheap classroom one from Rand McNally. Jane wrote *their world* over Eurasia with arrows going in twelve directions (twelve was how many birds she saw fly past her small window that day). Sometimes she'd spin it and pick a country and for the rest of the day pretend she was living there. But she didn't know how to do an accent from Singapore or Ghana, the two countries she last picked.

Aunt Jane?

Be quiet, said Jane, losing track of who was saying what. *Can't you see I'm feeling sick? I'm feeling silky. Arguing keeps me warm.* Jane's teeth were shuddering and her words came with different volumes, like someone was turning her louder and softer. Lost again, and Lucy really thought she'd had her for a moment. Reticent, Lucy told herself never to trust the idea of sanity ever again. Especially when it came to Aunt Jane, but probably when it concerned anyone.

a charitable meal

Sawyer was visiting his ex-wife by himself for the first time. They'd never been alone in the same room before. Claudio usually served as a buffer, in case Jane insisted on any nonsensical, tall orders. Nonsensical, such as *so if you're my husband why don't you ever kiss me?*

Two nights ago, Noah had confronted him about his marriage to Jane and kicked him out of the apartment until he was ready to trust him again. *It could be never*, Noah had warned him.

Thank you for being honest, Sawyer said, solemn. He packed a suitcase and moved in with Claudio and Mathilde, who welcomed him with open arms (and Claudio, with dreadful remorse, feeling it was all his fault). Sawyer seized the opportunity to force himself to focus on people other than himself. He made this visit alone, feeling it was necessary and maybe overdue. He wasn't sure what they'd talk about, but perhaps in some cosmic way if he could spend time with the person who unwittingly caused this, it would bring him a sort of peace, or better yet, bring Jane some peace, as she needed it more.

Hi, Jane, Sawyer said, opening her door. Light poured into her room.

Um, said Jane.

Sawyer held her hand and she let him. Her palm felt mildew-hot, like an old attic in August.

Sawyer dawdled. He gulped from his bottle of water. He picked up a picture frame and then set it down. Claudio had brought the picture frame over and put a picture of his daughters inside, but after he left, Jane had replaced it with the paper underneath featuring stock photography models. A brunette couple with a mackintosh-yellow dog in a garden. The soft glow of a calla lily made the frame's silver appear dull.

When Lucy got sick, Sawyer and Noah had been in the middle of planning their wedding. They'd already been talking about adopting, or maybe finding a surrogate. A baby! Sawyer needed to believe this would be his future. But who knew now? When he got divorced, he'd thought the hardest part was over and that his ex-wife would stay in the hospital for the rest of her life, if she needed to. He should have known, like so many other couples: trust and forgiveness were much harder to obtain than a divorce.

Would you like to leave for lunch? I checked you out for two hours. Sawyer said such nice things.

I guess? asked Jane. Her cheeks smoldered an inflammatory brick.

I know a good place nearby. Do you like croissants?

Who doesn't like croissants? All buttery and crusty, said Jane. She sounded like she could have a lot of conversations about casual subjects.

Jane put on her jacket and her shoes. They walked to the parking lot. Sawyer opened the doors to his bisque-tinted M3, and Jane slid into the passenger's seat. *Hot car,* she said, clicking her seat belt in place. Sawyer drove about ten minutes. The radio played the Four Seasons, "Walk Like a Man." He stopped in front of a coffee shop called Lulu's. Next to it was a day care center. They could see toddlers through the windows, playing with blocks and paints. Jane had never seen so many babies in her entire life.

It's a great place, said Sawyer. *We can come here again, if you like it.*

Nobody knows we are here, said Jane.

So? asked Sawyer.

He knew she wouldn't try to do anything like kiss him, because Jane was afraid. She would let anybody do whatever the hell they wanted with her body, but no way would she try to get something she actually wanted, even from the man who married her. That was why holding her hand was okay: this Heartrending security. Deferential Jane, whose vicious tendencies only veered (by the first degree) inward, didn't expect anything from Sawyer, for those with no self-worth don't expect anything from anybody.

Still, it was somehow true that Sawyer really loved this woman, but in a way no man he knew loved his wife, even the closeted gay men who still managed to have sex and best friendships with their wives. His connubial love was retired, safe. He compared it to the *god moment* he imagined surgeons experienced during surgery. A filial love, a kind of love for a baby.

Two pain au chocolats, please, Sawyer ordered for the both of them. Jane felt charmed by Sawyer's display of control. *Do you want anything else?*

He still hadn't let go of her hand. - *My companion*, - Jane thought. She said, *one orange juice and one pineapple juice*, distending her arms like a yogi or stretching cat. *I get really thirsty.*

I do too, said Sawyer. *Make that four.*

What could they talk about? He scrutinized Jane's hair, chin, collarbones. Was she sexy? Could she be? He'd never thought of it before. As he studied his ex-wife he wondered what was afflicting him, not a falling in love but a changing of outlook. Her blues bathed, diluted in the room. Her excruciating sincerity. Her damage. The endless, simple equation of time that she had for him. He felt a glimmer of something that was not pity.

I made a friend yesterday.

Jane, that's extraordinary! Who? asked Sawyer, expecting to hear all about another invalid with a fugue for a life.

Our niece. Lucy.

Okay, said Sawyer. She was slipping back into her mirages, poor girl.

She told me she's sick, said Jane, *too. That she needed surgery.*

Wait, what? Where was Jane getting this information? Wasn't it another secret they were supposed to keep from her?

For her Heart.

So Claudio told you?

Claudio told me nothing. Lucy did. A couple of days ago, said Jane. *I didn't know what to tell her. Everything she or I said. It was all awful.*

Sawyer swallowed his buttery mouthful, wondering why in the world Claudio would ever tell his sister about Lucy. The more knowledge Jane had, the more she'd disfigure it, have her way with it.

Maybe for our next visit, said his former wife, *you and I can visit Lucy in the hospital. The other kind.*

Maybe, said Sawyer. For a while, neither Sawyer nor Jane said a word. Sawyer didn't know if it was a *together* kind of silence or the clumsy kind.

What were you thinking, leaving me alone? Jane spoke with a drowning look on her face. She pushed her hands into her knees and looked deep into their pink pores, like she was trying to find a little god in herself.

I don't know, Jane, said Sawyer. His Heart buoyed.

We could've taken care of each other.

Sawyer thought about Claudio and for a moment hated him. He'd pressured Sawyer to take vows with this woman. They'd made a mockery of marriage. Jane was his partner in crime, and she didn't even know she was a criminal.

It seemed like they had all the right things for you in the hospital.

Jane gave a humid and insulted look. *The medicine helps*, she said. *Not all the time. But I could be a lot worse.*

I know, sweetie pie, said Sawyer.

I know a man who can't even speak, said Jane. *He drools. They have to wipe up his shit.*

That must be terrible, to have nobody know what you're thinking.

Sawyer thought about Noah. What was he doing now? Likely reading his e-mail or eating. Maybe he was on the subway. Dear Noah. The love of his life.

The waiter came by and asked if they needed anything else. Sawyer said, *that will be all, thanks,* smiling his faux-smile: enticing, incredibly stylized. Nearly mocking, like he was amused to be alive.

Maybe when I get better, hoped Jane, *you'll come pick me up, and then we'll pick out a house? And maybe have a kid?*

Maybe, Jane, said Sawyer. *Maybe.* He found her revelations attractive and wondered if she herself believed them, even at her maddest. They were shiny and flat, like magazine cover girls, more airbrushed than alive. He wanted to tell her something true and appalling for once, sick of lying to her, even if it was for everyone's own good. But instead he kept his mouth shut and drove her home.

When Sawyer walked Jane back to her room, she'd already reverted back to her passive self. *Maybe I'll see you soon?* she asked.

Definitely, Jane, yes, hustled Sawyer. *But I'm really busy this week. I have work.*

Everyone is always doing work, said Jane.

I'm sorry, Jane, said Sawyer. *I really am.* He looked for a moment at Jane's bed, which she'd share with nobody. The bed was unmade, and he could see the dent of last night's body, a Jane-shaped dimple. He walked away, looking forward.

Jane, making no sound, walked into the room where she'd spend the rest of her weary life. Thinking about the entire happy day, now that she was home, made her blue. She shoved the light on and hung up her jacket. She liked feeling her pulsing in the hand he'd held. She made her way to the bed and to the curtains, to her dresser and the picture frame and back to her bed. She touched everything her husband had touched. She picked up the picture frame, remembering how he'd bowed his handsome fingers around it. His fingers: gentle, like mini-cigars. With zigzaggy, zooty strokes on his palm. She kissed the frame. She tried to press it to her soul, but she didn't know where her soul was.

minion

Claudio received a telephone call from a doctor at Lincoln Mental Hospital, who'd transferred Jane to the emergency room at Good Samaritan Hospital. Jane needed a blood transfusion—twenty minutes prior, she'd slit her wrists with the soft golf pencil her hospital had allotted her. She'd been bleeding to death for only ten minutes before a nurse found her in her bathroom. *Cutting an artery with a pencil is nearly impossible*, the doctor told Claudio, sounding like he had some strategical power in his knowledge but only to a degree, like a broker explaining the stock market after a queasy, unanticipated plunge. *You'd have to try really hard.*

I see, said Claudio, and he tried to cry, pressing his palms into his heavy eyes. But it had been so long.

The more the doctor talked, the more Claudio spaced out. His sister, dying the same deranged way she had lived. If she was to spend her whole life being punished, Claudio would too. They were like identical twins in that way. *Holy*, he whispered, having no energy to say *shit* (the young brother in him would've) or *moly* (the father in him would've) or anything.

deficiency

november 2, 2010, 4:33 a.m.

Lucy's beeper erupted in sound. - *What in the world?* - Lucy woke rubbing her eyes, irritatingly locating the source of such noise. There it lay, there was the clatter it made—her salient beeper, epileptic on the floor. The instant felt like her birthday and the night before Christmas and she was in love, all at once. And softer—the disconnecting fizz of guilt in her ears. Somebody was in a hospital right now, being declared braindead. In the grand scheme of things, the luck that would save Lucy's life was nothing more than a frail silver lining. When she started this conversation on the way to Good Samaritan Hospital Medical Center, Natasha interrupted. *Don't think about that. Focus on the good vibrations.*

Lucy felt herself sweat in the dark. *It's sad he or she died*, she added.

preparation for the surgery

november 2, 2010, 7:02 a.m.

Another name for a Heart donor when (s)he's brain-dead is a *beating Heart cadaver.*

The cardiologist had warned Lucy long ago that sometimes the donor's Heart may be deemed unsuitable. Lucy waited to hear the bad news, wanting to assume the worst. That way, what she heard would either be good news or something she already knew.

A string of hours passed, thumping rain and dead leaves visible through the window. After the cornflower-into-marigold sunrise, this Heart was reckoned proper for Lucy, this Heart from Oxford, Mississippi. This southern Heart was all they knew. Hospitals had rules to respect its donors' privacy. Just as well, for Lucy had nothing in her that could find out any more information about the body. - *A body*, - she thought. Nothing could be worse than calling the body a person.

They waited and waited for the new, sad Heart to ship south to north. Lucy knew that it probably wasn't a good idea to name it, just like how she shouldn't have named her old Heart, but she did anyway. She named it Dirty Martini, since she'd always wanted to try one (imagining it bitter in a sparkly way), always felt the tense desire to be an adult. But maybe it was even a worse idea to name her Heart something with the word *dirty* in it. So she renamed it Kitten. Kitten, the alive, southern Heart from Oxford, Mississippi.

trust

november 2, 2010, 10:16 a.m.

The paramedics and doctor-specialists and nurses rushed Lucy to the emergency room, ready to take out Face and sew in Kitten. They'd done transplants before, which was so bizarre for Lucy, who felt the same empty she felt in the past flipping through a stack of scenic vacation pictures with no people. This was her life. For the professionals, it was one day's work. Everything was platitude with high-stakes jobs. Lucy's old Heart palpitated, one of the last times Face would be doing this. Face!

Trust and communication levels between doctors and patients weren't just reassuring, they were essential. Consent, or lack thereof, was a way of utilizing language to feel the effects of an action, whether that action was wanted or not. Lucy could feel the pressure from the surgeon when he asked her, *are you ready?* Would she ever be? The anesthesia evanesced, made her vanishing and susceptible. The surgeon told Lucy he was only there to help.

auf wiedersehen, good-bye

S aying good-bye wasn't Natasha's forte. Her family hugged and kissed her sister. Natasha latched her cheek to Lucy's cold hamlet of mouth, and instead told her she'd see her soon.

I don't want to go to sleep, said Lucy. *I'm scared. Please.*

I'll see you soon, repeated Natasha, reductive. - *Is there a better way of saying good-bye?* - she speculated, after Lucy was wheeled out of the room.

See you later. In a torpor.

See you later, alligator.

See you when I see you.

See you later—never good-bye. It was always, see you later.

(sound) effects

The year before, Carly and Lucy helped Natasha study vocabulary for the SATs, and every day Carly picked a new favorite word. One, *onomatopoeia* (how Carly loved that downy, near-negative letter *O*!), classified words that were technically also the sounds they made. Words like *crunch, pop, boing, buzz, wham!*

There had to be storms of sound on Lucy's operating table. *Thump, thump, thump.* The sound of a beating Heart. *Beep. Beep. Beep.* The sound of the cardiac monitor when the person's Heart was working. *Beeeeeeeeeeeeeeeeeeeeeeeep.* The sound of the cardiac monitor when the person's life came to a shuddering stop.

In movies, surgeons kept their speech simple. *Scalpel*, they'd say, and the nurse would get the surgeon the scalpel. Regarding life-and-death situations, Carly guessed that there wasn't enough time to dillydally. You had to make politics of words, preserve each one and keep pace, hold on to its utmost importance. So while her sister was getting her Heart replaced, Carly didn't marvel much about words. She wondered instead about sounds.

folly

november 2, 2010, 3:26 p.m.

On the operating table, Lucy dreamed of the beating Heart cadaver, deciding he was a boy. He smelled scummy and animal, like sheep. *It's a boy*, Lucy said, like he was being born, recognizing Kitten nesting bluish and strictured among his ribs. *Drip, drip.* He reached inside himself for his Heart and plucked it. There came a light sound of ripping, for his Heart actually had strings. It wasn't just something people said. Things were all happening the way people said them.

The boy pushed Kitten through her throat, past her collarbones, let his hand hang still for a shattering second down her esophagus. Shelving it like a bottle of Riesling. She didn't choke, but his arm tickled. The Heart pulsed, nuzzling Lucy, dwarfing her body. The beat felt heavy and collective, a curlicued round of applause.

You.

Have such.

A big mouth, the boy sniffled. Then the generous sucker played her bones, one at a time, like a pianist pressing keys or a cancer inflaming her. When he kissed her humerus, they both started laughing. She looked down, and she was clothes-less. Such an emblematic, a clichéd, dreamer. Then she looked at the boy. He was even more naked. His body was carnage, a lather of color, a meaty confetti. His insides reflected off her: elucidated, clocklight-toned. Lucy felt something complicated, like love.

surviving

november 2, 2010, 5:25 p.m.

Lucy woke up: victory! Hymns draped over the room. Not traditionally religious songs, just the songs she loved so much. Stevie Wonder, Simon & Garfunkel, Joan Baez; not the lyrics, the actual music. Had she lost her most primary senses, or was she hallucinating a synesthesia? Perhaps it was a dream she was leaving. Startled, she looked down at her feet, and thank god she recognized her squashy toes, the mini pears she'd used her whole life to kiss the ground when she walked. *Princess toes*, her mom called them, feet where the big toe is biggest and the rest align in a slope.

She was alive, with somebody else's Heart inside of her. - *Hallelujah*, - she thought. Then - *thank the lord*. - Though she didn't consider herself religious, she had so many pious words and phrases engrained in her mind during her most despairing times, often invoking the word *god* without consciously realizing whom she was talking about.

The Heart is in, said the surgeon, whose name she couldn't remember, though he'd already placed her Heart(s) in his hands. He had tourmaline skin and a dazzling accent, and was buried beneath scrubs and a mask. *Your body passed with flying colors.*

Lucy loved so much that he used these words, words with merit. She loved the surgeon's face. She loved the room's ceiling and floor and its satisfying, snow-shaded walls. She loved the feeling of her body on the bed, and she loved the feeling of having a body.

The surgeon told Lucy that she'd remain in the Intensive Care Unit until likely the next week, when her body would be safe to leave the comfort and sanitization of isolation, strong enough to survive on its own. He told her that at the moment, her condition was *good*. - *Doctors and teachers are similar*, - thought Lucy. - *They categorize in gradients*. - Excellent, good, fair, poor.

Lucy sneezed, felt the pleasure of winnowing effluvia, but nobody else was in the room. *Bless me*, she said.

surviving: reprise

I'm sorry, Jane said to her brother, who was standing across from her bed.

For trying to kill yourself or for not succeeding? Claudio asked his sister.

Succeeding? asked Jane, now among the micro percent of the time she could be cogent, even clever: *you have a pretty cheap idea of success.*

I didn't do anything, dodged Claudio.

It doesn't take very long to bleed to death. Jane had cut a main artery, and minutes had counted. Now she was safe in the hospital, had gotten her arms stitched up in the ER. They were in a ward just two floors above where Lucy was recovering from her surgery. Jane was unaware of their proximity, which gave Claudio a perverse feeling.

I was thinking about how it's my birthday next month, said Jane, *and how I so badly wished I never had one.*

The notion of his sister without a birthday made an endearing and terrible sense to Claudio. He made the choice not to picture the strange idea any longer, instead thinking of her moment of birth. How stupid and happy his family must have been. How much like a family. *Mom always used to tell me that right before you were born*, he said, *I had told Mom that I changed my mind and didn't want a sister anymore. And then I saw you. And there you were. And I said we can keep her, but let's give away any others.*

Precious, derided Jane.

What on earth triggered you?

Life gets to you sometimes, Claud, she said. *You of all people should know that.*

I have children, said Claudio. *It's a different way of thinking.*

Like how?

It's easier to forget what your favorite food is or what color you look best in or what makes you depressed.

I would love for forgetting to come easy.

You just don't have the time for yourself. You realize you don't really even need that time.

I see what you mean, said Jane. *But a child is never fully safe.*

You're right, said Claudio, and this was the saddest truth he'd ever confirmed.

You're a good man, Jane said to her brother. *If I ever had children, I'd be scared of hurting them.*

Come again?

Like you said, you think of them before you think of yourself.

Claudio closed his eyes. Jane was sick. Life was hard for her. Naturally she'd want to spare her potential children the suffering. It wasn't because she wanted to hurt them. In the hospital, too frail to touch, lying with her arms in white bandages for shackles, it wasn't that she wanted to be damaged. He had to keep reminding himself of this.

Why didn't you ever want my nieces to meet me?

Claudio was not expecting this. *I always told you, I wanted you to. It was just a matter of finding the right time.*

What time would that have been? Jane looked at her ripped wrist as though she were wearing a watch.

As soon as you felt better, pivoted Claudio.

Lucy came to visit me.

What?

She told me she was having trouble with her Heart. Why, with that timing, you'd think god had some big idea for our family.

But how? Claudio asked in the voice of a small boy.

Her mother told her. Lucy said.

Claudio had no more means of continuing this conversation with Jane, for now. He wouldn't interrogate her over the petty details—this pickle called for more difficult conversations with different people. So he said the only words left he had for her.

Please, just stop hurting yourself. And stop letting yourself be harmed.

Easier said than done.

Do something nice for me, he said, *and Lucy. Keep yourself alive, if only for that.*

If only for that. Jane laughed.

You know I don't mean it, said Claudio. *You have lots of other reasons to be alive.*

Give me one. Please.

The way you sing.

What Jane didn't know about the day Claudio picked her up from New Orleans was that Claudio had arrived at Otis's house earlier in the morning, watching from his car as Jane left, holding her tin can. Claudio had followed Jane to the French Quarter, watched her sing Tom Waits, and listened to her because she was so lovely. He'd listened all afternoon, and she'd had no idea. She hadn't seen anything.

Let me sleep, said Jane. She reached for the cup of water on her nightstand. As she sipped, one of her bandages flipped open, exposing a skin-fizzling bruise. It looked fake, like a special effect.

You've slept enough.

I don't like being awake.

You're afraid of being awake, he said, in a way that made them both want to cry.

Claudio felt his phone buzzing. It was a text message from

Mathilde: *I need you.* She always thought she did. Claudio sat down on a visitor's chair and played with his hands, moving his wedding ring up and down the knuckle. Sometimes it was so sad to be needed.

Sleep tight, he told his sister. *I have to go. I'll be back tomorrow.* Then he looked at her for as long as he could stand it.

Before you leave, said Jane. *I wrote a note. Before. It was supposed to be for you. You can still read it, if you want.* She motioned toward her nightstand, where the staff had moved her measly belongings. *Open the frame. Underneath the picture of those people I don't know.*

Claudio did as he was told, without asking any questions, and without reading the note just yet.

I just wanted somebody to understand, I guess, even for just a little bit. But none of that matters anymore. Nothing is how I imagined. For one thing, I'm alive. I had no idea that would happen. So night night.

Good night, Jane, said Claudio.

Jane crossed her arms, wrapping herself in her elbows. Her brother had good intentions, but really, that was it. And what good did it do her anyway? *You're not my hero,* she announced to the shut door, because Claudio had already left for his other family, the family that mattered to him. She scratched one scarred hand with the other, then switched. Residual blood on her arms flaked asymmetrically, like batter.

A few minutes later, she heard a rustle at the door, but her brother hadn't come back, of course. It was her doctor, who asked her how her arms felt. Jane said, *they're the only things that still hurt.*

aftermath

Natasha opened a plastic tin of mini cupcakes. *From your math class.*

How do you feel? asked Carly.

Still froggy groggy, purred Lucy. The drugs made her act bafflingly, yield to impulses such as sticking her hair in her mouth, trying to eat it.

The number of flowers, candy, and stuffed animals Lucy received from her classmates and neighbors was tremendous. She named the animals after references in Elton John songs: Blue Jean Baby, Tiny Dancer, Norma Jeane, Mona Lisa, Mad Hatter, Johnny Empty Garden, Little Jeannie, Crocodile Rock, Bennie, Honky Cat, Nikita, Daniel, Levon, and You. You was the *You* in "Your Song." You was a stuffed giraffe from Natasha. Lucy sometimes pointed at the giraffe and said, *hey, You.*

How wonderful life is, when you're in the world.

During her recovery Lucy finished all of her "get-well present" books, even the campy commercial fiction where the author thinks (s)he's a good writer just by using big words from time to time. *I can't not finish books* was her justification. She watched movies, categorizing into marathons by theme: straight-to-video Disney sequels (*Cinderella 3* was her favorite), wintry movies with religious/atheistic undertones (like *Narnia* or *The Golden Compass*), inspirational music mentorship movies

(*Mr. Holland's Opus* or *August Rush*), sports movies with racial ties (she wondered, - *does a movie exist with Denzel Washington that* doesn't *have a message?* -), period pieces, bad movies with animals, worse movies with talking animals. She also started a journal.

The summer before the surgery, Lucy's cardiologist gave Claudio and Mathilde the name of a psychologist. *Lucy may think it'll help to voice her anxieties to somebody who doesn't play a role in her life.* Lucy refused them all; it wasn't that she didn't believe in therapy, she just could identify her feelings with much fluency and felt tacit about life not being reasonable. She lived in a world where most of her country wasn't ready for Uncle Sawyer and Uncle Noah to get married and where her aunt Jane couldn't speak like a normal human being and where Carly's biological parents abandoned her most likely because of a government's policy and where her very own Heart was failing. She understood all of that and didn't feel like she needed to talk to an objective stranger with a degree about it.

So Mathilde bought her daughter a notebook, and Lucy filled it with poem after poem about pain. This was her therapy, and it was sacred, and it was free. The day she arrived home from the hospital, Lucy tattooed her body with Bic pen—one vertical ode on one arm and another on her leg, pressing them together to make a collaborative horizontal poem. She called it,

Donor to Recipient

A good story   anyway: this is
where they harnessed   the bad Heart, cut
it out,   harvested us into severe
                            oneness
where we were   hunted by
surgeons,   squatters
a Bartlett bruise   insides being pardoned,

engorged   evidence
an opus   of crescents. transcen-
                                dence:

a form of lying?   would you rather:
go out (of) style   go out (in) style
deeply discounted   cheaper than fodder
given the options   how would you (de)file
                                yourself: body colliding
with body,   nothing more method
                                than
tried and true   humans
nothing more human than
t(r)ying   could be more
to the story   than this
?   this is where
the bad   Heart could've
ruptured: pocked fear the   engorged
torch song together   we're
more   human
than dying

The form of branding had a low ante, as she could let the marks die in the bath. They were nothing like the scars on her chest: there forever, or at least until shortly after the rest of her life.

Decanting her soul into words created a wall of protection around it. Once she put a feeling into a poem, the sensation became at once immortalized and less real—a story, as there was no way she could have possibly captured every feeling and sensation she had. Writing things down detached Lucy from them.

What's new, peanut? Her father entered the room holding two decaf lattes.

Dad! yelped Lucy. *You scared me.*

Sorry. Don't you look just like a rock star this morning?

Can I be Robert Plant? Lucy set two fingers on her neck. The pulse of her new Heart bounced.

He wishes! Which reminds me, I saw a girl who looked like you at the coffee shop. Only of course, she wasn't as beautiful.

Lucy lifted the top and sipped the crème, musing. *What about her reminded you of me?* She very much enjoyed when other people thought about her during moments she had no participation in. It reminded her of the tightened impact she was leaving on the world.

She was reading The Invisible Circus.

Dad! That's one of my favorite books!

She also kept yawning.

Yawning reminds you of me? It was incredible. Lucy couldn't control what about her sparked associations for people. *I yawn a lot?*

Kid, you do, her father insisted.

So, what else is new?

Claudio handed his daughter the evening papers. *I have to warn you, though, it's mostly bad news.*

Lucy looked at the front page of the international news. *Another war? Again?*

It's the same war, said her father.

It's always the same war, said Lucy, shivering at how dreadful wars were. One side would do something terrible, and then the children of the victims would do something back, and then their children would remember, etcetera. Fear and loyalty.

What can you do? said Claudio. *As long as love exists, war will exist.*

I can't believe that.

I'm glad you can't.

I've been writing poetry.

Poetry, eh? Claudio nodded, then winked as he clicked his throat, making a cozy typewriter sound. A dad kind of noise.

He knew very little about poetry. The last time Claudio had

read a poem, the Clinton administration had been in office. He wasn't a born reader. Mostly since he was far-sighted—reading came as more of a struggle than, say, catching a movie or playing music. Whatever he read, Claudio came across like he was suffering, like he was carrying all of his troubles in his face.

Do you remember when I was a kid and you'd read me to sleep? I loved L. Frank Baum and Lewis Carroll best. Oh, and Roald Dahl. Charlie and the Glass Elevator. *You'd read to me in a tired voice to try to get me to sleep quicker.*

I did?

You really don't remember?

Your old man has a lot of stuff he has to remember. Claudio tapped his brain like an eggplant from the supermarket about to expire.

Dad, I wanted to talk to you about something.

Me too.

About your sister.

I know, said Claudio. *Mom told you,* remembering the prior night, when he'd had one of the worst fights he'd ever had with his wife. *You selfish fuck,* he'd called her, and cringed to himself, recalling this. He'd never spoken to her that way before. He couldn't help it—he may have betrayed her trust, but at least he'd done it with the intent of protecting their family.

It wasn't that Mathilde told Lucy the truth about Jane that infuriated him either—more Mathilde's impulse to call out other injustices merely due to her egocentric inability to bear being duped. He knew she wasn't looking out for Lucy's best interest, no matter how much she said she was. But they'd made up, and forgiven each other, because they had to. All massive issues are diminished during the time of one's kin dabbling between life and death. (In this regard, weren't Sawyer and Noah lucky—or unlucky, depending on how you viewed it—not to have children yet, to have more freedom to carry out their divergences?)

I'm sorry. It was the worst thing I've ever done to you and your sisters.

That's what's bothering me. Why did you think it was the right thing to do?

I didn't. I thought it was the only thing I could do.

I just can't believe she exists.

She does.

Yes. I saw her with my very own eyes.

I'm sorry I wasn't there to, uh, protect you. But I guess that's my punishment.

I didn't need protecting.

What did you do?

Well, she showed me the pictures you've given her of us. And she talked about how you told her I love English class. And she told me she's also a writer, but she didn't show me anything she wrote. She also said some odd stuff about Carly's birth parents taking her back to China. But, uh, mostly she was good. Good and sweet. I really wanted to love her.

I love her too, Lucy. Tears tethered to the nooks of his eyes. He swallowed.

I'd like to see her again.

We can see her as much as you want.

Do your sisters know?

I told Natasha.

Okay, so Mom and I will tell Carly tonight. There won't be any secrets left.

the natasha who researched

Lucy came home from the hospital a week and a half after her surgery. The night before, Natasha figured out who had died so her sister could live. In Oxford, Mississippi, on November 2, all of the town obituaries were written for people old enough to die from age but for one, whose name had been Alan Douglas Rachmones, who'd been withdrawn just one week from his twenty-second birthday.

The Internet was a sea of lethal knowledge. After further research, Natasha connected that he died in a motorcycle accident. Dead on impact. That wasn't bad, was it? A splash of pain. - *Like it didn't count,* - Natasha wished. She studied his picture. Cute—panoramic jaw; a godly nose, dimples. Gorgeous eyebrows—Natasha, who always noticed eyebrows, felt ludicrously jealous of the ones he'd had.

Time told the truth: he died the evening of November 1. Natasha closed the newspaper. It killed her that she couldn't tell anybody. She went to the guest room, where her uncle Sawyer had been staying for the past couple weeks, ever since Noah had kicked him out of their apartment.

I have a little question.

What's up?

What's your biggest fear?

That's a little question? Sawyer exhaled liberally. *I don't know if I have much of those anymore.*

You have to be afraid of something.

I mean, aside from the typical human tragedies of losing family, being lonely, feeling Heartbroken. His voice shifted. *When I was a little boy, I used to fear money. I'd have nightmares where I would swallow, then choke, on spare change.*

Natasha had to laugh. *I beg your pardon?*

Dimes weren't bad. They were tiny, easily digestible. Pennies were a little rough going down because of the copper, but still okay. I mean, it was no cup of tea, swallowing change, but in my nightmares, who am I to complain about the pieces that didn't kill me? It was the quarters that were the worst. The size of eyes.

Natasha said nothing. Uncle Sawyer said, *something's wrong.*

Nothing's wrong. Her sister was alive and she had a new Heart and she was going to live a long and healthy life, knock on wood, and god bless her, god bless the doctors, god bless their family. It was impossible for something to be wrong. She told her uncle thank you, and she loved him. She left him with a steady ache in her mouth, feeling as though she had just swallowed a pocketful of quarters.

That night, Natasha fell asleep to a Dylan record, *Blonde on Blonde.* Some lyrics sunk into her dreams.

The ghost of electricity howls in the bones of her face.

Natasha closed her eyes and opened her eyes and recognized the boy in front of her, eating a cruller, his fingers syrupy. He was a handsome fellow, and she was in love. She called him Jonathan Taylor Thomas, the name of her childhood celebrity crush. This boy looked nothing like him, but she wanted to christen him with a name she knew was familiar, one that had given the child-Natasha the chemical, synthetic representation of love. Besides, she knew his real name, but wouldn't admit it, even to herself and even in her own dreams.

He didn't ask her how her sisters were. He might not have even known she had sisters. He said, *it hurt. It hurt so much.*

What hurt?

The accident.

Oh man.

You know what the worst part was? I was all alone when it happened. He put on a suit and a tie.

Where are you going? asked Natasha.

Nowhere, his voice floating. *I'm extinct.*

A rope fell out of the ceiling. J.T.T. handed her the rope, then left the room. Natasha grabbed the rope and pulled and pulled. She felt something in between a tremble and nuzzle inside her pelvis, a flicker that pounded into her like somebody flicking a light switch on and off. Natasha met a happiness that could only be discovered through sleep. She felt like a guitar that somebody could play.

She felt herself wake up, calcified. Four a.m.—morning, technically. What a start to the day. She was alone, bathed in scattered technological light—her phone, her laptop, her tablet all on. She heard the hallway bathroom faucet go off—somebody else in the house was awake! She opened the bathroom door. Carly was filling a cup of water.

I just had a really good dream.

Congratulations. Sloe eyed and soporific, Carly plopped her willowy ass on the toilet to make room for her sister.

But those are the worst. Natasha bit her thumb. *You wake up and remember your real life.*

What happened?

It was all a dream, repeated Natasha.

You used to read Word Up! *magazine,* quoted Carly, not missing a beat.

I was in love with this boy.

Who?

I don't know. She was so ashamed of who he was. *I called him Jonathan Taylor Thomas, but it wasn't actually him.*

What did you do? In the dream.

Ate donuts. Well, he did. I didn't.

Even your good dreams sound boring, teased Carly. She scraped her finger along the edge of her cup. Her sister was right, yet Natasha was strangely fulfilled by her dream's humdrumness.

A metronome purr came from Lucy's room. Lucy was laughing in her sleep, nascent against her deliberate fort of pillows. It was the kind of night where they had nothing to prove she wasn't happy, nothing to prove she wouldn't survive this, and nothing to prove they weren't all dreaming this.

lucy's reverie

Lucy had been dreaming of Carly and Stephen. She thought she felt Kitten pulse almost hesitantly as she lifted herself out of her body and into her sister's.

Lovebirds. The warmly woven, pluperfect voices. One belonged to her, stippled with laughter. She could now enjoy her life, occupying this house of a sister's body.

He said, *remember that time I kneeled down and reached into your throat to grab all of the softballs that were staying there?*

She said, *it was terrific not to have a stomachache.*

And remember when I accidentally reached into your lungs and punctured your alveoli?

I love the way you kisskiss me. It's always plural, knowing exactly what type of love Stephen harbored for her, a mineral kind of love.

Stephen said, *plural kisses accompany a singular desire.*

Remember that time we turned my room into a schooner?

Stephen said, *in the ocean, the fattiest parts of you get the coldest. They're the first to lose circulation.*

Carly said, *you know what kind of love ours is? A fungus love.*

Indeed, Stephen said. *It grows and it grows, and it never runs out. Well, good night, Schnookums.*

Night, Porcupine, she said.

They said good night as Lucy woke up.

misconceptions

Good morning, said Carly. She checked her cell phone to see if Stephen had left her a text message in the middle of the night. He indulged her with texts of whims and little importance. Sometimes just one word: *hello* or *you!* or *baby* or *mornin'*. They messaged so succinctly and so often, Carly's fingers contained the muscle memory of all the words she wanted to say. She could have been blind.

The three sisters met in the kitchen for breakfast. Lucy was waiting for her tutor to arrive. Her doctor told her she wouldn't be able to return to school for another two months, at least, until her breastbone finally healed. Natasha ate oatmeal with blueberries. Lucy made a smoothie with coconut oil and bananas. Carly buttered toasted sunflower bread.

We heard you laughing in your sleep last night.

You did? Lucy avoided Carly's gaze. *I don't remember what I'd been dreaming about.* She looked at Natasha. Natasha took out a wand of mascara and gave herself big, gluey eyelashes, twisting the wand like a miniature orchestra conductor.

Every day, Natasha had driven her sisters to school. Then she'd tell her sisters, *have the best day*, a compulsion stemming from elementary school, when they'd reported to the same schoolyard. Ever since her first day of third grade, when Carly started kindergarten and Lucy was in first grade, their parents entrusted Natasha to see her sisters off at school.

She'd hug them and say, *have the best day.* Sometimes she had the urge to kiss her sisters on the lips and both cheeks and in the parts of their heads of hair. And sometimes she wanted to hug them both so hard she would knock them over and even maybe hurt them accidentally. Sometimes she wanted to hurt them because they were so much smaller than her. Because she could.

On Natasha's first day of third grade, she saw her two little sisters off in their matching yellow jackets and satchel backpacks. The instant was historic. - *They could get hurt so easily.* -
- *At lunch, somebody could spill their juice.* -
- *Somebody could push them.* -
- *Somebody could break them.* -
Man, they were small. She was supposed to protect them. *Wait!* They turned around. Carly was wearing shorts, and Natasha could see her goosebumped shins.

This is the very last second we'll all be together before you start school. Natasha picked up two rocks in the schoolyard, one zeppelin-shaped, one jagged. She handed Lucy the long stone and Carly the rough stone. Then she picked up a tiny pebble. She placed the pebble in her pocket, a house for her irresistible feelings.

Keep these in your pockets.

When her sisters left for the second time, Natasha took her pebble out and placed it on the ground. She kicked it around. She felt sweat conglomerate at the V of her T-shirt, as perceptible and delicate as raindrops or a string of pearls.

In high school, Natasha still smiled at both of her sisters and said, *have the best day.* But she couldn't hug them anymore. She wasn't in school anymore. She was in purgatory, better known as the real world.

I love you, Tash, her sisters both said at once, like they were one girl.

Me too.

As they all grew up, Natasha had felt it hard to contain her love for her sisters.

I love you so much I could eat you.

I love you so much I could kill you.

I love you to death.

Words so devoted they were hideous.

As the eldest sibling, Natasha felt the closest to being a parent, with the imperialistic gift of hurt-love. Her sisters were there when she felt most irritated. She had the most expectations for them. At any time, she was able to pick them up and hurt them. She was given a power she felt nobody deserved to have, even a type of god.

the city

Claudio and Mathilde let Lucy take the Long Island Rail Road into the city for a Saturday afternoon with her sisters.

I wouldn't want to live in the city, said Carly. *Too much crazy stuff going on.*

Sometimes the craziest things happen in the suburbs, pointed out Natasha.

Like a kid getting sick and dying. Lucy said the thing they were all thinking.

That could happen anywhere, Carly said.

They took the E from Penn Station to the West Village, and saw a woman lying on the floor. Next to her was a bucket filled with garbage. The whole train smelled of cleaning solution. She was crying. *They're coming! The plane with the suitcase full of gods lands in ten, nine, eight, seven, six, five, four, three, two, one*, she bawled.

This is a World Trade Center–bound E train, said the automated conductor. The doors closed and the train sighed.

That's eerie that they still call it that, said Lucy.

Why not? They were there once. That means they're there, said Carly.

I want to give her money, said Lucy, pausing for concern, tilting her head in the direction of the woman, which was also the direction of the floor.

Why? asked Natasha.

Because doing good's a muscle, said Lucy, *and I'd like to bulk up.*

Don't give her money, argued Carly. *She'll spend it on drugs.*

Why do you think it's drugs that are making her crazy? asked Lucy. *Maybe drugs are the only things that can keep her sane.*

No amount of money we give could really help her, pointed out Natasha. *We aren't her parents.*

But didn't you hear the story about the homeless man who fell upon some hard times, and then he went on the radio, and people donated a house to him, and now he does voice-overs for radio commercials?

There are two kinds of true, said Natasha. *Stories, and everything else.*

I want to believe the story's true.

That's your problem, agreed Carly. *You're stymied by hope.*

Once I gave money to a homeless kid on the subway, said Natasha. *I was on the six train with Molly, and we had just come from one of Mom's shows, minding our own business, when this kid with uncut hair started begging. He looked and sounded like a normal kid. He could've been one of our friends. He said he wasn't really trying to bother anyone, but he didn't have a family who could help him out. So I gave him ten dollars.*

That's not fair, said Lucy, *to older people.*

Hey, said Natasha, *life's not fair.*

What is life, asked Lucy, *anyway?*

A song by George Harrison, said Carly.

He was just a kid, repeated Natasha.

The worst part about crazy people is how they're everybody's problem, you know? Lucy rehabilitated their discourse.

Even so, said Natasha, *I can't imagine what it must be like to be crazy. You may be the entire world's problem, but* your *problem is the entire world.*

lucy's birthday

The night of Lucy's seventeenth birthday, her sisters threw her a secret party in their basement. Claudio and Mathilde went out to dinner in the city, giving their daughters the house for the evening. They probably wouldn't be home until at least midnight.

The Simone basement was 1970s style: shag carpeting, Claudio's record players and vinyls in the corner. Another generation arrived through the boxes filled with teen magazines from the early 2000s, that maudlin decade when "Dubya" Bush was in office and Paris Hilton ruled the media. The three sisters collected *Seventeen*, *YM*, *Teen Beat*, and *Tiger Beat*, and they saved them all. Occasionally the girls still thumbed through the publications, nostalgic for *The O.C.* references and advertisements for Smuckers chapstick. Antique periodicals.

Natasha announced they'd start off with a game of spin the bottle/seven minutes in heaven. The spun bottle decided who kissed whom, but instead of a small peck on the lips, the couple would go into the laundry room for seven minutes to kiss more.

The ratio was perfect and intentional: five girls and five boys. Natasha, Lucy, Carly, Molly, and Leora. Stephen, LJ, Matt, John, and Sloane.

John, a ginger with nostrils the size of cherry pits, wore a suit and a tie to the party. John—homeschooled, smug, and nearly mute—was their neighbor from three houses away. Lucy, in the same way she always assumed nerdy people were really nice, liked boys with no game. He greeted her with an envelope. Then he went around the basement introducing himself. *Hello, I'm John. The thing that you need to know about me is that I wear a suit and a tie to a party in somebody's basement.*

Lucy opened the envelope to find a twenty-dollar bill, a ten-dollar bill, a five-dollar bill, and a one-dollar bill inside. He'd spelled her name *Lucie* on the front envelope. This was odd. How could you mistake spelling a name like Lucy? Maybe he thought she would think of him more often, and perchance endearingly, if he made a mistake.

LJ had started dating another girl, Leora, the week of Lucy's surgery. Lucy felt obliged to invite her too, and she came with him. Carly and Natasha joked that she had an IQ of twenty. Lucy knew that they were doing it for her benefit, but she thought Leora was nice and smelled like popovers sometimes, especially mornings before homeroom.

Sloane, with his harsh hazel eyes, walked the walk. He was six-four. Half black and half white, *like a diner cookie*, he liked to say. In middle school, he'd believed that it was not only his job but also his god-given duty to give every girl their first kiss. He never reached Lucy, who at the time wasn't interested. Then, of course, puberty happened.

Birthday girl goes first, said Natasha.

Lucy thought to herself, - *be cool or something*. - She twirled the old-timey glass Coke bottle, empathetic for the tiny carbonated particles left, clinging in droplets to the side. They'd never be drunk. She gave an exaggerated spin, staring at the knees of her friends who still had their regular Hearts in their bodies. It landed on Carly, sandwiched between Stephen and Sloane. - *Stephen!* - Kitten squirmed vigilantly through Lucy's rib cage. Carly nudged the bottle in Sloane's direction.

Laundry room's thata way, pointed Natasha.

I live here, snorted Lucy, annoyed.

That you do. Sloane, touching her arm, was as handsome as Ricky Ricardo, the type of toxic boy who would probably never have to take a girl on a first date in his entire life. All he needed to do was find a girl and a bed, where they could lie next to each other and talk for hours about anomalous, private things until they fell asleep.

Lucy was still thinking about Stephen, her eyes clouding with sinister energy. - *Be quiet, mind! A mind is a terrible thing to waste. Does thinking that make me racist? You know a mime is a terrible thing to waste.* - She hated her mind. - *What if I die right this second?* - The second ended. She'd been feeling this pathological depression all week: a floating and vaporous foundation, one that seeped through her. Depression wasn't like fear or anger or panic—a body didn't go into alert mode when it was depressed. Lucy's depression was a cold Saturday afternoon with no obligations, and instead of relaxation feeling dread—like wanting so badly something that wasn't there.

Lucy's kindergarten class once had a lesson in floating and sinking, where Lucy's teacher dropped objects into a bowl of water to predict what would sink and what would float. Everyone in the class predicted that the penny would float except Lucy. The teacher kept a tally, and for the PENNY row wrote everyone else's name in the FLOAT column. Lucy stood alone under SINK. Of course she'd been wrong.

She didn't know why she remembered that. - *The brain is interesting*, - she thought. She reflected about how every time she washed her hands she'd sing "Happy Birthday to You" to herself twice, since she heard somewhere that's the suitable length to remove all the germs. Lucy hated germs. - *Happy birthday, dear Lucy.* - She always ended this brain-ditty with - *and many more, 'til you're twenty-four, and your parents kick you out the door,* - like Cody from elementary school, who would always add that tag and make everyone laugh. She wondered about Cody, who had moved away, and how funny it would be if he knew she thought about him every time she washed her hands.

Your hand's soft, Sloane said. *Like you've never worked a day in your life.*

I work. These words squirted out of Lucy's mouth. She washed dishes and made her bed and wrote until she perspired. *Did you know that our initials are each other's, but backward?* Lucy asked. She needed her sodden hands to stop and just be her hands. She felt like a good song after being used in a commercial.

You okay, Lucy? Sloane asked, then accused. *You're nervous! No I'm not.*

- *He'll see my scars. He'll touch my hideous torso. Think comfortable thoughts, brain,* - Lucy ordered herself, like the smell of her sister Carly's scalp when she'd been an infant or the song "Do Wah Diddy Diddy" or her neighbor Mrs. Meyer, who spoke in Yiddish to her husband and who let Lucy pet her pet cat De Pudge, calling it *giving her a snudge.*

Sloane tapped Lucy's nose. *Come closer.*

What's your favorite condiment? Small talk failed Lucy in this situation, so she resorted to asking bizarrely specific questions, trying to find the clue to Sloane's psyche, believing creativity to be her only wealth.

Honey mustard, he said. He didn't acknowledge the arbitrariness of the question in the scope of where they were, what they were about to do. *You're so cute.*

Thanks, and you're interesting, she replied, bewildered. Man, she said the word *interesting* too much. She thought to herself, - *next time I say it I need to put a quarter in a jar.* - She thought again about pennies. She sang the birthday song to herself again and thought about Cody. What Lucy needed was more mental hygiene. Sloane's eyes perfectly fit in his face. Looking into them felt like trespassing. Holy mackerel.

Why don't we kiss? Sloane suggested, which was about the coolest thing anyone had ever said to Lucy.

Why do we kiss? asked Lucy. *In AP psych class we learned there's no evolutionary value.* In fact, there were scientists who studied kissing. They were called philematologists. *The most likely theory is that it comes from primate mothers passing along chewed food to their toothless babies.* Evolutionary psychologists had also done tests suggesting that the fluid swap creates a chemical transfer that helps humans better understand if the person they're kissing would be able to better produce viable offspring.

They heard Jay-Z playing through the speakers outside. Sloane drummed the beat of the song on her waist. He massaged Lucy's shoulders with the base of his hands, rolling a finger around her shirt collar. He placed his hand on the skin showing, the color of Brie. *I like this part of you.* He lifted her shirt up to touch the small of her spine. *This part too.* Kissing the apple of her left cheek. Fake flattery. Her parts weren't all hers. - *Does that make Sloane a polygamist?* - she thought. - *If we ever fell in love, he would love another's Heart. Is he a necrophile? Half a necrophile? Brain, I hate you!* -

god, I love your body. Sloane swooned. His bear hugs; his quick tongue swishing around hers. She breathed into his neck and ear, smelling Nilla wafers, fresh terry cloth towels, sweat. This was what he was made of. And Lucy? Her body felt more like a vending machine, with processed snacks, shaken sodas, and spare change inside.

Do you? asked Lucy.

Lucy looked at his mouth, his bottom lip spooning the top. He said again, *god, I love it.*

She thought, - *but how could you?* -

wonderland

Lucy ushered Sloane to her room instead of back to the base-ment. *Nice place you've got here*, Sloane relished.

They kissed for almost an hour. The song playing in the next room was "Norwegian Wood," its lyrics misheard by Lucy. *Isn't it good, knowing she would?* He yanked out the chord on the light on Lucy's nightstand. She liked that he felt very comfortable in her room, that he had the audacity.

He took his shirt off. Lucy knew what she was supposed to do next, first with her hands, since she had never done it before. She was supposed to tread slowly like other teenage girls and do only what she felt ready for. She knew all about how her body was her property, and how young she was. Still, Sloane would be a fine friend in bed, and it was lovely not to be alone. Lucy's finely tuned sense of her own mortality only intensified her longing to be normal, to live. He put a cold hand over her crotch. A nocturnal act of mercy, of alchemy.

Be careful, she said.

I'll treat your body with the highest regard, Sloane said. That was the spirit. She let him touch her because why not?

lucy's wish

Progeria is an extremely rare genetic condition wherein symptoms resembling aspects of aging are manifested at an early age. The disorder occurs in an estimated one per eight million live births. Those born with progeria typically live to their midteens and early twenties. It is a genetic condition that occurs as a mutation and is not inherited.

Lucy watched a TLC documentary about progeria while eating dried mango slices in bed. TLC had reality shows about Siamese twins and families with nineteen children. It was just like the freak shows in the circus, only twenty-four hours a day, diffusing from anybody's living room.

- *How does living feel to people with progeria?* - thought Lucy, chewing a mango strand with her eyes closed. - *Like that?* - she wondered. - *Intensified.* - They aged in their bodies many times as fast. Like dog years: seven years to every human year. It was the opposite way of living from what she was used to. It would be the opposite way of dying than the way she expected to.

She pictured somebody her age with a face and wisdom of an octogenarian. The wisdom was the stretch: she could imagine someone like Sloane with a wimpled face but not with the matching placid nature. She couldn't imagine somebody her age being okay with dying. Even her hubristic peers who adolescently theorized, *I won't last past twenty-seven*, their predictions were more glamorous than sincere.

How Lucy wanted to be an old lady, wanted her teeth to loosen in their sockets, wanted a head of caulking-textured hair, wanted a shabby hairline bent like an upside-down smile. She wanted nobody to touch her hair or to even think about it because her husband, god bless him, would be dead after fifty-some-odd years of marriage. She wanted legs practically all vein and frilled age-ripples, senescent skin. She wanted it badly, but eventually.

She even kind of wanted the type of elastic bigotry that old people have about other groups of people, and how she wanted people to forgive her for being set in her ways. She wanted to find children and teenagers irritating, because she had been one and raised several. One by one she wanted her grandparents and parents and aunts and uncles and older friends to drop off gently like smacked flies, and she wanted to say to herself at their funerals, while looking quaint, *see you*. How she wanted it badly, but eventually.

It's never good-bye. It's always, see you later.

She wanted to live until she forgot where she was. Who she was. How she was. Wanted her memory to expire before her body. Until she rambled gnomically and forgot her way home and her huge family of at least three or four children and at least ten grandchildren took her to a nursing home and told her how lovely it was, how beauteous the facilities, how nice the staff. She ached for it. Eventually.

She wanted them to go to bed every night with a tinge of guilt for leaving her there, but she wanted their spouses to soothe their anxieties by bringing up the selling points of the nursing home. *Remember their game nights? Remember the fountain by the side? And the indoor pool. Even though Grandma doesn't swim, should she change her mind, she could do water aerobics any morning she wanted.* Should she be so lucky. She wanted it badly, and she wanted the years in between them more.

on holiday

People out there got sick, then inspired to become doctors. Lucy felt the opposite and wanted to separate her body from her purpose as much as possible.

You're recovering, her cardiologist told her.

Lucy had one more month before she was able to return to school. She was bothered by the fact that she hadn't been a sporty girl before the surgery. If she hadn't been in recovery, she could have played basketball, even though she had mediocre hand-eye coordination. Indoor track or volleyball. And was it too late for her to be a ballerina? - *Certainly,* - she thought, clustered with woe.

She still took effort to dress for her tutoring lessons in her noisy pants and shirts, but everything that handled her body itched her, reminding her how much better life would be if she weren't so frail. Alone in her room, she took off her clothes. Her sutures encrusted in sugary-purple bruises reminded her of a long rain, or nerves.

She whispered prayers every night before bed. These private liturgies weren't long—usually she just needed to say, *bless me, bless my sisters, bless my parents and family. Bless Kitten.* Then she always said five Our Fathers, which her priest told her to say during a recent reconciliation. Lucy had started going to Catholic Mass every week. She and her sisters had been raised

Catholic and received the sacraments but stopped going to church years ago, after they finished religious school and were confirmed in the faith. Claudio and Mathilde were never pious, but they raised their daughters in this community. *Communities get you through. Someday, they might need one*, had been Mathilde's validation to her husband.

She loved the services, the priest and incense and chapel interior, but was still deciding whether or not she could believe in god. She was almost there, except for the times her brain told her - *uh-uh. Not this god, not this one. Not with what I know about science.* - Nevertheless, Lucy took comfort in the confidence that the miscellany of Catholic mores would always linger within her, like vestigial organs.

She told this to Natasha, who told her that *not everyone thinks about prayer.* How prayer probably made no difference whatsoever.

Sure, said Lucy, *but it fixes my blues.*

As a baby, Lucy had a habit of prefacing her sisters' names with *my. My Carly, My Tasha*, claiming them. This led to all three sisters marking their territory on everything they loved, claiming certain music the way they bought pairs of pants or jewelry. However, the only kind of possession involved was a type of familiarity, a fidelity. Everybody knew that Bob Dylan belonged to Natasha and that the White Stripes belonged to Lucy (Elliott Smith to the blue Lucy) and Van Morrison to Carly. In terms of the Beatles, whom they all adored equally, they divvied up the albums. Natasha had *The White Album* and *1* and *Let It Be*, and Carly had *Rubber Soul* and *Revolver*, and Lucy had *Magical Mystery Tour* and *Sgt. Pepper's Lonely Hearts Club Band*. They shared *Abbey Road* because they couldn't agree whom it was most part of.

After the surgery, Lucy reverted back to these ways, fretfully claiming small spaces in her house, searching for seizeable beauty, like someone with a new camera. Being a poet, she decided, was to do the things that everyone else did but a little more sensitively. She figured all one really had to do was give a clue to the universe and *voilà!*, there it was—a good poem. And the less fancy one talked, the better, because simplicity had more possibilities.

A poet, said Natasha. *That's kind of like being a dinosaur.*

There are still lots of poets out there, said Lucy. *Most people just don't read them.*

I think people just don't have the attention span for it anymore.

Maybe they're afraid poetry will depress them.

It doesn't all have to be about sadness and darkness, Natasha told her. *Why don't you write a poem about being healthy?*

So Lucy wrote a hale and Hearty poem. She wasn't bad at being happy:

(Inevit)abilities

The verb *to suffer*
has vanished!
No more fourteen hours
of sleep a night.
My body
now can be described as having hobbies
other than breaking down, my body
takes up
too
much
space!
I blink once for yes,
twice for no, thrice for always.
My hair is washed, two back-to-back
thunderstorms. I sleep in clichés
like *ear-splitting,* or *eyesore,*
remembering too well the amplified splits
and sores and a body that felt like it

was just as good bought or sold
as it would be dead. I could have been
a Chinese fetus, a prisoner's son. Now I feel
fire-splatters in my nerve endings, my body
turning counterclockwise and growing younger,
my awakened lungs, my soft Heart.

She thought of her sisters reading her poem, then crossed out *Chinese fetus*. Having an audience was scary. Her family went to the *Bodies* exhibit last year at the South Street Seaport in Manhattan, an exhibition showcasing dissected humans. Natasha had read in the newspaper that the bodies had all been unspoken for, from the Chinese police. People were wondering whether the bodies had been prisoners executed by the Chinese government.

They aren't exactly known for their human rights, Natasha had said, staring at the display of the man throwing a football, his preserved system displayed like a platter of hors d'oeuvres. Carly fell into a bad mood for the rest of the day, telling her sisters she was sick of them and that nobody knew what it was like to be her. Which was a widespread conundrum: nobody knew what it was like to be anybody but his or her raw happenstance of self.

It was December 23. Their parents were working late, again. They were always working. *A Festivus for the rest of us!* hollered Lucy. Lucy and Carly were fanatical with holidays. In June, they'd initiate a countdown until Christmas. They also tried to celebrate Hanukkah, Ramadan, Diwali, Tet, and Kwanzaa.

Dinner that night would be latkes, frosted gingerbread houses, reindeer cookies, hamantaschen, turkey sandwiches, pumpkin pie with graham cracker crusts. They ignored what would detach these occasions: religion and time. Carly was wearing a red, white, and blue dress. Lucy was wearing an effulgent party dress, along with novelty glasses that said *2000 Y2K* on them.

You're making a joke out of what a lot of people take seriously, said Natasha.

Nobody can see us, said Carly. *We aren't hurting anybody.*

It just feels wrong. Is nothing sacred anymore?

You're being old-fashioned, Lucy said, sizzling potato pancakes in oil.

They played dreidel as a drinking game, opening a bottle of their parents' Pinot Noir. When she landed on gimmel, Carly chugged her red wine with ice, stirring with a red-and-white-striped swizzle stick, sipping from a stripey straw.

Split shades of pink and crocus-colored wax melted in pearls over the copper menorah they'd stuffed with birthday candles. They lit them and sang "Happy Birthday to You." When it was time to sing the name, Carly said *Jesus* and Natasha said *Mr. President* and Lucy whispered *Face*. What had become of Face? She pictured her corroded Heart out in some field alone, covered in lacy snow. Maybe Face had been donated to medical science and was lying on an operating table, penetration through its piping. Maybe there was an unsentimental medical student, deciphering what had gone wrong with the Heart that had been born into Lucy.

what holiday?

Mathilde and Claudio's holiday was Groundhog Day. They stuffed the house with banners: *Go Punxsutawney!* They took garish bets on whether Phil would see his shadow. When their daughters were younger, they'd cast groundhog shadow puppets, trace them with crayons on paper. They'd have Bill Murray movie marathons.

Mathilde clandestinely felt bad for Groundhog Day, and that was the reason she fêted it. Growing up, she felt bad for the sneakers that never got worn, the ugly hangers hanging in her closet, the lunch she watched a classmate throw out instead of eat.

A few days after Groundhog Day, which had fallen on a Wednesday that year, Claudio was alone while his wife was at work. Mondays were his day off. He clipped down the homemade banners, unplanted thumbtacks. The Groundhog hadn't seen his shadow. Claudio didn't know what to do with himself. At some point, both Claudio and Mathilde had ceased to function best on their own. They were themselves best as a couple, which was emblematic of a dear marriage: a couple first needs only each other to love, and with enough time they need each other to live.

His sexy, small wife. His nightingale wife. Unlike their two biological daughters, who'd inherited Claudio's height (Natasha at five-eight-and-a-half and Lucy at five-nine), petite Mathilde barely topped five feet. He loved her baby bones, alluringly undersized muscles. She'd played no sports in her life but still got injured a lot, spraining her wrists even from opening pickle jars. His darling wife, his emotional creature. Fragile in every form. Like a flute of champagne. Like a discontinued brand of Dreamsicle.

Claudio and Mathilde tried to role-play once, sexually and months ago, sort of after Lucy's transplant.

Let's try something new, Claudio had said. *Something new in bed.*

Yes, and when the girls go to college, let's also turn our basement into a sadomasochistic dungeon. It could serve two functions: love dungeon in the nighttime, Pilates studio in the daytime.

That actually sounds pretty fun, said Claudio.

They tried that afternoon. Nobody could say that they hadn't tried. Mathilde was Little Red Riding Hood, and Claudio was the Woodsman. After two minutes, Mathilde said, *this is bizarre.* By *bizarre* she meant - *a smidge difficult.* -

You're making it bizarre, said Claudio. *It doesn't have to be bizarre.*

Playing pretend gets people off? asked Mathilde.

You say tomato, said Claudio.

They kissed, and Claudio was just Claudio and Mathilde was just Mathilde.

But after they finished, as Claudio started to snore like a finely tuned locomotive, Mathilde buried her hand in her underwear and thought about Milla from *Textbook Case* and Frances from *Make a Living* and Liesl from *The Sound of Music* and imagined each of them having sex with her husband. A fanfare of women besides Mathilde. Claudio bent them over and loved each in a way that he couldn't love her. Milla needed to get fucked to stay warm. She'd satisfy Claudio in trilling ways. Desperate, greedy Frances would carry Claudio's child, and *their* child would never get sick. Liesl would always stay sixteen. Claudio liked them young, didn't he? What man didn't love sluts?

Mathilde could be sick too. She could be a wolf of a woman, humiliating herself with ideas that would stun her husband. Who could conjure visions, the power to let herself disappear. Ghost sex. Interlude love. Injustices.

Her husband thought he knew the inner-Mathilde so well, emptied of all wanton theatrics. A common inflammation of insight. But how well can one know another person, really? She'd told him her darkest secrets, about the time she masturbated alone in the back of a cab and the shameful developmental stage she'd gone through faking a British accent to appear more cultured, but he still couldn't know all of her. And she could never know all of him. There wasn't enough time to.

What she had to admit, though, was that Claudio knew her own facial expressions better than she—both the ones she practiced in front of the mirror and her chance, authentic ones. They were as Mathilde as her signatures on checks. Mathilde would try to filter the latter into the prior when rehearsing for a show. *Jesus, kid*, said Claudio once. *Be careful. You don't want to turn into your character.*

Every time they'd hear about an actor dying young, Mathilde would blame it on art (of course, there were also always drugs, but art fed drugs). *Look at Heath Ledger. He tried to become The Joker, and it killed him.* His cause of death was an access of his darkest parts, and an inability to achieve the delicate balance between his character and himself. Actors who (insert vice)d themselves to death were a dime a dozen.

Among the years, Claudio had witnessed his wife live through Heartbreaking cycles of violence against herself. One of the first things that had attracted Claudio to Mathilde was her vulnerability, before he learned of its danger, became weary of its strength. Her death urge contended with her life urge, and they weren't always in equilibrium. Marrying her put Claudio in a complicated place. What if he enabled her? What if he could not help but be complicit? They were self-destructive in different ways: Claudio set flame to himself, but Mathilde only disintegrated.

calamity⁶⁰⁰⁰⁰⁰⁰

Stephen and Carly were on a study break, playing *The Sims 3* on Stephen's desktop, controlling the lives of their Sims, insipidly named Stephen and Carly. Stephen entered *rosebud !;!;!;!;*: the cheat that would give them more money in increments of a thousand simoleons. Their vicarious avatars spent all their time making love or painting together or moving up on the career ladders. They lived in their delightful big house together, cooking dinner and watching movies on their wide-screen TV.

Carly returned to her textbook. - *The worst part about the Holocaust was how organized it was.* - Her World History homework was actually on Westward Expansion, but Carly was reading ahead, to Europe and World War II. She wasn't trying to overachieve; she was only in the midst of this habit of forcing herself to mention the Holocaust at least once a day, as the magnitude of the word brought her troubles into perspective.

Her fixation began one month prior, when a Holocaust survivor spoke at a school assembly. *You are the last generation to hear about the Holocaust directly*, she reminded them. That stuck with Carly: this responsibility, this knowledge of a very bad thing. What could she do with it? - *I will always remember this moment. I better.* - She tried memorizing everything about the survivor, a ninety-three-year-old woman named Hannah, the crash of her voice, the shape of her earlobes—eggy and free, like ultrasound waves.

Hannah survived three concentration camps and more surgeries than she kept track of. German doctors had used her body for their medical experiments. As a result, she was unable to have children. She also suffered from post-traumatic stress flashbacks every time she saw someone in a white coat, making any of her lifetime physical calamities all the more difficult. She lived.

Stephen nodded. He'd told her early in their relationship that he was Jewish. Only his mother was Jewish, which, he explained to Carly, made him a full Jew. The Jews were the Chosen People, carried down by heritage and lineage, always on the mother's side. Carly was one quarter Jewish, but on her mother's father's side, so it didn't count?

Concentration camp prisoners received tattoos at only one camp: Auschwitz. Incoming prisoners were assigned a camp serial number, which was sewn onto their prison uniforms. Prisoners who were in the infirmary, like Hannah, or those to be executed were marked with their camp serial number across the chest with indelible ink. The prisoners sent directly to the gas chambers were not registered, receiving no tattoos.

As prisoners were executed or died in other ways, their clothing bearing the camp serial number was removed. Because of the mortality rate at the camp and practice of removing clothing, there'd been no way to identify the bodies after the clothing was removed. Eventually, the SS authorities introduced the practice of tattooing in order to identify the bodies of registered prisoners who died.

Why did they need to do that? Carly asked. What sort of status could these bodies hold? What dignity? She read further.

Stephen said his grandfather had a tattoo on his left arm, which was the number he was assigned as he entered Auschwitz.

Stephen's grandfather had been a survivor of five concentration camps. He'd lived to eighty-six.

Stephen said, *Jewish law says no one with a tattoo can be buried in a Jewish cemetery.*

That can't count, said Carly.

Carly's only conceptual acknowledgment of concentration camps prior to that moment had been when she saw the movie *Harold and Maude.* Carly loved that one second in the movie that showed Maude's concentration camp tattoo and how it was never mentioned again.

People brand themselves every day, said Stephen. *A tattoo is the most permanent form.*

Branding, like clothing? asked Carly.

Yeah, said Stephen. *Clothing. Doctors and other medical professionals wear white lab coats. Nazis wore swastikas on their sleeves. My grandfather wore hats with floppy ears.*

My grandpa wore handkerchiefs, said Carly. Her mother had always talked about that.

So did mine, Stephen said.

Everybody did back then, I guess.

It's funny. I remember, what troubled me the most during my grandpa's funeral was that I didn't know if he had a handkerchief in his pocket. Jewish funerary tradition requires ripping a piece of clothing to profess one's grief. He'd rip up his own entire wardrobe if it meant knowing his grandfather was safe with his handkerchief. Not that it really mattered—of course, it hadn't been his grandfather anymore, just his body.

Stephen looked away, at the clock on his wall, squinting, as though he were trying to clutch time. Like he could say, hold on a second, and mean it. *He always wore a suit whenever we went to the theater. We'd all be wearing jeans and sweaters, and he would wear a suit.*

Stephen told her that if the Holocaust hadn't happened, his grandfather probably wouldn't have moved to America and met his grandmother. *I exist because of the Holocaust*, said Stephen. *I'd take it back if I could. I wouldn't be alive, but six million people would be.*

Maybe that's why they say god doesn't interfere with free will, said Carly.

Or there just could not be one, said Stephen.

But who knows, whispered Carly.

Right, said Stephen. *What do we know?*

precision

Carly started cleaning houses after school. She was first hired by her next-door neighbor, Mrs. Everstein, who wanted to clean out her basement. Carly became friendly with Mrs. Everstein's daughter, Dana, who chatted with her as she cleaned. Carly and Dana became Facebook friends, and some mornings before her job Carly would scroll through all of Dana's Facebook pictures. Dana liked to bowl with her friends on the weekends, enter silly names on the score screen, and then take pictures of the screen. Last year Dana had gone camping at a state park. Four years ago she had a boyfriend who looked cheerful in his profile picture and who did ethical pharmaceutical research at SUNY Stonybrook. She didn't seem to regret their breakup, if her cartoon *some-ee-cards* advocating singledom in a comically mocking way were any proof. *(I'd rather have a shitty boyfriend who forgets my birthday than a freezer full of Sixteen Handles, said no woman ever.)* Her favorite quote was *a girl should be two things, classy and fabulous.* But she had it misquoted, attributing it to Marilyn Monroe. - *People who call themselves classy usually aren't,* - Carly decided.

Two weeks after she was commissioned, Carly saw Mrs. Everstein cry after Carly discovered Mrs. Everstein's old Woodstock '69 poster huddled between two boxes of old fur coats. Carly felt the chronic sense of empowerment. She was using her hands to make people happy. Cleaning had to be her art medium, since she could use it to reach more people emotionally, even though she was taking things away instead of creating them.

Carly cleaned Mrs. Everstein's basement after school for almost three months, until she was commissioned by the O'Connor family, who had eight children, ages two to twenty. Mrs. O'Connor, with the crepey decade-holding skin under her eyes, was due with another in April. - *Worn, torn, and forlorn*, - Carly thought.

Four years ago, Mrs. O'Connor delivered Catherine, a stillborn baby. The summer before the birth, twelve-year-old Carly went to Mrs. O'Connor's house to feel her stomach. *She just did a cannonball!*

Mrs. O'Connor had three daughters and five sons and three children with freckles and eight children with recessively gray eyes and all of them with a startling sense of humor. Mrs. O'Connor had eight children, enough for a baseball team, whom she all knew very well (even if she sometimes whisked up the names, but it was okay, as people understood). Mrs. O'Connor, who had an exquisite baby girl named Catherine for an afternoon, whom Carly had predicted would be a good swimmer but nobody would know. Mrs. O'Connor had veins off the side of her face with a goopy texture like cold Bisquick in a pan, and she told everybody that it was okay and she would be okay because she never actually got to know Catherine. That was precisely the tragedy, but nobody could be cruel to Mrs. O'Connor and tell her so. *Don't worry about me. I never actually knew her.*

Or *worry about me. I'll never actually know her.*

Studying the O'Connors' crammed basement, Carly couldn't stop swallowing. She picked up a weathered dress meant for a baby either grown-up or dead. She stared at her mop, which reminded her of Janice from *The Muppets*, a kind of pretty mop, with soft, sopping curls. How could products be beautiful? Couldn't anything be beautiful, so long as it had some use to it?

Carly, true to her word, organized and scrubbed that basement for scores of afternoons. And then she quit cleaning for good. The whole week had been what did her in—every day, feeling more psychologically alone. She had never understood before how much junk was able to mar her Heart.

Carly decided to spend all of her earned money on clothes. Her favorite thing to wear was a pair of Parisian boots. She'd splurged full price, ordering online from Au Printemps. They didn't quit: showstopping, three inches. When Carly clicked them, she felt pretty, well versed, like a local weathergirl or TV personality.

Natasha told her that fashion was phony.

There are worse vices.

Carly didn't designate clothes for certain events like a normal person: clothes to go to work in, clothes to sleep in, clothes for the weekend. Instead, she categorized clothes by emotion— each article got designated to a certain mood stemming from the first time she'd worn it. She had her scared shoes and her fluky dress. She wore her near-gleeful slacks and surly headband. The day she found out Lucy was sick, Carly had been wearing white leggings, a lambs' wool skirt with anchor buttons, and a champagne-colored ribbed tank top. From then on they'd be her devastation clothes, with a thin shelf life.

Lucy also loved clothes—wearing them, buying them, talking about them, thinking about them. Before her surgery, Lucy dressed up. After her surgery, she dressed down: slips with ice chiffon clouds, sculptural textures, and cream silk. Pajamas with fuzzy linings, like the ears of a bear. Smock nightgowns printed with nightscapes, symphonies of stars. She used to spend money on bohemian dresses, lipsticks, and leather bags. Now she spent it on clothes to sleep in, for what else did she do, and what else could she do?

The night she found out her sister was sick, the basis of Carly's dream was a fingerprint of memory, the quotient of some drive from her brain, though her recollection looped distortedly. She was in middle school, under the swaybacked sun. Children called her names—*Ugly Chinese girl. Why don't you look like your sisters?*

She woke herself up, walked to the bathroom, saw herself in the mirror. Her lavender bedclothes, her blond face. Carly thought she made everything around her look better. It was self-esteem, she guessed. Like snowflakes, every girl's was different. She sat on her fingers. She wanted it all off with back-breaking speed: every invisible tattoo she had, every sacrilege she'd ever been called.

- *You're not* really *a Simone.* -

Carly drew a bath. She was a Simone. - *I love my family, and they love me. I've known them my whole life.* - She consulted her olive skin, stepping out of her clothes. Her clothes hid her body, her body hid her voice. She was a Russian doll.

- *You're not really a Simone,* - a cluttered defacement of property. Her body, was it really even her property?

- *I have to be a Simone. I don't know anything else.* -

She pictured Stephen as an old man, wrinkles crawling on that toxically gorgeous mug. It wasn't hard to imagine—he had the hair. Men were lucky to age with more poise than women. Carly let herself pee in the bathtub and sat for a minute in her cloistered waste. It almost felt good, the way some wanton things uneasily do.

Carly stepped out of the tub. She thought about wombs and how she couldn't see her own. She changed into a hoodie and flannel pajama pants, went downstairs to the kitchen.

It's too early for you to be awake, said Uncle Sawyer, sitting on a stool at the kitchen's island. He was wearing a bathrobe and had been growing a linty-gray beard for the past two weeks. He looked like Father Time.

Early? I thought it was late.

Depending on how you look at it. It's five-thirty.

It's hard to sleep.

Is your room too warm? Hot rooms give me sad dreams.

No. I'm just blue about Lucy. She found blaming her fear on Lucy the easy choice to make, since the distress their family felt about Lucy was the kind that took the cake. Even her uncle hadn't mentioned Noah since moving in, disregarding his different pain.

Are you sure? Nothing else going on?

Nothing else. Besides her foolish loneliness?

Her uncle peeled a banana the upside-down way monkeys do. *You're lucky you're the youngest.*

I'm lucky? Carly smiled, and suddenly Sawyer saw her in an objective way. The five feet of her, the weight probably close to double digits. You wanted to take care of her. She should have probably gotten braces. She had a bad tooth-to-gum ratio that maybe some people would think exalted her appeal, but probably not everyone.

You think you get overlooked, but really, it's the best. You have your older siblings making the mistakes you can avoid, before telling her a story of how he'd been bullied for liking boys in high school and how Carly's mother had taken care of him.

I'm really sorry that happened to you, Uncle. Why are people so mean?

We were teenagers. Most teenagers grow out of being mean. And you have your sisters to go through it all with together.

I guess, said Carly, thinking of how poles apart her plights could be from either of her sisters'.

That's not to say you won't make mistakes. But you also have Lucy and Natasha there to comfort you, who know what it's like. You're lucky not to be alone in your troubles.

We're all lucky, said Carly.

That's right, said Sawyer, as if he'd only just realized this. *Any day above ground is good. And many days are less good, but many are also more.*

Maybe the adoption agency matched me up with Mommy and Daddy because I looked—I mean, seemed—like the type of baby who would grow up into a girl that gets hurt. Maybe they looked like the type of parents who knew how to help me.

Don't say such nonsense about yourself. But you're right about your parents.

mass

Natasha took Lucy to Mass only because Lucy had asked her to. *You don't mind?* asked Lucy.

None of my business what helps you, said Natasha.

I like the sermon, Lucy said to Natasha. *The priest can say whatever he wants.*

Probably not anything he wants.

Church could be nice, I bet. Why didn't we go after we finished our Sunday school years?

Because you have to believe in god and I don't think Mommy or Daddy did, or do.

But why did we go in the first place?

Because I once heard Mom say that tradition and communities get you through. Whatever that means.

Get you through what?

Beats me. This world, maybe?

This horrendous world.

It's not such a bad place. First off, we have life in the first place. It's more the universe's fault. After all, it's cold, and nobody knows too much about it.

Lucy looked at her sister. *Not my universe. Maybe yours. Tell me, Natasha, where's your universe?*

Natasha parked the car.

I believe in god, Lucy continued. Their father believed in rock and roll. Lucy believed in god. *Would you ever?*

It's too hard for me to.

I'm sorry.

Don't feel sorry for me. It's just that, how could a loving god smite people all the time, à la the Old Testament Yahweh?

Well . . .

At least Jesus was a little nicer?

It's not the point, persisted Lucy. *Do you think that most of the people who go to church these days believe in the bogus details anyway? About homosexuality being an abomination or Eve sprouting from Adam's rib? Well, maybe some, but I think most people go to church, or temple, or mosque, because you can turn to each other and go,* peace be with you, said Lucy, taking a seat in the back pew.

Or because rules make them feel safe, murmured Natasha.

- *Here is the church, here is the steeple. Open the door and see all the people.* - The people, who were there for a reason, sitting down and craning their knees and taking Communion and sitting down again. Lucy received Communion, even though she also knew that technically she couldn't take Communion unless she'd recently been to Confession and absolved of her sins. But the last time Lucy had gone to Confession, the priest had told her to say a bunch of prayers. And she'd probably sinned since then—temptation from Sloane, gluttony over cupcakes, futile envy. Would these infractions matter to her god? The oddest and worst parts about religion were the technicalities.

Lucy opened her mouth. The priest slipped a dry wafer inside and said, *the body of Christ.* She thought back to her first kiss. Sloane had handled her mouth with his and said, *god, I love your body.*

Abruptly Lucy considered: what if he'd not been talking to her in the warmth of the moment, but to god? In which case, Sloane loved god's body, not Lucy's. The thought was incredulous but almost relieving. - *Sloane loved someone else's body. Some divine body.* - This abdication of responsibility, the idea that she could consume somebody else's lovable body, felt good.

The service ended with *Amen!* and consolation in the certainty of the final word. Lucy wondered what her final word would be, her Heart moving in her fishbowl of a body. She felt terribly unholy. The god Lucy believed in probably had nothing to do with the Catholic Church, but she didn't know how else to find him. (Him? Her? her? It? Like polytheists or Shakespeare conspiracy theorists, them?) she said, more to herself than anyone else, *heavenly father.*

the other doctor

G*uess what?*
     You're pregnant, Natasha joked.
Uh, almost.
Huh?
Stephen and I. We did it! Carly heard herself saying *it's a long story*, while smiling, the casual way an acquaintance would say *it's a small world.*

Whoa, said Natasha. Her little sister, sexually active? How could Carly have time for boys? Natasha couldn't imagine having time for anything but the constant jeopardy game in her head.

The next day, Natasha made an appointment for Carly with her gynecologist. Natasha had her appointment on the morning of her eighteenth birthday, a few months prior. *You have to go when you turn eighteen or lose your virginity. Whichever comes first,* their mother had explained to Natasha.

Dr. Pendleton was middle-aged, her own figure akin to a loaf of focaccia bread. She said, *it would help if you pushed your bum down and made like you were going to pee*, sticking something cold that felt like a giant doorknob inside of Carly. The instrument made a snapping noise. While examining Carly's reproductive atmosphere, Dr. Pendleton made chitchat.

What is your favorite subject?
History, said Carly, *even though it stresses me out.*

How's your sister? When Carly asked her how she knew, Dr. Pendleton said, *your other sister.*

At the end of the appointment, Dr. Pendleton asked Carly if she had any questions for her. But Carly had a fear of being defective, so she didn't speak a word, not asking even the most timid or softball of questions. It wasn't until the ride back home when Natasha asked Carly how it felt to be loved.

I don't know, said Carly. Carly was used to sharing her opinion in slim lines, mostly affirmative and in reaction to others.

You don't know?

He's not only my boyfriend, he's also a really good friend. One of the best. We draw together, and read out loud to each other. I know it sounds kind of stupid, but we also listen to cassettes together. He was on the basketball team, but the season just ended. I've met his parents, and I like them. I don't know what his dad does, but he works on boats. It sounds totally obvious, but I have an enormous crush on him.

Segue into how you guys met. How did your first kiss happen?

Carly yanked her sleeves down. How *did* it happen, anyway? The body had made plans, that was how. What more could Carly say? How could she endeavor anything? They were just two girls, really. They couldn't be more than this. Carly wouldn't be more than this.

A few months ago, Natasha had read an article with the word *segue*, of which she thought she'd only seen in print. She'd heard people say it out loud, *segway*, under the impression that this was an entirely different word. She understood *segue*, as written word, had the same definition, but thought it a word she'd never heard, pronounced *seg-you*. Natasha understood that she had more intelligence certainly than most people her age, but she understood that there were bushels of things she didn't know. And when you don't know, it doesn't mean you're wrong. But this means it's probably your responsibility to learn.

I don't think I like feeling so much about somebody else. It makes me feel needy and old.

Well, we're both kind of old souls, said Natasha, with frugality. Girls their age, bouncy and directionless, were the kind of girls who had high school sweetHearts. Not Carly, not Natasha. Girls going through their kind of scrapes weren't supposed to waste their days being in love.

Carly brought over a pint of butter pecan ice cream that evening from Stephen's kitchen freezer to his living room. In her other hand, she held two spoons. She lay on top of him. It was like he was wearing her.

Why two? asked Stephen. They were watching *Friends* on Nick at Nite.

I forgot, said Carly.

That we're lovers?

Am I you? asked Carly.

What? asked Stephen.

Carly spent most afternoons-into-evenings at Stephen's house. His mother would come home from work and always say *oh!* like Carly's presence still surprised her. Still, she was a kind lady. Nobody mentioned it, but Carly started to notice more of her favorite snack constituents in the fridge, like pesto and Fuji apples.

It was Passover. Stephen was giving up bread with his family. *It's kind of fun. Like we're all in it together.* Carly learned how to make matzoh ball soup and matzoh bric and matzoh pizza. They talked like weak and visceral dieters about rye loaves and baguettes, cake and crepes.

- Auschwitz survivors were given only one piece of bread a week. - She wondered, had she been a Holocaust victim, if she would've received a tattoo and been sent to work or else sent directly to

the gas chambers. How would Carly have been viewed? What would her worth have been? In many ways, though, Carly believed that being sent to death was not the worse outcome—at least there was a finite future. At least there was no more worrying about survival. At least she could've died with her own name.

the most dangerous
word of all

april 30, 2011

Slightly Lucy insinuated the word - *Alan* - to herself, handling the name beside her sisters.

A week later, Lucy ordered a framed map of the United States
and put it up in her room. *Pretty*, said Natasha.

Just before bedtime, Lucy pressed her fingers to the map,
dwelling on *Allentown*, Pennsylvania. *Alan*, her lips wreathed
the name. Then Lucy concocted the words, *tis of thee*. It sim-
mered in her throat. *Tisoftheetisoftheetisofthee.*

Even if Lucy hadn't consulted the newspapers at the time of
the transplant, Natasha realized, archives ghosted online.

They were eating peanut butter and jelly sandwiches with
the radio on because they were tired of all of their records.
A Jackson 5 song came on, "The Love You Save," and Lucy
mused, *I love the radio.* Natasha said there was something to be
said about serendipity.

If we were PB & J, who would be who? Natasha asked Lucy, even
though she'd already come up with an answer herself long ago.
They knew every answer to each other's questions. If Lucy was
peanut butter (enduringly glorious), Carly was jelly (wobbly, sac-
charine), then Natasha was the seven-grain bread their mother
made them eat to assist their digestion. Their dispositions
called the shots: Natasha was responsible, and her sisters stuck
to the ribs. And if they were colors, Natasha would be bone and

Lucy would be flamingo and Carly would be sea green. Then Natasha risked it, the issue backstroking out of her. *Do you ever think about where your Heart came from?*

I know where it comes from, said Lucy. *I looked it up.* She took a spoonful of indigo jam from the jar, then licked it like a lollipop.

You did?

I did.

Natasha nodded, tentative. *Fuck, well, so did I. Don't hate me.*

You would, smarty-pants. But I love you, said Lucy. *I love my secondhand Heart. And I love Alan.*

The fact was, just one week after she'd come home from the hospital, Lucy had too furtively looked up the obituaries online, then searched for Alan Douglas Rachmones on Facebook.

Lucy loved Facebook, posting digital pictures and joining groups like *BRB . . . I'm not going anywhere, but this conversation is.* She'd declared herself in a faux-marriage with one of her platonic girlfriends from school and wrote her religious views as *are you there god? It's me . . . Lucille Margaret.* The morning of the surgery, Lucy had even told her sisters her Facebook password. *It's crunchyelevator7,* she told them. *Do whatever you want with it, if something happens.* She was saying, - *log into my life and make it last.* - Forbid.

Lucy had typed, her new-fangled pulse nudging through each finger vein, *Alan Rachmones.* And after she'd pressed enter, her fingers ran out of things to do. She'd been able to do nothing further but read his horrible Facebook page. How it existed, was public, and by that time had already become a shrine of sorts. The page was being maintained by his family as a grievers' forum. Anyone on Facebook could see how Alan had been rich in family and friends. *Miss you Alan . . . thinking of you every day. Kiss Bubbe and Milkshake for me. / I miss you Alan. I wish you could be here to celebrate everything in our lives. / Love you Bro . . . Thanks for sending me happy signs. You are the world's best angel.*

Alan had just graduated college that summer, Lucy learned.

The profile picture of Alan smiled, wore a graduation cap. Ultimately her fingers broke paralysis, and she logged out of the family computer and erased the Internet history, having never in her life before absorbed so much information.

His mother was one of his Facebook friends. Barbara Rachmones. Lucy couldn't help herself. Over a matter of hours, opening and closing the same tabs, she gained an awful courage to find the mother's phone number and enter it into her phone. Then she called.

Hello? the mother answered, and Lucy said nothing, but her Heart called out, accelerating, rattling. She pressed end and felt relief. - *It's your mother, not mine,* - Lucy thought, pointing between her breasts, addressing her torso, feeling small and spooky. She felt like she'd just risked everything, but this did not stop her from jotting everything else she learned about this once-mother, this retired mother (Alan had no siblings, at least none on the Internet), on a pad of paper. Her address, her e-mail—both work and leisure.

What to do with this information, other than hide it? Lucy wasn't sure, but she felt slightly better having it in her possession. She was the type of person for whom the ultra informative approach surpassed all other worths. If god had offered Lucy a piece of paper with her date of death on it, Lucy would take the paper. It didn't mean she was necessarily stronger, or better, or unhappier—she just had a kind of personality. Knowledge comforted Lucy no matter how embarrassing or maddening it could be.

The night he stopped being a secret, and every night that week, Lucy dreamed of Alan. One night she had even gotten into bed two hours early to dream earlier, for (what she twinged to believe) their harmonized sabbatical: hers from her conscious life, his from his death. She had made a mistake in telling her sister. It was obvious now.

Guess who I dreamed I made out with last night.

Uncle Jesse from Full House.

No. It was strange.

Someone like Mr. Johnstone? Mr. Johnstone was the creepy technology teacher everyone joked about being a pedophile.

Alan. We kissed in the dream. Lucy, erring on the side of honest.

Oh my god, Lucy! This poor boy! Natasha's mouth sweated, keeping her own secret. She could never tell Lucy of her own dream. Alan wasn't hers to dream about. Also, appearing in more than one person's dream somehow made Alan seem more alive.

Shut up. And fuck you. This came as a fright for Natasha, given how rare swearing was of Lucy. Lucy's treatment of language was delicate and not because she had anything in common with banal vanillas like Perry Como or Disney Channel child stars before their discovery of Hollywood nightlife. *Why curse when you can use more articulate and powerful words?* she frequently said, saving her curses for the times she had nothing else to say. The times she said these words, she meant them. Their father was the same way—he treated words with reverence and a varied palate, a connoisseur.

All Lucy knew of her dreams was how they led her thighbones in an achy trance. How every morning she woke up with her blanket off her body, arms enswathing the bed. Whenever Lucy used to have a crush on a boy, she'd daydream for hours about what they had in common, like membership in a band or an aptitude for math or their ethnicity. She almost felt the same way about Alan, loving him distantly and urgently, like a celebrity or venerated idol.

- *Nobody understands, so screw everyone,* - Lucy thought. Nobody understood how it felt to graze the After. Lucy's journey had been (was?) a lengthy dredge. Alan's had been walloping and hopefully with little pain. Alan didn't come back. Lucy did. Alan saved her sorry body. His lovely, uncertain Heart beat inside her, and she couldn't imagine anybody else meaning more to her.

In her favorite dream, Lucy and Alan roomed together in

a city where all the lost children, children who died too early,
went. A nirvana run by lost children, neither living nor dying.
The city was an island, and Alan floated up on a canoe, offering
her a seat.

Where are we going?

Leaving, said Alan. *I want to go back.*

Back?

I miss my mom too much. Alan sniffed. He twirled his oars,
dipped them in and out of the shivering sea. She fingered his
spine, sure to stroke zithers of cartilage, a tundra-framework
of cold porcelain. But nothing remained except bedrolls of air
through her fingers.

That shattered in the accident, he told her. *How could this thing
have been so important?* he asked.

What thing?

You know, he said. *My body.*

Lucy hugged Alan, breathing jaggedly, for only when she and
Alan made love did she have a Heart. They could be one unstop-
pable body, sharing Kitten. They had to be one body: sex was as
necessary as it was carnal as it was ritual. Face was the lukewarm
moon in this city, and even here it had trouble working. Face,
who was supposed to heat up the whole night and nourish the
planet with its crinkling light. The city as dark as a shearwater
wing, except for Kitten, who heated Lucy and Alan in halves.

Lucy couldn't tell anybody what it felt like to be in love.
She had nobody living to love. There was LJ, but he was with
Leora, and even his love felt conditional. He romanticized her
circumstance, which was even sadder than not having anyone
in love with her at all. As for Sloane, well—he was too playful,
seemed like he had no faculty for sadness. Lucy felt guilty about
her feelings for him. And speaking of guilt, there was Stephen,
who Lucy coveted in her confidential way.

There were so many boys, too many boys, none of them fit
to adore. Lucy loved the only boy she believed she could. In the

conscious world, they couldn't share his Heart, and he'd given it to her. - *Well*, - Lucy thought, - *maybe* give *wasn't the right word*, - since his Heart had been taken and forced into her, the living deciding someone needed it more than he.

Lucy researched sexual fetishes the next day, learning about frotteurism, sexual sadism, sexual masochism, telephone scatalogica, necrophilia. She studied partialism, zoophilia, coprophilia, klismaphilia, emetophilia, erotic asphyxiation. She went to websites looking up pyrophilia, mammaphilia, narratophilia, olfactophilia, salirophilia, somnophilia, sthenolagnia, teratophilia. Why were people erotically charged by such different things? It was just probably association. Getting turned on in a blue room just once sometimes led to being turned on, for the rest of your life, by blue rooms. The mind could be astonishing or sinister.

Somewhere in the midst of her investigation, Lucy read about the idea of *safe words*, sometimes a term that people used during sex. *A safe word is a code word or a series of code words that is sometimes used to unambiguously communicate physical or emotional state, typically when approaching, or crossing, a physical, emotional, or moral boundary*, she read. Saying a word or term out of context like *platypus* or *umbrella* brought the two consenting adults back to reality if one or both went a step too far.

- *How can words be safe?* - Some words, c-words and n-words and k-words and w-words, edgy and fluid words, were dangerous when they stood alone. Other words, like *child pornography* or *snuff film*, were dangerous only in combinations. But what if one used them with irony? With sarcasm or insincerity? What if one tried to reclaim the history of the word—was that even possible? Was it possible that maybe every word had the potential to be dangerous?

Was it possible no word was safe?

A year before, Lucy had attended a high school weekend retreat with Carly in a cabin in the woods in upstate New York.

It was called Common Ground, and the point was to inspire dialogue and discussion about heated topics. Carly's history teacher and the Common Ground faculty facilitator wrote LOADED WORDS on a whiteboard. *People, I want you to think. What words have you heard that make you upset? What kind of power do they hold?*

Her teacher transcribed a list as students shouted out words they'd heard before, names and labels they may have been called or heard somebody called. Words they may have called others. The teacher divided the room by race. First, the students who considered themselves black left the room, and everyone else stayed in the room, and both groups started lists of every derogatory name, every stereotype for this race. Then all of the students who considered themselves Asian left the room, and both groups repeated the exercise. Then the students who considered themselves Latino left the room, and both groups repeated it. This was repeated for kids who considered themselves to be Middle Eastern, and then white. Each time after the lists were made, both groups took turns reading from the list they each compiled. *You must look into each other's eyes the entire time you read the words,* the teacher said.

Certain words affected only certain people. Lucy hadn't felt that with any of the words they mentioned, though Carly did. *I have eyes that work just like any white person's. I don't eat dogs. I know I don't look like my family.*

At Common Ground, when they'd finished compiling the list, with all the misguided hurt in the room, Lucy had realized that the same hurt had been in the world for much longer. She'd thought, - *where do we go from here? -*

happens

Lucy caught a series of colds. Collected fevers thawed into her head like parasites. *There are some complications.*

Shucks, said Lucy, lightly and at liberty, trying to make what was happening funny.

I'm so sorry. It's a sign of rejection.

The *I'm sorry* caught Lucy off guard. Doctors weren't supposed to mix feelings with business, and they weren't supposed to admit to being sorry. Lucy read somewhere that a doctor saves an average of 525 lives a year. What about the people who couldn't be saved?

I'm sorry, Lucy's cardiologist told her again. *This sort of thing just . . .* The cardiologist made eye contact with Lucy and then did something strange: blushed. *Happens*, the cardiologist ended.

Lucy thought, - *doctors feel sorry and sometimes things just happen.* -

The cardiologist started talking about the idea of a second transplant. Somebody else's Heart. Lucy could barely believe this. - *Somebody else dying so I could have a third Heart?* - It suggested such selfishness.

Lucy made a phone call when she arrived home.

Uncle Noah, she said, her voice catching on his title. Was he even still her uncle?

Lucy. He recognized her voice.

I just got some bad news.

Oh no.

The new Heart doesn't like my body.

Baby. What are they going to do?

I'm not sure. Look for a third Heart?

Okay. Well, they got you a second one, so don't lose hope.

Are you going to forgive Uncle Sawyer?

I . . . Noah coughed or laughed. *Does he know you're calling me?*

No. But I wish you would so much, because he's been miserable. I love you, and he loves you.

I'm not sure. But it's brave of you to tell me.

I'm not being brave. It's just the truth.

That night, Noah drove to the Simone house and forgave Sawyer before he proposed to him. When they told the rest of the family the good news, Lucy feared she'd pushed Noah through guilt, which was why he slyly handed her the receipt for the two gold rings he'd bought for himself and Sawyer, from this January, in hopes of marrying in Massachusetts or Connecticut. *I was taking my time,* he explained to her, when they had a minute alone together. *I'd never want to rush into a marriage, or to do it for the wrong reasons.*

how do you like them apples?

Mathilde drove to the supermarket, following all of the right-of-ways. *Yield.* Mathilde yielded. *Stop.* And Mathilde stopped. She was a decent driver, she thought. Nobody had ever told her otherwise. She thought of all the other skills she assumed she had just because nobody ever told her she didn't.

The worst kind of headache throbbed in the back of her head. A growl slinked out of her stomach. She knew that she wasn't supposed to go food shopping on an empty stomach, but this was Saturday, and her dangling idleness infuriated her. She needed to be useful. If she wasn't useful, she couldn't understand what she was, or that she was.

She had two hundred dollars cash in her wallet. She could have anything: this was America. But it had become such an unpleasant task to feed her family, her three girls, none of whom had appetites. Tougher than one would think, to buy only what was necessary.

Had it not been so long ago when she was the college Mathilde, who once rascally ate nothing but pineapple for a week because her roommate told her it would make her taste good down there, whose supper often consisted of string cheese and a box of Entenmann's cookies? Maybe she could slither and slink back into the old-school, livin' la vida loca Mathilde for the night, whose spirit animal was Stevie Nicks and who would try anything once, thrice if it felt good. What could she choose? A bagel with a container of guacamole? Some pomegranate seeds? A jar of Nutella? She'd have to eat her dinner in the parking lot, but this would be okay. Maybe she'd put on the radio, and a happy song would be playing. Listening to her body could be so nice. She liked her body in general, which wasn't too bad for a woman who had given birth to two children. - *Not too bad*, - she told herself. - *It could be worse.* - It could always be worse.

The supermarket the Simone family patronized was the Whole Foods on the west side of their neighborhood. They had a favorite everything in town—supermarket, pizza place, bowling alley, beauty salon—calling their places by their names as though they were people they had relationships with. This time Mathilde noticed herself driving to the dingier side of Babylon, north of the Southern State Parkway, parking at the Foodtown. She held her own hands as the automatic door stopped lackluster, halfway in its tracks for her.

- *I'm an asshole*, - she designated herself, resisting the yen of reaching for her hand sanitizer. She should've eaten lunch with dirty hands just so she could say she knew what it was like. But hurting herself wouldn't help anybody. It wouldn't make poor people rich, stupid people smart, nor ugly people beautiful.

Mathilde looked for fruits to bag without bruises or incisions. Her family wasn't supposed to be a family who bought their fruit at the supermarket. They went to the farmers' market because they liked to support local businesses. Being this kind of family was a luxury, she knew, and this consciousness of privilege close to shamed her.

When Lucy was a baby, she called grapes *guppies* and peaches *pizzas* and avocados *chumbawumbas*. Lucy loved saying the word *often* from the moment she learned it. *We don't often eat while watching TV.* She'd also drank from a bottle until she was six, but only at night. *I don't often go to school without my sisters.* After she started kindergarten, Lucy raised her hand at home sometimes because she was so used to doing it in school. *I don't often get sick.* Lucy was afraid of doctors, people sitting behind desks, this one episode of *Sesame Street* where somebody jumped out of a tree, and whenever Mathilde had to leave her.

Why are you going, Mommy? You don't often leave me.

Mathilde made her way to the ovo-lacto section and picked up a gallon of milk. Letting the condensation drizzle on her sullied, minute hands, she picked up a pint, then a quart. She was having a brain lapse—how big was her family? Did they all drink milk? - *Obviously,* - she told herself. Milk was good for the body; there were public service announcements for it. But now they were saying it was all propaganda from the milk industry, that farmers were feeding cows estrogen. As a result, girls as young as six were hitting puberty. Soy milk? Soy was just as bad. Almond milk? Too much sugar. And which kind of milk was the kind with the links to cancer? Camel milk? Coconut or cashew milk?

- *How soon does milk go bad? How much can we consume before then?* - The tiny procedural grooves in her brain, the memory of birthdays and shoe sizes and who liked what food, felt murky. She was replacing them with her emotional memories, the ones she liked more, the ones that belonged to her family.

She fingered her mind: - *think, Simone, think.* - Over the past year she'd habited talking to herself in her head for clarity, referring to her fractured psyche by her surname. It made her feel like a boy. Tough. So often the name Simone felt strange to her. Out of everyone in the family, Mathilde was the only one born without it. (Except Carly. One could argue that Carly was born without any name.) She thought of Spicer, her maiden name. Life without her husband. Mathilde Spicer felt like a different person, an old acquaintance she'd want to avoid running into.

This Mathilde Spicer person would hold her arm as they caught up, chummy, making Mathilde Simone feel even smaller than their talk.

Your daughter is sick? So sorry. Marriage was never that important to me, Mathilde Spicer would say. Mathilde Spicer would be earning six figures, married to her career. She would've kept her Tony Award in her china closet. She would not have considered Mathilde's acting history anything significant: one stint on Broadway and several *Law & Order* episodes and a stand-in role on a midtier NBC show. She would've had a lover younger than she was and had a stomach you could bounce quarters off of: the tight body of a woman who's never carried other people inside it and the wardrobe of a woman who could afford to spend all her money on only herself. Mathilde Spicer would smoke jazz cigarettes and say *me, me*. Mathilde Spicer would be pure bullshit.

In the bakery section, Mathilde lifted a loaf of artisan bread the way she would a baby, in the Hearts of her palms. Mathilde couldn't resist desserts, drinks, and indulgent snacks after meals, after she was already satisfied. But she craved bread only when she felt truly, feebly hungry. It was the case with most of what she needed to live. Why did people always rush, sometimes riot over milk and bread and eggs? Why were mangoes, artichoke Hearts, smoked salmon not considered staples? Why not scones or lamb shank? What economic delicacy could one possibly conjure up on solely milk, bread, and eggs? - *French toast*, - she thought, resourcefully.

Tomorrow would be Sunday. They used to make pancakes on Sunday mornings, with fruit faces. *I'm making a polar bear pancake, with banana eyes*, Natasha had said once, and *I'm making a man named Simon*, Lucy had said. *He's like us but without the E. He has a mustache and goes to the prom and to the bank. He likes to say*, kiss me, baby. Carly had said, *I'm making a woman named Ziggy S. She plays gee-tar.*

In college, Mathilde read a fable about a man stranded on a desert island with his parents. He cooks his own flesh, orders them to eat what remains of his body, and at least his parents are able to survive. - *Why would they let their only son do that?* - She remembered the Greek myths and literature she'd studied and how cannibalism seemed to be a constant theme among parents. There was Titan, Polyphemus, Attila, Iphigenia, Atreus. There was Tereus, Procne, and Philomena.

A memory came. Mathilde often thought she remembered things in a different way from everyone else. *My brain is sand,* she liked to say. *What happened to me is now either a dollar or a crab. And each grain is another distraction.* She'd call trying to re-member something *digging,* and forgetting something *building a sandcastle.* This memory was a question her college room-mates used to ask, when they'd challenge one another, asking thorny-scenario questions like *is it worse to lose an arm or a leg?*

The question in question was, *if your spouse and your child were both about to fall off a cliff, and you could only save one, who would you save?*

Her girlfriend had the audacity to answer without ado. *Save the hubby. After all, we could always make more kids!*

You're sure of this, Mathilde confirmed, unsure herself.

As sure as anyone can be about anything.

A number of years back, Mathilde had watched a documen-tary on the Discovery Channel about a polar bear mom who had cannibalized her cubs in a German zoo. *As humans, we tend to think of parental care as a very loving and nurturing behavior, which it of course is most of the time,* the voice-over narrated. *But sometimes there is a darker side to parental care, and understanding behaviors such as this often requires a very close look at what's going on.* The show had taken note of the reasons parents might eat their young, none of which were mutually exclusive. For in-stance, they could be weeding out inferior offspring, or they could very well be hungry.

- *Just hungry*, - Mathilde had thought.

Quickly Mathilde imagined herself on a desert island. Lucy was already dead, her dead legs resting like two cold pipes on Mathilde's shivering, frantic, alive lap. And Mathilde was starving. She got farther than she should have. Then a stupefied pain clutched her between her lips and stomach. She looked for a hand mirror, a tabletop surface—anything that could show her own face. The ocean! A manic glance into the ruminative foam showed her the grotesque avatar of maternal contrast. Her entire mouth, throat, and belly were layered in thorns. Too weapon, too succubus—scarcely mother.

Mathilde closed her eyes, considering the notion that she had been coming to so ghoulishly often: - *how could such a terribly wrong thing be allowed to happen?* - leaving the supermarket holding two peaches and a bag of grapes. Pizzas and guppies clothed in plastic. How could they be shrouded in plastic and still be living? How was it that they could live and not move?

Ma'am, you're going to have to come back inside, said a bag boy. His nametag read DIRK. Mathilde looked around and realized she was outside with the peaches and the grapes and no daughters.

Excuse me?

You didn't pay.

Okay, said Mathilde. *But who cares?*

Dirk guided her by the elbow inside. Inside, where the air was faithfully cold and the speakers blew The Five Stairsteps into the aisles. Like a prelude, the walls wooed with: *Ooh child, things are gonna get easier.* Dirk picked up the phone.

Besides his acne scars and the message he was sending to her with his posture, Mathilde noticed he was handsome. A well-built chin and snowflakey lashes. Maybe Mathilde could hit on him, even sit on him, exercise her flirting like a lethargic muscle. Even in the early days of being married to Claudio,

Mathilde would love to go out with her single friends and wing-woman. It just did something to her, filled the candid louvre inside whining - *nobody will ever like you enough.* -

Who are you calling? asked Mathilde, thinking - *Ghostbusters.* - Their whole family loved that movie, grew up watching it on weekends while eating chocolate soufflés. Claudio would say, *wifey, tell me again what we did on Saturday nights before the girls?* Mathilde would say, *you know, city stuff. Not much.* Claudio would ask her, *why did we waste our time?* Claudio used to say, *can you believe we have all this?* Claudio used to say, *how can so much beauty fit into one room?* Carly and Natasha and Lucy would give mouthy laughs and make funny faces to be less lovely. Mathilde would make the soufflés, which would take all day. Nobody in the family would seem to realize all the effort it took her. Her husband and daughters—they were always asking her for more.

The manager, said Dirk, *who will probably call the police.*

I didn't do anything wrong, said Mathilde. *My daughter Lucy used to call peaches pizzas. I would have taken her food shopping with me, but I'm afraid she's dying.*

Dirk made a ribbiting, Kermit the Frog–like sound as he spoke. *Ma'am, you're going to have to calm down.*

Okay, said Mathilde.

He laughed, breaking his own character. *You look like you could use a nap and a bottle of vodka.*

And my husband, Mathilde said, unhappy with him for being right. She took out her credit card. *I'm really sorry. I promise I'm an okay person,* she maintained. She paid for the fruit, took it in a paper bag, and called Claudio.

Can you take off in the next hour? I'm blue, peddled Mathilde.

Just briefly she thought, - *I could leave right now. Leave the family that makes such a mess of me and never look back.* - Claudio would never know, though it would always be an atrocious thought that existed, and would proceed to exist, albeit cloaked. But there was no sense in taking precautions about thoughts because, Mathilde had realized long ago, thinking cannot be controlled nor helped.

Yes, said Claudio. *We'll order Chinese. Watch a movie.*

Yes, said Mathilde. Claudio was good that way. He'd talk with her—if she pleased—about their daughters or about themselves. But likely, for both of their sakes, about nothing that might be important.

crime part 2

When Claudio walked into the kitchen and saw Carly sitting on the counter with Stephen touching her eyelid, he screamed.

His whole life, Claudio hadn't understood why people screamed. He understood a kid screaming at his or her mom during a fight, fine. When else should people ever have to scream? Grown-ups should never gratuitously scream, was his conviction. Never scream at all unless it was an extreme situation. Like an emergency.

What the fuck are you doing? Who was this dumbass kid, trying to hurt his little girl? Stephen. Some kid who claimed to love his daughter. Nobody could ever love Carly more than Claudio.

He was still coming to terms with the idea of his daughter having a boyfriend. Stephen seemed like a passable kid, but up until then Claudio hadn't had to worry about boys. He couldn't resist every time the situation seemed to germinate: once, when he caught Lucy looking through LJ's Facebook pictures, he said, *he looks like a psycho.* Once, when he picked up Natasha from school, he saw her talking to one of her classmates, John. *Who was that geek?* Claudio had asked.

He didn't like that Carly had a boyfriend, though he knew this revulsion was illogical. If Lucy had been healthy, he didn't think he wouldn't've minded. Carly's handling of Lucy was different from Natasha's—she seemed sympathetic but not as involved, spending nearly every afternoon and evening at Stephen's house. And Claudio hated this. He knew it didn't make enough sense to articulate but felt the loathing all the same.

Daddy! What's wrong with you? My contact fell out. Stephen was just trying to put it in.

Claudio's ears went flannelette-white. Had his own, grueling eyes been so insistent? *I don't understand.*

Why did you freak out? asked Carly.

Yeah, is everything okay, Mr. Simone? asked Stephen.

I'm sorry for yelling, son. It looked . . . Claudio bit the top of his lip, swallowing his philippic. god. What his daughters did to him.

Strange, from where I was standing. Claudio had never told his daughters about the time in the pool. He hadn't even ever told his wife. They just assumed Jane's illness was chemical. And of course it was, something carried through genes, like other illnesses. Claudio could not have been a trigger, but that didn't help his guilt. Claudio went into his bathroom, looked at himself. How revoltingly relieved he felt for having one daughter of his be adopted. Should anything happen to her genetically, the blame would be placed off him. He was a sick bastard, wasn't he?

Jane had gone off her rocker. When would he? Could it be a matter of time? Could he too surprise himself with his capability? He'd been unable to stop Jane, after all. They shared genes and a history. Given the circumstances, he was sure he could slip into lunacy just as effortlessly. He took off his shirt and stared at his forsaken torso. - *The shirtless criminal is never soft. He has no bad genes. He is a man. Be a man,* - Claudio told himself. *Just* a man, but a man. There was only so much a man could do, but there was a lot a man could do.

Claudio dead-bolted his dominant hand into a fist. He was left-handed, and none of his daughters were. Where had his other genes gone? His cleft chin. His attached earlobes. His thick calf gene. His sweet tooth gene. Were they still carrying them all, recessively? Would it matter if Lucy even was? He thought about all of the little useless eggs inside of his daughter's body. His wonderful half-portions of grandchildren, the grandchildren with Lucy's eyes and mouth and toes, who'd never be born.

Claudio was certain his Heart would turn blue if any of his daughters left him. He thought about all of the times he made sure they wore their seat belts. All the times he made sure they took their vitamins.

- *Surviving,* - he thought, - *is different from living.* -

Mathilde rested her head that night in the soft cup of her husband's lap. *How could our daughter just get sick the way she did? And what does a mother do?*

It's not your fault, said Claudio. *It's god's fault.*

Since when do you attribute things to god? Who is god, anyway?

god? asked Claudio, cracking his knuckles, staring at the ceiling. Mathilde didn't know whom he was addressing until he said, *god's a word.*

Mathilde glutted a tissue. It was so safe of people who said things like *it will all work out* because, fuck, it didn't. Right after Mathilde's father died, she'd told her mother that she decided she didn't believe in god. And her mother had asked her if that made her sad. And Mathilde sat and felt about it for a while. And then she decided no—if anything, she felt relieved. god was like a taxing family member.

You know what my worst fear used to be? asked Mathilde. *It used to be that one of the girls would disappear suddenly, and that we wouldn't know what happened to them. We'd put their pictures on milk cartons. But you know what I'm thinking now? Maybe it's worse to know.*

Hope can keep most people going, agreed Claudio. *But it doesn't work for me.*

Why not? asked Mathilde. This thought sliced through her conscious: - *I'm having an abortion, seventeen years and six months too late.* -

Claudio looked at her. *I never said I didn't want it to. I've tried. It just doesn't.*

In this teaspoon-moment they kissed.

Did you know, Mathilde asked Claudio, *that you smell exactly the same as the way you did when you were twenty-three?*

Stop it, said Claudio. *We can't be silly.* He thought about how when they were younger, they'd spend selfish hours just chasing each other around their apartment. What did they think was so funny? How had they been so happy?

I'm not being silly, said Mathilde, eyes splintered with tears, recalling her former splendor of crying, when she pushed it on herself. The good old days. *I'm being serious.*

a space

For her final history project, Carly chose to write a paper on Judaic history in a contemporary Christian-dominated European city. *Find history in what's been destroyed,* her teacher had said. *Find meaning in what isn't there.*

Carly picked Venice, Italy, with *only two rooms* in its Venetian Jewish historical museum, because most of its artifacts had been destroyed in the Holocaust. - *Pathetic,* - thought Carly, studying its pictures on the Internet.

Stephen read over her paper and edited it. *The ideas were all yours,* he said, *I just cleaned them up.*

Thanks, said Carly.

Stephen said, *at my grandfather's funeral, a six-year-old neighbor of mine asked me if my grandfather was history.*

History could be safe or devastating in its finitude, like math or medicine or science. Carly thought about doctors, understanding it was their job to separate themselves from the emotional component of their work. But how were they able to desensitize themselves? How could Lucy not manage to break everybody's Heart, including her surgeons and nurses? Maybe they cried in secret, like in the janitorial supply closet. Maybe they felt very great pain efficiently, getting compassion out of their systems as pragmatically as taking cigarette breaks.

Stephen and Carly went into the kitchen. Stephen sliced two crumpets and two biscotti in half and toasted them. Stephen's family kept hip snacks: smoked gouda, baklava, wasabi peas.

I've always toyed with the idea of getting the same tattoo that my grandfather had. The same number. I had heard of some Israeli grandchildren of Holocaust survivors who'd done that. As a way of saying fuck you to history. Also, because I never want anyone to forget about what had happened.

That's intense, said Carly.

That's what everybody said, said Stephen. *My mother said it would have killed him. But we'll never know, because he died a couple of years before.*

Carly traced his hip tattoo: the word *lux* in cursive. *Lux,* meaning "light," in Latin. *The first word I ever said was* light, Stephen said.

I like this one, said Carly. *It reminds me of the goodness of humans.* The word had authority over the body, not as a form of branding, but a form of art.

In the end I didn't get it, because I'm not my grandfather. But the thing was, he wasn't his number, either. But I'm scared. I don't want anyone to forget about it. The survivors, they're all dying now.

People won't forget, said Carly. *And the Venetian Jewish History Museum is still there, even when it's barely there,* her hope leaking. At lunch, right after she handed in her paper the next day, Carly overheard the janitor say to the lunch lady, *somebody unplugged the ice cream machine as a prank. I have to clean it out. All the ice cream's melted by now.* And Carly cried, her eye-whites runny as *oeufs au coque.* Untoward how she'd arrived at the point where crying felt routine, like brushing her teeth or tipping a waiter.

She left the cafeteria, felt a blueberry seed in her teeth, and was fishing her pointer inside as Molly, a high school senior who used to be Natasha's best friend, turned a corner.

Help me, said Carly.

Molly took her outside, put her bossy arms around Carly so that Carly's head was clutched between her funny-bone muscles. Molly's arm hair, the tint of curry, tickled Carly. An archangel. *Sorry I have such a small head,* said Carly. *And a small brain.*

What are you talking about? You and your sisters are smart as whips. You legit are.

I'm not really a Simone, said Carly inaudibly.

Molly, though sensitive to sound, tactfully ignored Carly, accustomed to not acknowledging everything she heard (one of the requirements of her teenage-girl strength). She opened the door to the warm inside of her boyfriend Matt's car, a Lincoln. *It's his dad's,* she told Carly. *I know. It looks like it's straight out of* The Godfather.

Molly drove to the neighborhood diner. Their sides touched as the host led them to a booth. Then came the waiter. *A turkey burger, please,* said Carly, and within minutes it appeared before her on a plate. She lifted the seeded bun and dumped ketchup all over it. The food shifted from teeth to tongue to throat to stomach, where her bolus would digest. Her stomach growled, like the wheels of a penny-farthing were caught in her ribs.

They weren't comfortable with each other yet. Carly cared about such technicalities, aware of how cumbersome she felt. Social anxiety whitewashed her tragedy. *Sorry for crying.*

Please! Don't worry about it. The words seeped from Molly's mouth.

Carly kept thanking Molly, pleased and disturbed at the same time, challenging her memory to unearth the last valuable time she'd spent with a friend. Not Stephen or a family member. A girlfriend to go to lingering lunches with and talk about teachers they didn't like. Carly suddenly felt a wide need for friends.

What happened? asked Molly. They'd been eating in silence for almost half an hour, but Molly noticeably must've classified too long a silence unsustainable.

Carly nodded in response to nothing. - *Nothing happened,* - she thought.

You know how she's not doing so well? Carly wondered why it was so hard for her to tell Molly, for she knew telling somebody had no effect on the probability of events. There were superstitious people out there, those who didn't throw baby showers until after the baby was born, but Carly wasn't like that. Superstitious notions to her were frightened ways to keep wishing.

The Heart is starting to reject her body. We'll have to call every-body we know and say she's dead. There are close to three hundred names in our family address book. I won't want Mom or Dad to go through with it, so Natasha and I will split the duties. I will have to call a hundred and fifty people and tell them.

Her voice loud, soft, loud. *Do you think it can be a hundred and forty-nine people? Can I just text you with the words* it happened? *It would help me. You know.*

You sure can.

Do I ask who they're with before I tell them? What if they aren't alone? Should I call them back later? And what if they are alone? What if being alone is worse?

Do I ask them if they're sitting down?

Do I say I have bad news?

Carly was a child: powerless, desultory, displaced.

Molly said, *let's eat some dessert.*

Carly said, *I can never eat when I'm sad.*

Shut the front door, Molly said, instead of *shut the fuck up.*

Carly made a laughing, *tssss* sound to break the silence, a noise she made with her tongue against her teeth. Her real laugh came from the base of her belly. It had been a while since she'd heard it.

We can go back now. I'll be all right, she lied.

bedtime

Outside, god held court, and there fell a thick rain. The clouds covered the sky like wallpaper, and they were all equal in the sky, as no overcast patch was heaviest. Mathilde picked up lunch from the hospital's Au Bon Pain, with its distinctive odor of zesty soups and salads. The indignity and injury of this strapping smell guaranteed that every time Mathilde would ever go inside a future Au Bon Pain somewhere else, she'd be reminded of the hospital.

Mathilde had been telling Lucy stories all week. Lucy listened in her skimmed way, sometimes not even awake. She told her mother not to look at her, alleging it was due to her self-consciousness. Her body exhausted itself, and yet she saw the therapeutic effect these costly cradlesongs had on her mother and didn't want to fritter it away. It was what she could do for her mother, to keep her from thinking. As long as her mother didn't have to think of Lucy, she'd be all right.

Tell me a story from when I was too young to remember.

How young?

Lucy said, *go back to the beginning.*

Lucy came into the world looking shriveled, like an old lady. *The first thing Daddy said when he saw you was a prayer. I was doped up on painkillers, but I still remember.*

Daddy, praying?

He kneeled down and said to god, thank you for that amazing music. *Those were his exact words. Like he had just left the Philharmonic. And then, together, we picked you up and looked at you from every angle to make sure you were healthy. We knew you were original because you had a little birthmark on you.*

This one? Lucy pointed above her wrist.

The very one. The one in the shape of an envelope.

Lucy smiled. When she was three, she had pointed and said, *does this come off or stay on?* Her mother had said, *that's a beauty mark. That's how we know you're one of a kind.* Lucy had said, *can you take it off? It won't hurt. I promise.*

Mathilde told true story after hyperbolic story after ghost story, all with happy endings (for the time being), her train of unfocused and inefficient thoughts fishtailing one another. After another hour she turned around to ask if Lucy needed another glass of water and found her sleeping smoothly, breathing, still living.

utility

As Kitten rejected Lucy's body, her organs meting out like crumpled petunias, Lucy read books about animals. She studied their rituals and losses. Elephants, such subtle and sensitive creatures, bury their dead and grieve just as consciously as humans. Not only that, if elephants recognize bones as elephant bones, they will stand for a long time near the gravesite. Lucy wondered why some animals, even domesticated animals like dogs and cats, given the opportunity, enter the forest to die. She was going to die in the suburbs, and probably in a hospital. This was implicit.

Claudio asked Lucy if she wanted anything.

I'd like to see Aunt Jane again, said Lucy.

Claudio drove to Lincoln the following day, signing his sister out. Jane looked at home in her clothes: gray parka, pajama bottoms, a secondhand T-shirt reading NOBODY'S UGLY AFTER 2 AM. They drove from one hospital to the other hospital.

Look who's here, announced Claudio.

Look at this place. Jane twirled around. *Your hospital room is even smaller than my hospital room.*

Yeah, said Lucy.

It wasn't long ago when I was here too. But I don't really remember. I don't like this place, said Jane. *It's where my ghost came out.* This phrase seemed to grip at a chilling profundity to Claudio, or probably he, as always, was interpreting some clarity among nonsense. *Can we go somewhere?*

I don't think they'll let me leave, Lucy said. Untimely lines gathered at her temples: thin, and so many more than anyone would expect, like bobby pins hidden in a large hairdo.

I just wanted to take you to this restaurant Sawyer took me to, said Jane. Her Heart flooded at the memory. *We had so much fun. We drank two juices each and ate croissants. The breakfast of angels.*

Well, maybe if we can get a pass, you can take me out in a wheelchair. Lucy hadn't been outside in weeks on her own volition—the air's cleanliness depressed her, the drippy clouds depressed her, the sun depressed her. Anything within limitation reminded her that it would be around forever, and she only temporarily.

Claudio was still in the corner of the room, gnawing his fist. He'd never been the kind of person to even consider an affair, but for once he thought he understood how it must feel to be a man whose wife and mistress meet, even conspire. *I'll ask the nurse.*

Jane clapped her hands like a little girl.

So, what's new?

Nothing much, Lucy's classically conditioned words.

Claudio poked his head in from the hallway. *Unfortunately, all of the guest passes are out for the afternoon, so we can't leave.*

We can't leave? Lucy and Jane asked simultaneously.

Not now. Maybe we can play a board game.

I don't want to play a fucking board game, Jane screamed, jarring her brother and niece both. *We are the Simones and the Simones don't curse* was something Claudio had been repeating for his daughters' entire lives. *Remember, those words are more unoriginal than shocking. It's like how gory movies aren't scary, they're just stupid. You want to really offend, choose smarter words.*

Shh. Claudio reached for his sister's elbow, but she pushed it into his abdomen. He sputtered and locked her body so she was not in pain but couldn't move. Instead, she screamed, *Fuck you, Claudio! You should be the one dying!*

Wait, Lucy said weakly.

She's not having a good day, her father said. *I'm going to take her back, and then I'll come back. I'll see you tonight, honey.*

Get off me!

Lucy felt surprised to wonder if it was the last time she'd ever see her aunt Jane. It wasn't like they were close, but for the first time Lucy understood she was lucky by comparison. Lucy would die, and the pain would stop. Aunt Jane would keep living, and the pain would go on for as long as she'd let it.

wedding day

Lucy's uncles were to wed at the Lighthouse at Chelsea Piers in Manhattan. With her finger, Lucy followed a curled vein up her shin. She'd lost her ability to walk stalwartly a week ago, and relied on a daisy-garlanded walker. Soon it wouldn't be *her body*, it would be *the body*. Not hers anymore, but the earth's. Nothing anyone worried about anymore, put out of everyone's misery.

During the reception, Stephen sat down next to Lucy.

Hey.

Lucy raised her frosted coupe.

Someday this will be me and your sister, Stephen emitted.

She's pretty crazy about you too, admitted Lucy.

One day, said Stephen.

I'll miss it.

Well, I could marry her tomorrow. He fretfully bounced his left leg, wrapping an arm around his girlfriend's older sister, knowing her jealousy was more than for just their health. He pressed his chin into his shirt and made a noise that could have been happy or sad. As they made eye contact, Lucy shockingly discovered which it was.

Why are you crying? What happened?

Well, he found himself saying. *I'd marry you tomorrow too.*

Please stop, said Lucy, *just stop.* The tone killed her, as it was such schmaltz, this patronizing idea of Stephen being able to love her. As related to her needs he thought this love was, deeply it was the opposite—just pretending, even more devalued than the truth, and the truth was a question: who could *really* love her in a patient and reliable way?

No. I won't stop.

Then for a second—she breathed—*can you call me Carly?* A proxy Carly. To dream of walking with her sister's legs, swallowing from her sister's throat, hearing high truths, and thinking with her sister's brain. - *This is the way love works,* - she thought to herself. - *Somebody falls in love with the person you want to be.* -

The DJ played "Shout!" Noah asked Lucy to dance. *It's spectacular here,* whispered Lucy, crouching low and breathing in flutters, during the *a little bit softer now* moment. *What a place to get married.*

Man, I can't believe how I've cried twice already. Once during the vows, and once when Sawyer told me how much easier this was the second time, said Noah.

Through the windows they couldn't see a foamy cloud in the air, and Lucy would miss this brand of blue. More important, she'd miss everyone else's celebrations. Weddings, babies, graduations, quiet nights at home. She'd miss all of the fun ahead of her family the most.

Through their complacent silence, Lucy wanted to find something that they had in common. *We are all kind of stuck in this web, don't you think? We'll all be gone in two hundred years. Our body temperatures and Heartbeats are all around the same. We all like someone who may or may not like us back. We all have a fear.*

They looked out at the guests they loved. *Besides,* Lucy continued, *we all know pain.*

Yes, said Noah. *Is there anything we can do?*

Maybe laugh, said Lucy.

You know how in Shakespeare, comedies end with weddings and tragedies end with funerals? In real life you never know how it will end.

Weddings and funerals don't even mean it's the end, said Lucy. What people called the end wasn't, except for the lucky or unlucky. - *This sucks*, - she thought.

Seven songs later, a prosperous mixture of Motown and current pop that'd date itself within a year, Lucy reached for her cell phone, dialing the number she'd memorized. She excused herself. *On the corner of the West Side Highway*, she specified.

The appetizers had been served, and dinners were brought out on silver plates. It was an eat-dance-eat-dance wedding, not eat-eat-dance-dance as she'd predicted, so it would be a little bit harder to slip away. But Lucy didn't need dinner, and if her timing went as planned, she'd be back in time for cake cutting. Lucy coughed into an embroidered napkin with a gold-calligraphic *SW & NW*. Sawyer would be taking Noah's last name, which was Whistler. Their initials were no different from directions.

Lucy abandoned her walker by the bathrooms. She wouldn't be walking too much where she was going. She reached into her silk purse for Natasha's credit card, which she'd lent to her the week before on Lucy's request. *Just need to take care of something small*, Lucy had told her sister. *I'll pay you back*, saying this just to say it.

She peered down the long undercurrent of highway. It wouldn't be long before people would start to notice she was missing, as feeble people are also often the center of attention. Finally, she saw what she needed, its yellow lights unblemished, and its window curled down.

Good evening, miss, said her driver.

will you walk away from a fool and his money?

july 1, 2011, 4:56 p.m.

Because Lucy couldn't leave the cab without a walker, the driver honored her few requests. *I can't thank you enough,* she whispered. He parked, walked inside, then came out with Jane. *This the woman?*

Lucy, said her aunt, *why?* Jane hadn't recognized the man who checked her out, with nutmeg skin and hair like ricotta cheese curling against his scalp in a cul-de-sac trajectory, but he told her he had Lucy waiting in the car. She didn't know whether to believe him or not, but she had nothing better to do, so she told the staff she knew him.

I wanted to see if you ate dinner yet.

Nope.

Well, asked Lucy, *you hungry?*

Where?

That place you were telling me about, said Lucy, *the one you went to with Uncle Sawyer. Do you remember the name?*

No, said Jane. *It was orange. It was next to a day care center.*

I'll look it up on my phone, said Lucy. She named some restaurants, and Jane recognized one, so Lucy gave the address to the driver, and the driver took the pair to their coveted café. He waited in the parking lot after Lucy promised to pay for his time. She'd pay for the entire evening.

What a pair Lucy and Jane must've appeared to be: the blind

leading the blind, with what Lucy had left of a body and what Jane had left of a mind. (With symbiotic choreography?)

This is the place! said Jane, glad to domineer, to have experience. *See the day care center next door? Get a load of all those babies. And here we are, with the orange walls. It looks like there are other waitresses this time, I don't recognize any. Did I ever tell you about my favorite restaurant in New Orleans? It was called Cloquet. They had this adorable waiter named Eddie. I loved his tushie.*

What's good here?

The croissants, of course. You can't pass them up, said Jane.

They ordered. The croissants arrived on ceramic plates, thin flaky strips arranged in a lattice art. They delivered their conversation in enriching, simple scraps, talking about their favorite songs and favorite songwriters and favorite words. Jane said her favorite word was *always.* When it came time for the bill, Lucy held out her sister's card, but the waitress told them it was on her.

Why do you think that is? whispered Jane.

We must look like nice people, Lucy told her aunt.

I like that, said Jane. *I love you, Lucy. god should bless you.*

Thank you, said Lucy delicately. *So. I don't want to go home after this.*

Do you have anywhere you have to be?

Well, said Lucy. *I don't have much time. So I'd rather be here.*

They walked back to the car, Lucy leaning against her aunt like they were doing a trust exercise—building a team, just the two of them. *Drive us back to the city, I guess,* said Lucy. *But would you stop in front of the highway by Fifty-ninth Street? By Hudson River Park. There's something beautiful over there.* When they got there, they stepped out of the car, anticipating the sunset. The sky was a carnival of ruby and salsa, suffusing into a low point of cobalt. This could have been a nice place for a picnic.

Look at this sky, insisted Lucy. They looked at the sky and listened to the city.

Lucy, is there anything I can do for you?

You had this evening with me, said Lucy, *and that's more than enough.*

I mean, to help you heal.

I'm not sure.

I tried before, said Jane, *but nobody would help me.*

Tried? asked Lucy.

Well, said Jane, *I know my brain isn't too good, chemical imbalance and such, and I wouldn't trust my lungs or my liver, on account of my drinking and smoking way back when, but I think my Heart's okay. Nobody ever told me there was anything wrong with it. And I figure, why not give a perfectly good one? They have those operations nowadays, don't they?*

What? asked Lucy.

I mean, it wouldn't be so bad, I even tidied up before I did it and wrote a little love note, saying good-bye, in poem form. In the poem I don't write about what I'm about to do, I write about other things. That's how you write a poem, you know, it's a kind of code. Of course you know—you're a better poet than I'll ever be. Before I was even allowed to meet you, your father would always talk about what a brilliant writer you were. How you loved your English class. You made me want to write. You made me want to get better. Better at writing, I mean. The poem's still underneath the picture frame in my room, the one with the couple and the dog. I slid it behind the picture so those hospital worker fuckers wouldn't steal it. It's still there because I'm afraid to move it.

Anyway, I wrote the note and there was no other weapon in the room, they're real strict about that sort of thing, so I used the only thing I could have used. Next thing I know, I'm awake in a hospital I don't recognize and your father is there, telling me I disappointed you and the whole family, and I just can't fucking explain a thing. I hear you're in the hospital too, two floors above me, and I don't know why. And I think that maybe god's decided to punish both of us because I tried to take care of my dying and your living all on my own.

Lucy trembled. Earlier she'd figured this was going to be the last time she'd ever see Aunt Jane, and wanted to make it special, and now there were too many things she had to understand. Most important, that this was what Jane had been trying to do last time. The time she was almost successful, but the doctors found her and stitched her up in the hospital before she'd been able to die. Jane hadn't hid this. Anybody could have found out the reason why Jane tried to kill herself was to save her niece, but as it was, nobody had asked.

sitting on the sofa
with a sister or two

July 1, 2011, 5:28 p.m.

L *ucy is gone,* Mathilde noticed nearly right away, *anyone see her?* *She'll be back,* Carly knew. Lucy had briefly told her sisters of the plan, and they'd honored it as confidential, for what else is sacred if not a secret kept among blood? At once Carly felt the thralls of a widespread alarm throughout her body, her legs jellied. - *Will she? No. Lucy can't die. She's not going to die. She'll come back. She has to come back.* - Every moment that Carly had spent with Stephen had been a moment away from her sister. What if Lucy and Carly had a finite number of moments together, and this stretching out of discrete events prolonged them, separated the seconds? What if Carly's actions were selfless, not selfish? What if Lucy came back? What if she could always come back?

And then Lucy came back.

How'd it go? asked Natasha.

It was very sad and wonderful, said Lucy. *And I'll never forget it.* She yawned.

They're just about to play the last song, and then we'll call it a night. Daddy's calling a car service to take us back home. You almost missed dessert, said Natasha. *Instead of a bride's cake and a groom's cake, they just used two of the grooms' favorite desserts. I saved you a tiny pie and a cupcake. Which one do you want?*

Lucy took one in each hand, alternating between bites. The

cupcake was drenched in fondant and sprinkles. She felt drowsy, thinking, - *everybody loves me.* -

Did anyone ask where I was?

Mommy and Daddy, but Carly and I calmed them down. Because what else are sisters for?

A lot of things, said Lucy. *Last wishes are just one of the things.*

jane's night

Good night, ma'am, said the driver, parked in front of Lincoln. But Jane didn't leave the cab.

What's wrong?

What else do I do? asked Jane.

Your friend took care of it, said the driver. *We're all good.*

Are you sure? asked Jane. There were a lot of things she would have done. She didn't even know what she would have done them for.

I'm sure. The driver laughed stormily. Jane didn't like him laughing at her. *You take care, and have a nice night now.*

Okay, said Jane. *I did, and I'll keep trying to.* She shut the cab door, and she traipsed back to the hospital, and she got home alive.

note for a suicide that never happened

november 1, 2010

Love

The night of the party, at three am, nobody knows if you're using the bathroom or lying in a ditch five hundred miles away. You call 9-1-1 and hear she's leaving home after living alone for so many years. You call Sanctuary but you can't use electricity today. Shabbat Shalom. The ditch looks like you can fit two or three people inside. Writing this means you're not healthy anymore. It's a pretty good party. Everyone's drinking gin buckets. The last time they made gin buckets you lost your underwear.

—Jane (Simone) Spicer

final poem

Four days before Lucy died, the trifling time came for god, and then it was over. During that point of severe poverty, Carly prayed to every god she ever heard of and knew in her life: Allah, Jesus, the Jewish g-d, Buddha, Confucius. Eventually the only god left was the passive god, which is maybe all that god is in the first place. Carly read the last poem her sister wrote, in her tireless and sans serif scrawl, back when she was conscious, attached in a note for her mother. - *Written like there is no tomorrow*, - she thought.

What Makes Me Anxious

the sound of sneezing, the fact that the Heart
is slightly inclined to the right. I'm right-handed. I
   have just a few hours
to live. Stephen has a crush on me and he thinks
   I'm joking.
Come on a date with me, he keeps saying. *Young people*
   don't die.
The life expectancy test told me I'm going to die
young because I sleep ten hours a night
and keep my thermostat high. That was in the midst
of my eighth-life crisis. I decided to change,

and re-spelt my name with only consonants. It wasn't
    enough.
I spoke to Death before coming back once.
She told me she wanted a new name
for god. And the new name for god was
Alan. And Alan wouldn't start wars
or seduce suicide bombers this time.

—Lc(y) Mrgrt Smn

Sunday became Monday and Monday became Tuesday and
Tuesday became Wednesday and Wednesday became Thursday
and Thursday became Friday and Friday became Saturday and
Saturday became another kind of Sunday. Time took up space
in a discreet, votive way.

You should get sleep, peanut, Lucy's father said.

Don't go, said Lucy. *Stay. You need to stay.*

Yes, said Claudio. *I'll stay.* He lay next to her in her bed.

Don't leave me alone.

Never, said Claudio, all the while thinking, - *Isn't she the one
leaving him? -*

Don't go away. She yawned. *I'm going to go to sleep. I'm scared.*

I'll stay with you, said Claudio. *You're safe. And you have me,
and you had me, and you will have me.*

So good to know. Lucy smiled with her eyes closed. *But Daddy.
I already knew that.*

The day is Tuesday. - *Do I still have it, this heavy Heart? How
long does it remain broken in me? -* Lucy thinks.

two kinds of sad

Carly and Natasha held hands beside their sister's grave. Everything outside and far away seemed to be moving faster than they were, like the moon was a bell being swung in the air by fingertips, like the stars were pieces of change pockmarking the night.

There are two kinds of sad, said Carly. *There's regular sad, and then there's the sad that comes with knowing that the person you love most is underneath your feet.*

Sometimes I believe that Lucy is a ghost, admitted Carly. *She comes around and tells me to break rules.*

Natasha laughed. She was twenty-five. Carly was twenty-one. Lucy would have been four months shy of twenty-two. She'd slipped into a coma the way one would a sweater. A few days later, they buried her, they buried Kitten. That day, according to the newspaper, forced disappearances were a growing problem in Mexico's drug war. A movie with Meryl Streep was released in theaters. An earthquake hit the California coast.

Carly didn't remember much about the two weeks in between, except that Natasha called Lucy by her oldest nickname, White Cat, and their friends visited. LJ and Sloane and Molly and everyone. They ordered pizza and passed it around and talked and laughed. Mathilde made sure everybody's drinks were filled. Claudio passed out napkins, and when people asked him how the business was, he raised one shoulder and said, *it's okay.*

The funeral was two days later. Lucy's fingers begemmed with her mother's pink gold ribbon and Italian cameo rings, her rich and retro striped bodysuit, tweed blazer, and solitaire heels, one of her clutches beside her. Carly wore Lucy's black cigarette pants and black halter top, dropping them off at Goodwill the next day because nothing was worse than funeral clothes. Mathilde and Claudio had bought a deep family plot with one gravestone, big enough for three people. Lucy had the grave on the bottom, and if they were lucky, Claudio and Mathilde would be buried above her. If they were lucky, Natasha and Carly would have families of their own to be buried with. Everyone would end up in the same place, and it would be justice for the time on earth her parents spent doomed.

That night, Natasha and Carly read their sister's diary together, about Face and Kitten and the whale and Alan dreams. They cried and cried and laughed every so often because their own Hearts demanded some laughter. And then some poetry.

The last words in Lucy's diary were *I'll send you a sign. Drop some face-up pennies from the sky at 11:11, or make some dandelion fuzz go up your nose. You'll sneeze and think of me. Peace be with you. I'm sorry for leaving you all. I didn't want to. You have to believe me.*

Everything after the transplant was just borrowed time, Carly would say now to console herself. That too was something Hannah the Holocaust survivor had said. *Everything after the Holocaust was just borrowed time.* According to plan, Holocaust survivors weren't supposed to live. Carly figured the same about Lucy.

Pictures of Lucy lived in every room: some lit by candles, some framed, most candid. Lucy in every room of their house, smiling and flat and from another, healthier era. Their family didn't know if the pictures made them happier or sadder, but most important, they didn't feel okay without the pictures around. Grieving was like this. Or this: Natasha texting Lucy's phone the other day with *I miss you*. What did she miss the most about her sister? Her nose, she decided. Her little pointy nose and her long, marsupial feet and the way she thought she was all alone until she wrote a poem.

Stephen broke up with Carly a few months into college. He told her that it wasn't her; it was a problem coming from his insides, and that he was going to his school psychologist.

My sister died, and I don't go to therapy, said Carly. *In the old days, a lot worse shit happened, and nobody went to therapy*, refraining from the mention of any precise parcel of history.

That night, Carly called Natasha and they talked about high school. *And we were happy and nobody was dead*, Carly screamed into the phone.

Then Carly lived without Stephen, dating a boy named Thomas who sang opera and drank a quart of olive oil once a week, and then a boy named Alexander who played football and gave Irish good-byes and when he saw pictures of Lucy, would always squeeze the wrinkly pit of Carly's elbow and told her how much he missed her even though he'd never met her.

Natasha studied economics at Princeton and graduated summa cum laude. Carly double-majored in history and art history at William and Mary. They came home on summer and winter vacations and listened to Claudio's records, old records of bands that still toured but with one original member, such as Creedence Clearwater Revival rechristened Creedence Clearwater Revisited.

Still a band, even after most of them left, said Natasha. *Still playing their same old songs.*

It's sweet, said Carly. *Romantic.*

I think it's pathetic, said Natasha.

You know in Disney World, they don't call janitors janitors, said Carly. *They call them cast members. As if that makes their job better.*

They watched the cadences shake the wooden floors. *Who will stop the rain?* the music asked.

Claudio set down a new record, dropped the record needle, and instead of playing from start to finish, which he believed was the only way you could play *Abbey Road*, it fell in the middle of "She Came in Through the Bathroom Window." Because it had started in the middle, they were going to play it to the end.

Didn't anybody tell her? Didn't anybody see?

Carly had always thought the song had to do with a young girl, somebody like her, believing she was a criminal. A girl who broke into a home, stole something, then gave it back. She'd pictured Sunday and Monday and Tuesday as police officers (*Tuesday's on the phone to me*), but coming to think of it now, she realized that the song had to be more than that. She still couldn't grasp it entirely but knew that the lyrics had something to do with time, and this congested her with a quiet, though spectacularly faithful feeling.

The record continued onto "Golden Slumbers," "Carry That Weight," "The End," and finally the random "Her Majesty." They heard about a pretty nice girl without a lot to say, and there was no reason to anything. Paul McCartney needed a bellyful of wine and they all listened very hard and nobody said anything and then at the end, Claudio finally let himself say, *I miss her.*

Sometimes Carly grieved for Alan the donor and Lucy together, and every so often just Alan. Sorrow was water, the way it could pour or wave over more areas than one could anticipate, flood the most unsuspecting places. She'd think of Lucy's last months, the prize months, the months they both deserved and didn't deserve, with Alan's Heart, the Heart buried with Lucy, the Heart she wished she could give to someone else, the Heart that belonged to everybody and nobody.

Some water fell from the sky. Tiny bits of rain on the dirt above Lucy. *Remember the time when everything was okay.* Natasha's voice fell slick at the end of that remark, turning their *remember?* game into purged conclusions rather than light-Hearted questions.

Carly stared at the grave, then up at her living sister. *Sometimes things were okay. Sometimes things got better.*

Coda

It's gorgeous out, Claudio said to Mathilde. *Can I take you on a date?* Every time they were alone, Claudio called it a date. They walked down their own block, both retired now, Claudio making good money after selling the store space to a dry-cleaning service. Now they could do things in the daytime without feeling guilty, like catching movies or doing Sudoku. Mathilde linked her arm through Claudio's. She was wearing makeup that looked like she wasn't wearing any at all.

I made reservations this morning for Purple Lune Bistro, said Mathilde.

Good, said Claudio, his nails to his illicit chest, scratching his blue Heart. *You know me.* Purple Lune Bistro was their favorite restaurant in Carly's college town. They were visiting her in two days. Carly's art collective had a show that featured three of Carly's oil paintings. The first was a portrait of her and Natasha and a headless body for Lucy. The second painting featured Lucy's face to the best of Carly's memory and blank faces to signify Carly and Natasha. And the third, entitled *In Abstentia,* was a blank canvas with three pairs of eyes. There were nine eyes and there were three girls. Once. And Claudio loved them, just as much as he loved their mother, just as much as he loved their aunt, and much more than he could ever love himself.

Speaking of, Carly called this morning.

I miss our baby. The sun was in Claudio's eyes.

She wanted to know if we would be okay seeing it this weekend.

You won't cry? asked Claudio. He looked down at the little tattoos on his thumbs. The one on the left said *Lucille*, and the one on the right said *Jane*.

No promises, said Mathilde. She probably wouldn't. It had been years, and she knew she would never get over it. Frankly, tears gave her a headache and she could exercise some control over her body.

They saw a penny on the ground, and even though tails looked at the sky, Mathilde picked it up. She was feeling less superstitious and more frugal these days.

What else did you tell her? Claudio held his bride's hand and studied her eyes, her sutures of cheeks. Sweet Mathilde.

I told her to stop worrying about me and Daddy. That we're fine. That life is finally beginning to leave us alone.

acknowledgments

I started *Sunday's on the Phone to Monday* as a book of poetry when I was nineteen. Most of it has changed—all but the Heart. Thank you to G. C. Waldrep and Shara McCallum, the two best teachers I have ever had. For the rest of my Bucknell teachers—thank you.

For Lucy Rosenthal, for guiding this novel through its early drafts at Sarah Lawrence. I will never forget your grit and wisdom. For my Sarah Lawrence poetry teachers, especially Jeff McDaniel, Victoria Redel, Marie Howe, Kate Knapp-Johnson, and Dennis Nurkse.

For my friends at Sarah Lawrence, in particular Daniel Long, for writing the most wonderful letter I have ever received; if not for his eye, this book would not be in your hands.

I thank all of the writers in my life who have dispensed infinite insight: Panio Gianopoulos, Alethea Black, Lisa Shea, David Gilbert, Joanna Fuhrman, Dylan Landis, Parker Marshall, Pamela Erens, Amy Shearn, Katie Arnold-Ratliff, Kim Stolz, Michelle Miller, and the good people at *Tin House* and the Gotham Writers Workshop.

For my colleagues and students at the Dalton School, City and Country School, Collegiate School, and the Professional Children's School for teaching me how to be a teacher.

For my agent, James Fitzgerald, for the conversation and laughter, and for treating my characters like human beings. For

Sally Kim, who saw this book exactly for what it was and pushed it to be the best version of itself, and for the Touchstone team, particularly Etinosa Agbonlahor.

For Robby and the Cecot family, especially during the Brooklyn years. For all of my best friends, my muses: growing up in the Five Towns, at Bucknell, in New York City. There are too many of you to name, but you've probably already seen yourself on every page.

For New York City.

And, finally, for my own family: my grandparents, aunts, uncles, cousins, and Kenny, Paul, Mom, and Dad.

index

CHRISTINE REILLY lives in New York City. She has taught at Sarah Lawrence College, the Dalton School, City and Country School, and Collegiate School. She received her bachelor's degree from Bucknell University and her master's degree in writing from Sarah Lawrence College. *Sunday's on the Phone to Monday* is her first novel.